the *journey*
series

The Dangerous Journey
The Lost Journey

the
journey
series

W. Lenore Mobley

Pleasant Word
A Division of WINEPRESS PUBLISHING

ISBN 1-57921-703-6
Library of Congress Catalog Card Number: 2003107321

Table of Contents

Preface

Four decades before the beginning of the twentieth century, Idaho was still primarily a mining area. Its mineral and cattle interests were strong and dominated the land. The coming of the railroads changed that in two ways. It brought more people to the area, along with needed supplies for starting new settlements, and it took back cattle and sheep that the East Coast cities needed.

Many of these early pioneers were great, adventurous people looking for a new life. There were the first homestead acts that began as early as 1850, but rapid transfer of the land to private individuals was near the railroad lands. The settling of the less expensive land was often several hundred miles from these railroad towns.

The 1849 gold rush in California brought miners and others West. There was influence from Mormon Utah, mining Montana, and pioneer Oregon, much of which came from the influence of the Whitman missions. Gradually many of these pioneers turned from mining and lumbering to livestock-herding and farming.

Fort Boise was a bustling town in 1863. Many of its inhabitants were ranchers and their families, along with Basque sheepherders and their families that were brought here from Spain and Portugal. The sheep barons expanded their grazing from Nevada into the high Idaho plains.

There began to be battles between the sheepmen and the cattle ranchers. The cattlemen claimed that the sheepmen encroached on farming and cattle territory and spoiled the land for future use. The region had to be made safe and accessible for settlement. This led to new communities with self-government to combat violence.

Idaho became a territory in 1863. At that time, silver was purchased by the government to be minted into silver dollars. Placer mining was being replaced by more elaborate processes requiring heavy machinery. This required heavy capital. As a result, profit went more often to absentee capitalists than to resident prospectors and would-be miners. Better transportation was provided by the stage coach, the pony express, and, finally, the railroad was developed and heavily used.

Along with these came the telegraph, opening communications from East to West. Ranchers discovered that the treeless grasslands were ideal for grazing livestock, although before the railroads they had to drive cattle to cow town rail centers as far away as Nebraska. When the Desert Land Act was enacted in 1877, families could start homesteading for as little as a dollar and twenty-five cents an acre for a section of ground to call their own. They came by the hundreds and required safe and fast transportation. With this expansion, the railways—and the settlers they served—expanded further and further West.

Acknowledgements

I would like to say "thank you" to my beloved husband, Bill, and to all my family for their help and encourage-ment.
Ben and Janell put up with my English questions.
Beth helped with computer problems, as did Cliff at CJG Designs.
I love you very much!
Win Lenore
www.lenoremobley.com

I also want to thank Creation Studios for their help with the picture on the front cover. Please contact them at 208-764-3522.

Part I:

The Dangerous Journey

Chapter One

Molly Newman never knew what was grand about this place, until on this fall day she looked across the great abyss to see the colorful grandeur that was below her. A large, emerald lake lay against beautiful forested mountains. These mountains, topped with dark, weathered granite, shown brightly against a clear, blue sky.

The waterfall at the end of the lake below fell perhaps one hundred feet, misting the shrubs and flowers with its spray. In the morning's sunlight, it created a beautiful rainbow.

The days had fallen into their autumn routine. She hadn't been here in the late summer to see the change of colors, although Molly had often come to this overlook to meditate and pray when there was a crisis.

"I felt a little sorry for myself today," she thought, "and I believe it is time to search my soul. I know the things I want for my life are not at the end of the world; they can be within my reach."

She spoke to herself as she sat alone in the shaded pines. She breathed in deep the cold, damp air, which made her feel better. It seemed just yesterday she had returned from her trip to Kentucky.

"Boarding the trains and visiting friends in the East last month allowed me to go from isolation to spheres of influence," she cried out in her heart as she remembered. "Did it help me? Or did this visit just remind me of heartaches? My mother thought it would help to rid myself of unresolved pain, but I'm not sure it did so."

Seeing the school and a few classmates was nice, and Molly did enjoy their company. Perhaps if she had left out the lonely rides along the river where she and Thomas first met she would not have had this pain. She remembered that time in her life now.

It had been the beginning of a new semester and she enjoyed riding along the beautiful pathway near the Ohio River. When she first saw him coming around the large hardwood trees into open view of the river, he was accompanied by a classmate of hers. Molly might not have stopped except the classmate hailed her to stop and say hello.

"Was it the magnificent thoroughbred horse the stranger was riding, or the way he gave her a tip of his hat?" Whatever it was, it was clear to her that he was a virile and exciting man. The emotional tide of the introduction left her enchanted and bewildered.

Soon, Margaret (Molly) Newman and Thomas Bernson were the talk of the university and considered a serious couple. One memorable time as they rode along the river path, the evening was delightfully calm and the air near the water refreshing. They discussed their different worlds, their lives, and their paths. Sometimes they rode along without talking, just enjoying the green lane and being with each other.

Their horses, slowly moving along, seemed to sense the serious attitude of their riders. She had known for months he was in love with her. The last day she had seen him, they were riding here when Thomas reined in his mount beside a park bench. Swinging to the ground, he reached for her to dismount, asking her to sit there beside him. There was tenderness within his look, as he asked the familiar question once again.

"Please, Molly, come with me as my wife. I have to leave next week. We have time to be married." Molly remembered this same conservation, which they had had last week, when she tried to discourage him from going. But he was determined to take this job and would not listen.

Sadly, she shook her head *no*. The week after he left, Molly was sitting out on the big veranda of the women's boarding house. She did not look up from her task as the sheriff rode up and dismounted to the tie up his horse in front of the house. It was not until she heard her name called that she realized he was there to speak to *her*. As he told her the terrible news, she felt her vision blurring, her throat closing, and her heart breaking.

Her need for air was urgent. She walked out into the sunshine and turned to quickly walk away, as if she could run from the shocking news of Thomas' tragic, accidental death. Molly spent the days that followed with her grandmother, who lived near the university. Here she learned the sympathy of God as He began to restore her broken heart.

Grandmother's wisdom had helped her, too. She had said to her, "Death can hide, but it cannot divide. When one knows God and when answers are not enough—there is Jesus." Molly clung to these words in the following months. After graduation, she turned down several opportunities to work in Louisville. She knew she needed to go home to help resolve her sorrow.

Now, six months later, Molly was at home at her Idaho mountain ranch. Sitting there in the morning shade, Molly became aware that she had company. It was very quiet; there was no sound that came from the hole in the side of the rocks, but a movement flickered. Along the side of the slope downwind from her, a red fox came out of this cavity and was cautiously sniffing the air. His red-tail plumed, fringed in white.

He took several lopes away from the safety his home provided. He had not gone very far when a slow growling came from deep out of his body. It was answered by another low and frightening growl that came from something just beyond the trees. All Molly could see in the shadows were amber-colored eyes, cold and drooping, until it came out into the sunlight. Then she noticed that the two looked much alike, except one fox was bigger and had a bitten ear with a ragged edge.

The fight did not take long as the young fox was quicker and had longer sharper teeth. He decided when it was over, and that was not until his enemy lay bleeding on the forest floor. Then the young, male . fox trotted back into his place at the rock ledge.

Life and death go on, Molly said to herself. *Sometimes even nature sits and chooses. And today the wind of death did not moan through the trees as it has done before,* she mused.

Then, when she connected back to the passage of the morning, she understood that she was whole again. "Today I am enjoying the freshness of the mountain wind and the odor of pine. For the first time this year, the spirit of the wilderness gave me shelter. I had a friendship with you, Thomas that came along once in a lifetime. I thank you for it, and I thank God for blessing me because of it."

She sighed as she lifted her hands up toward the heavens. "I steadied my course through storms, and now I'm here, Lord. What do you have for me next?"

Leaving this place of prayer, she went to find her horse, Copper, whom she never had to tie up or hobble. He was always there for her.

A "people horse," Shadow had once said about this animal when he helped her train him. Molly found the horse where she left him, relaxing in the shade with his shining hair glowing like his namesake.

"It doesn't matter whether good company walks on two legs or four," she said. "Come on, Copper, let's go home."

When Molly returned to the ranch, she put Copper in the barn and began to give him a good brushing.

"Thank you for a very good outing, Copper, but I think you enjoyed it as much as I did."

She spoke to the young horse with much affection. As she led him out to the pasture, she noticed that Shadow's horse, Scout, was not there.

"Where are you, Shadow? I expected you yesterday. If it was not so late in the day, I would go look for you now. Oh, I fear something has happened to you," Molly thought, as she hurried to the house to see if there was any word of him.

Chapter Two

Harris Davis had broke jail. He was a killer on the loose. His flight from the posse in Fort Boise had led him higher and higher into the northern wilderness. Then he headed east, where he planned to hop a train near the town of Naples and flee from this part of the West.

I had to kill that sheriff, but my arrest would mean a hanging, he thought to himself. *The powerful cattle interests that obtained my hire won't save me now. Just the opposite; they would like to see me dead,* he reasoned. *I need a place to hold up for a week or two 'til the hunt to capture me slows down. It will need to be somewhere I can survive. Maybe a large ranch will hire me since we are into the roundup season. Winter comes early this far north.*

He was talking to himself as he often did, a lone man riding apart most of his adult life. He was a person who had always taken more than he had given: an individual with a devious soul, ready to kill, as he had done many times if it profited him.

Broken sunlight flickered in and out of his eyes, showing his deep, inner hatred. For the next few weeks he thought he would hide out in the mountains and live off the land. He turned in the saddle of his worn out horse and looked back across the range.

The woods were well behind him as he headed toward the rolling, open country. Giving the land behind him a thorough scrutiny, he missed nothing. He was looking for a cloud of dust, for he could see about a mile down. He saw none.

It would be dark soon and Harris knew he was in no danger. He would go on down the trail for a half mile toward the thick trees, then double back to watch this trail. He slouched easily in the saddle and the big horse made a gentle pace across the lush country. He planned to make a dry camp but didn't care if it was wet or dry because he was callous to hardships.

Here was fine land with rolling hills and rich valleys, well-watered by streams, fully capable of supporting and fattening vast herds of cattle.

First I'll need to steal more supplies to get me through several weeks. Then maybe I'll steal a horse or two before I travel to that railhead east of here. It should be easy as these ranchers are very trusting around their places. Maybe this person who made these tracks in the trail today will return before nightfall, and the first part of my plan will be completed, he mused.

Before long he heard the sound of singing, as well as hoof beats on the trail, becoming louder. This made Davis retreat to the cover of some large pine trees, where he could carry out his evil plans. All he had to do next was cock his gun and wait.

On his way home, Shadow watched the late afternoon sun fall upon the infrequently used upper trail. He was a day's ride from home.

Home, he thought. *Our "Three Circle Ranch"—that's where we live, Scout. We are so fortunate to have a place to call home. I could be confined to a shabby reservation and would probably still be fighting against my white man captors if it weren't for this!*

"It will be late before we get back, and Molly and the others will worry about me," he said to his horse as he nudged him into a fast trot. The horse responded, his ears moving back and forward as he listened to his teacher.

Why do I take these long trips out in the mountains alone? Shadow questioned himself, speaking out loud. *At nearly eighty-years-old, do these hills still call me as they did when I was a young brave and I went by the name of Sun Runner? Can I still hear the cry of the hawk and the growl of the bear?* Yet, he reasoned in his mind . . .

This is God's handiwork and it gives me peace. He'd needed this when he'd lost his wife and child. That was a low time in his life.

Then He gave me another family to love and those who also love me. It all happened when I was guided to rescue Molly, he remembered. He smiled at the thought of her, as she was like a granddaughter to him. He thought of the nearly twenty years he had been with the Newman family.

What a blessing they have been to me, he mused. *Comfort in my old age.* Shadow went on thinking back. How he loved them, not only Molly, but also her brother Dalton, who was such a fine young man. The Newmans had shared a lot of love bringing up those two.

Molly was so much like her mother, a very striking likeness of the good-looking light brown haired, blue-eyed woman whose father had come to this mountain country and helped them settle here.

"Yes, so much alike," Shadow thought, and then he smiled, "except 'mama' is a lot better cook! Of course, Molly is a better horseback rider—cause I taught her."

He began a chant, one that reflected great memories and happiness. As Scout began to descend the switchbacks along the most dangerous part of the journey, he slowed. Shadow knew that it was normal for Scout to be cautious—but the horse hesitated in his walk with his ears alert. Then he stopped, and now Shadow became alarmed.

Shadow crouched low in the saddle and began to direct the horse into the trees. Before they could escape into the trees, Shadow felt the impact of the tearing bullet just as he was deafened by its loud report. The pain was sharp and there was the sound that told him bone might be damaged.

The bullet's impact had nearly knocked him from the saddle. He tried to hang on as he moved deeper into the forest. The burning pain in his side was intense and he was fighting a losing battle to stay on the horse. Somewhere in the thicket, he fell unconscious onto a bed of pine needles beneath a tree.

Chapter Three

It was a wild and rocky land with scant brush between bristling peaks. The mountains were high, with glis-tening white tops that lay against a sky of deepest blue. Molly looked down to see that between the peaks lay canyons of valleys luxuriant with grazing land that looked as if the grass had never been touched.

"This is the wilderness whose fierce beauty has claimed my heart," she thought as she released a sigh. Her youthful spirit had been transformed into mature courage by the pioneering years she and her brother had spent in these mountains.

Indeed, she'd been born here. Her parents had come to this remote central Idaho wilderness the first year of their marriage. Her Uncle, who had come to mine silver years before, had told them about the tall grasses in the valleys that would support herds of cattle. He said that they could make a good living ranching here—and they had.

Today, out riding Bourbon, her faithful horse, Molly took much pleasure in observing the beauty of the land. It seemed a long time since she and her friend Elizabeth had returned from school in the East. Molly was now of age to homestead land of her own and could not wait until her father and mother would return from the East with the grant that would make it possible.

Winding up the trail, she hoped that today she would find Shadow Runner, their old Indian friend. He had not been to the ranch for three days. It was not like him to go off without letting them know how long he planned on being gone. He had only taken a day pack with him, and although he could stay more than a day with little supply, she had a vague, strange feeling that an accident had prevented his return.

Shadow had no other family besides them. *Where had he gone?* Molly mused. She had to find him for she felt responsible for his life. At his age, he did not need to be out in early winter storms with no means of protection. She prayed for his safety and health daily. *Why?*

Besides her love for Shadow, she owed him her life. With every fiber she could gather, she would continue her search for him. It was cool and still in the forest. This was easy riding and ahead. There were miles of gradual ascent before the trail entered one of the canyons. Here it was more open, with scarcely any brush. Molly saw deer but no cattle because she was out of the cattle zone.

Within a few miles the forest changed and thickened, and the tall pines obstructed her view. There was a charm in this part of the forest. She could occasionally see the lofty gray crags of the Sawtooth Mountains through openings in the trees. Soon she would begin climbing in steep earnest and must use more caution.

Suddenly a rifle shot, loud and sharp, was fired close by. It gave her a violent start. Molly realized Bourbon had stopped, transfixed, waiting for his master's signal on what to do next.

Who fired that shot? She knew it had to be a stranger. It couldn't be her brother, Dalton, as he had to remain at the ranch with the expectant mares. The birth of Mickey's foal was long overdue. This being her first, they knew she might need help. Their only other neighbors were to the west more than twenty miles away from where she was.

Molly drew her horse behind a dense thicket of pines and waited. She was so glad to find cover, and she breathed a prayer for guidance. To meet strangers alone in these mountains frightened her. Once she had experienced a bad encounter with a miner who did not have good manners. Remembering her escape from that one made her shiver.

She was now more cautious, carrying a rifle when she rode. Now, she held her hand over her horse's nose and turned him away from the trail to keep him quiet. After a long wait, she heard hoof beats. She crouched with her rifle in her hands as she watched the approaching stranger.

He was a lone rider with a small, slain deer strewn in front of the saddle over the neck of his horse. When she could see him more clearly, she was relieved that the encounter on the trail with him did not happen.

It was the look of him that frightened her. He was a lusty, unkempt lout with deep, narrow eyes that pierced like live coals. He was a hard-looking man; his face had an unkempt beard with a large, eagle-beaked nose. His wide shoulders hunched over the saddle as if he had been there a long time.

The horse he was riding was branded with a brand she did not recognize and moved with laboring steps. She wondered where this man's camp was and hoped she would not run into it on her way home. After waiting a long time, she got back on Bourbon and spoke softly to him.

"Come on, it is time to go home," she said in a disappointed tone. The horse traveled at a busy pace on the downhill trail. She could see the other horse tracks ahead of them and prayed that when they came to the fork in the trail these unwelcome ones would proceed north. When they did she sighed with relief.

Her survival as an outdoorswoman had gained Molly much respect among the pioneers of the valley. She certainly had pulled her load around the ranch after finishing school two years ago. But to have trouble alone in this remote area was not what she needed.

The late afternoon shadows seemed to stain the tall pines an inky green. Here she had a feeling of contentment that she never realized in the big cities of the East. *Oh, I miss some of my school friends,* she was thinking, *and some of the good times we had . . . . But I would never go back there to live. This is my home, and God fills my loneliness as I communicate with him. He is my personal friend and He understands how I feel. He will provide a companion for me when I am ready.*

She smiled as she crossed the small stream and looked up to see the falls above. There were broken rainbows covering the higher falls. She looked at the foam beads glittering as they caught the late afternoon light. It was awesome to see such colorful beauty.

"I must come back here again at this time of day and bring my oils and pad," she said out loud to her horse. "This scene needs to be put on canvas."

As Molly began the long descent down the trail, she heard a coyote howl a wild, lonesome sound. The echo of it was drowned out by the sound of water falling on the smooth, washed rocks. She gave Bourbon his head and again began a running walk off the mountain toward the ranch. He needed no coaxing; it was where he too was born, and he could have found the place where they were going in the dark.

The roan proved to be a good traveler. Refreshed by an hour of rest and some fresh grass, the big horse kept the road gait steady for the next two hours. His stride ate up the miles easily and then they began to climb.

The tall stranger on the roan thought about the fact that this was not his country, not the country he knew or liked. It was a stern country, demanding much from those that lived in it.

The things he recognized in this land were the huge expanse of space and the cool, windy emptiness that seemed so strong and silent. *So, why doesn't this country appeal to me?* He wondered. He had spent long hours brooding, as his brother called it, of wanting to be alone. He experienced wonderment that his wealth and business dealings no longer gave him satisfaction. Even the women friends he knew back East lacked something for him. He had to find something to do that gave him significance. Was his unrest because he was lonely? Did his soul need peace?

"Is it my soul, Lord?" He questioned again, aloud. Then he asked himself, *who was Jim Russell, anyway? Was he the same person that had been raised by godly parents in the good Bible churches of the mid-west?*

Since his father had died, he had only thought of God occasionally and that was when he did not attend the worship service on Sunday morning at his home in Kansas City. This country made him acknowledge his Lord more often, and if he would be honest with himself he did not know when he had seemed so alive.

"Perhaps it is the prayers and acknowledgments I have had with you lately, Lord that is bringing up these questions within me. Thank you for this, and I pray I will be more open to what you have in store for me."

When James completed this simple prayer, he seemed to acquire a position of expectancy of *something* that was about to happen. The trail they were on was thin and curled against the slopes of the Sawtooth Mountains like the thong of a whip.

He hoped he was on the right track and would arrive at the mine before dark. His trips to these mining towns had been fruitful for his engineering firm. At the Galena lode near a place called Big Camas the man in charge had also referred him to a new find west of there, somewhere near Stanton Crossing. They said it was a day's ride, so he had supplies only for that day.

Usually Jim traveled with a pack animal loaded down with a lot of necessary camping equipment. After his stay at the mine he was eager to catch the stage coach that would take him to the train at the town of Naples. Kansas City seemed a continent away while he had been traveling, but with the railroad, trains could connect them all within a week.

The map showed only a trail over the Sawtooth Mountains that would have to be taken to reach his destination. He had left the clear wagon trail in the early morning. Now suddenly the roan stopped. His ears moved back and forth, alert, listening, and his eyes were wide with a lot of white showing. Something ahead that the animal could hear was warning them to be cautious.

Jim touched his rifle down in his scabbard with his hand as if it were an old friend, wondering if he should pull the Winchester out and ride with it in his arms, ready for trouble. The man at the outpost where he'd acquired the roan told him to look out for an escaped murderer loose in the valley.

As they moved slowly around the bend, Jim became very alert, not eager to walk into an ambush. Then he heard what the horse had heard. It was and eerie sound like a chant—or was it the cry of a hawk that he heard?

The sound was coming from the direction of the dense trees just off the beaten trail. The sun, which had dropped behind the peaks and clouds, drifted in to obscure the thin, jagged pinnacles. There was snow up there, he remembered, and this storm could be a serious threat for him to get back to catch an eastbound train.

Soon there were fresh tracks of a lone horse on the trail and he could smell smoke from a campfire.

We are not alone in this wilderness; that's for sure. He said to himself. He looked around cautiously and wondered: *Do I want to go there?*

He awakened as suddenly as if a voice had called him or a hand had shaken his shoulder. It was cold, but he knew it would soon be daylight. He smelled an odor that he recognized as sulfa water. Could he be at the hot springs above the ranch?

He lay very still and listened with the nerves of his body. He felt a vibration of a sound, and then heard a noise. He thought it was the beating of drums—drums beating softly as they often did early mornings in his village when he was a young boy. By some miracle was he there?

The urge to chant the Wah-kon-tah prayer, the rising prayer, was so strong. He turned his face to the East—the place of mystery. He formed the beginning words with his mouth. "Ah, hooo," asking "Let the sunrise bless this day," and continued the chant. Then there was another sound and he knew that he was not alone. It was the sound of wood crackling and footsteps on the earth. He could not see beyond the rock opening of the cave. He tried to rise, but found it difficult without any strength. On his knees he was able to crawl forward and peered around to where he heard the noise. A young man was building a fire nearby.

This stranger, dressed in a winter coat and wearing a wide-brimmed hat that did not completely block the view of his kind looking face, busied himself with his task. His long, slim legs were covered with a pair of buffalo chaps worn over dark, wool pants. His riding boots looked worn and wet. James looked up and saw the old Indian with his long, gray hair streaming into his face, starring at him.

"Good morning. I heard your chant so I know I didn't wake you," Jim said. "How are you feeling? Soon we will have some hot tea and I will bring you closer to this fire," he continued.

There was kindness heard in his voice as he spoke to the injured Indian. The sound of the crackling fire and the friendly voice gave the old man much relief. He sat there and for the first time realized his wound had been bandaged and the blood stains were dried on it.

"A good sign," he sighed. "This must be good medicine." With this thought, the aged man sat back against the rock wall and praised God that he had been rescued from near death. James helped Shadow out of the cave and laid him near the fire.

"Some storm we had last night! And you had your own personal storm with the fever. Do you remember?" He spoke to Shadow as he handed him a cup of hot tea.

"Aowaha, and yes I do recall some of our trip here, but do not recall last night. You have rescued me again. I prayed for you to come and find me, you know. God has answered my plea," he answered with broken words.

"Yes, I too believe it was God's leading that brought this about. I am glad to be a part of *the rescue,* as you called it, Shadow. God gave me courage to find you and to find what He desired in my life. Perhaps this is why I am here in these parts." James replied.

"It is best not to question; sometimes I just try to follow," faintly the injured Indian uttered. "You get some rest here by the fire, and we will talk some more about getting you home—maybe tomorrow." James said, as he too relaxed beside the fire.

He trusted he would be able to find Shadow's home. He knew it might be a long walk with only one horse, but he would take one day at a time. Last night he had listened as Shadow, in his high feverish state, rambled on about his life. Much of the story was not clear to him, especially the part about the training of a brown bear and his "companion," hawk.

The story really got confusing when he told of finding, "his Estelle," and releasing the bear in exchange.

I imagine this man has many interesting legends to relate, he thought, *and I would like to hear them sometime. I also know this godly man has real depth in the Christian faith and is the man I would listen to in many situations. I wonder where he calls home, and if I'll get a chance to really become his friend.* With these thoughts, James smiled and wondered how this might be possible.

Chapter Four

Molly felt the cool wash of the vagrant breeze as she stepped out the door of the log house. She loved this place but could not put her mind on why she felt so restless this morning. The late October rain in the night left a freshness on the earth. The gray dawn had moved aside to let the first fingers of sunlight lift over the mountains. After Dalton had left she wondered what she would do by herself again today.

They usually rode the hills together, but this morning, he had offered to help Bert move some bulls to a winter pasture, which would take most of two days. She knew her brother liked to go to the Blazer ranch so he could spend the evenings with Elizabeth, Bert's daughter, and her good friend.

On her way to the barn, Molly saw Price feeding the animals in the corral. He had returned from his ride last night before she had. The rugged cowhand waved hello to her, and said, "I'll be in for breakfast shortly."

"Good," she replied. "Check the mares frequently today, will you please? I may be gone all day."

He nodded in agreement as he watched this pretty young woman walk out to where the horses were. He knew she was going out again to look for Shadow. They were all worried about Shadow not returning home.

Molly went to the corral where Bourbon, her sorrel gelding, was walking around in the morning sun. She stroked the muzzle of the gentle horse, and then she spoke to him.

"Are you as eager as I am to ride out into these hills?" His ears went forward in an answer only she understood. She often talked to her horse, and he responded with much affection as he nuzzled her cheek.

"Good then, come on, let's get ready," she said with enthusiasm. They walked together into the barn where the riding gear hung. Shivering slightly against the dawn's chill, Molly rode the horse along the well-worn ruts that showed heavily in the native grass.

These reminded her of her Uncle Jess, the prospector of the family. He had lived here when the immigrant wagons passed this way and saw the settlements spring up from the floor of the lush valley. He often talked of these mountains and of places where no other had ventured, where warm water bubbled up from the ground and the warmth from the steam melted the snow.

Remembering the hot springs north of the ranch, Molly wondered if she could travel there and still return before nightfall. Saying a silent prayer, she pushed Bourbon into a faster trot, which they continued for a long time. They had begun a steep climb when she eased Bourbon up from his fast stride.

When the trail turned east she saw the dawn splash its deceptive softness on the mountains. It added an atmosphere of loneliness to this remarkable view.

"Loneliness?" She said aloud, even as she questioned why she had called it that. Was she totally honest with herself, she wondered.

I am still young, and a woman with dreams. Was giving up the only man who might ever love me worth all of this? I chose this life instead of a life in the city. Am I doubting myself again?

Oh, I was not sure I really loved him, but I do believe he possessed the qualities I am looking for in a serious relationship. My father and grandfather were such great examples as godly men. I have vowed I shall not be attracted only to physical looks.

Then the answer came to her.

Oh, I am just lonely today without Dalton or mother here. When the horse slowed, she realized they had come to the stream called Warm Springs. This stream, which rolls down from above, washing rocks immaculate for ages, has its origin near a cave where they plan to stop to rest.

"It will be a warm location to get out of the wind," she said to Bourbon. So the horse and rider began their ascent up the mountain following the warm stream. Ahead Molly could see the thick stand of cottonwoods where the overhanging cliff jutted out. She thought it was so beautiful!

The grass around the stream in this small alcove was such a vivid green it was startling to the eye. She remembered that Shadow had talked of the special medicine the hot springs seemed to have. He said it contained a mineral that God had placed there and one soaking in it could receive healing.

Startled and surprised, she heard voices and quietly got off the horse to tie Bourbon up. She took her rifle from the saddle and, staying in the cover of the trees, began to walk in the direction from which she heard the talking. When she got closer she peered around a tree, and what she saw nearly caused her to cry out.

Lying on the ground with a blanket over him was her beloved Indian friend, Shadow Rider. The stranger that was bending over him appeared to be applying a white cloth to Shadow's side. Molly gasped under her breath.

"He's hurt!" She saw red stains on the bandage but still waited and watched. The stranger spoke to the injured man with a kindness she had not heard since her grandfather had lived with them. She saw the stranger's hands tenderly work over the wound and saw Shadow respond with an agreeing nod.

No longer could Molly contain herself. Now that she felt it was safe, she ran up to their camp, shouting out an Indian war hoop. James jumped up, surprised. He stood to intercept her coming directly at the injured man on the ground, not seeing the smile on Shadow's face because he was too busy looking at the most attractive woman he had ever seen.

Molly had lost her hat and her flowing light hair danced over her face as she ran. He caught her seconds before he thought she would have fallen on the wounded man.

"Stop!" he commanded, "You must go easy because the wound could begin bleeding again."

He held her in his arms for a moment. She gasped when she looked into his warm, blue eyes. Then she replied, "Oh, yes, I . . . I will."

He released her and she knelt down beside Shadow Runner. Molly reached for the hand of her Indian friend and they sat like that for a long moment, smiling at each other.

31

"Oh Shadow, tell me, how are you? How did you get here? Where is your horse, Scout? What has happened," she asked breathlessly.

"My Estelle," he began. "So you have found me. I knew you would come. I am better today, but this kind man has saved my life."

He pointed to the tall stranger near the fire. Molly turned and looked again at the stranger Shadow was talking about. This time she really saw him.

A smile lit across his steel blue eyes as he gazed back at her. His eyes upon her face made her heart skip a beat.

"I'm Molly, and I am indebted to you for your care of Shadow," she said breathlessly as she held out her hand, offering a friendly introduction. His long stride carried him quickly to her.

"Hello, Molly, I'm James Russell," he said. The stranger's voice was soft and his eyes were steady. His hand grasped hers as they stood looking into each other's eyes. A long fringe of Molly's hair fell into her face. She withdrew her hand from his to push it back, but before she could, he raised his other hand to do the delightful task.

"You look perfectly lovely, Molly, whoever you are," James stammered as he backed away. "My name is Molly Newman of the Three Circle ranch."

She was still blushing, wondering why she felt so shy. This was not like her, and yet he did not make her feel uncomfortable. "I have been out searching for Shadow for the last three days," she continued.

"Our family's ranch is south of here, about a five-hour ride." She hesitated, looking down at Shadow.

"Now I must ask you, what has happened here? Did you injure Shadow? Was there an accident?" she inquired, looking into his handsome face. He held up his hand to stop the barrage of endless questions.

"No. No. I will tell ya'll what I do know and we will let him tell you the remainder. Two days ago I found the old gentleman nearly dead with a bullet in his side. He was lying just off the trail from the Camas Country Mine. I brought him here, at his suggestion, to get out of a storm.

"I dressed his wound, and took care of his needs. I knew I couldn't leave him. I was waiting until he could ride to take him to the nearest place where he could get care—but I don't think that is going to be until tomorrow or the next day." He said all this in one breath, not giving her time to interrupt.

"Oh," Molly said, "I *am* sorry. I didn't mean to be unkind. I am much indebted to you, Mr. Russell."

"Well, that's nice," said James, "and I can't think of a prettier girl I would want to be indebted to me," he teased. "But I would help anyone who was bushwhacked. It's such a low down thing to do to someone, then leave them alone to die."

His anger rose up in his voice as he spoke. Molly turned to Shadow.

"Now, tell me how you let it happen. "My Estelle," he began with a dejected face," I have much turmoil. My great bear has failed to step in my tracks and cover them with his as he had promised, so the enemy couldn't' follow my trail. Now I am afraid of the bear and I have no protector."

He sat with the look of a defeated man and rocked back and forth with his arms wrapped around himself. Molly was shocked because she had never seen Shadow in such a state. She looked at James for help. He spoke up at her silent request.

"Shadow, you all have been badly wounded, and are not yourself. After one more night's sleep and more of your pas-she-co soup for the evening meal, you feel better. Now lay back, and we'll fix us some food."

The old Indian obeyed and Molly covered him with the only blanket she saw in camp. She smiled at him and quietly whispered an Indian word of endearment. He gave her a hollow smile, then fell to sleep almost immediately.

Molly sat there for a while with his hand holding hers. James began to build up the fire and fix the evening meal. He glanced at the pretty young girl often—unable not to do so. Then he leaned back, studying her, and said, "Sure hope you all like this soup, it is about all we have left."

The smile held considerable charm, Molly thought, and his big shoulders added to his rugged appearance. He had a dark Irish look with a bony, bearded face to go with his lean build. His blue eyes sparkled and Molly noted when his eyes met hers they were very calm.

"OK Miss, I must ask you something," he said, pausing until he could get the words right.

"Your name is Molly, but he called you Estelle," he questioned her. I heard you speak Shoshone to him, but you are too fair to be Indian."

"I will answer you part of it and sometime you must ask Shadow the rest," she began.

"Shadow has given me back my life. When I was a little girl, I wandered away from our home. I had been lost in the hills for two days and was near death when he found me and nursed me back to health. As soon as I was well enough he took me back to the ranch and he has been there ever since. He called me *Estelle* during that time, so he still does. But what about you, James Russell? I note a tiny bit of drawl in your speech," she said, still looking into his handsome face.

James smiled at her question and began to tell her where he was from and why he was on the trail. Then he told her how he found Shadow.

"You heard strange sounds?" She asked him to repeat in detail how he veered off the trail and just *happened* to find Shadow. "I never thought much about it, until I just now recounted it to you all, that it *was* pretty unusual," he said thoughtfully.

"As I recall, it was the sound of a hawk that stopped me—a loud screech that stopped my roan in his tracks. This was followed by a deep chant that seemed to be accompanied by a drum beating. When I urged my horse on, he didn't want to go on down the trail. He snorted and moved sideways. His eyes were showing white and he was very tense, like he smelled a large animal nearby.

He hadn't shied all day at anything and I knew he smelled some kind of danger. So, I allowed him to move deeper into the trees a ways off the trail. I was very cautious because I was warned about a jail break from Fort Boise. The smell of smoke was stronger and I feared I might be walking into an unfriendly camp. Then I saw your Indian friend, lying nearly unconscious on the ground beside a small fire.

"It sounds like your horse led you to Shadow, and like he got some help from Someone or something," she said, then waited for his opinion.

"Oh, I agree," he replied as he watched her pretty, azure eyes sparkle as she talked about a possible miracle. The softness of her emotions showed on her face. And that face! How pretty she was with her full, red lips and straight, white teeth revealing a happy smile.

"You sound like you are in a hurry to get back east to your family," Molly said, suddenly changing the subject. She wanted him to talk so he would take his eyes off her mouth. It was hard for her to think with him so close to her as they sat beside the fire.

"Yes, I guess you could say that," he said, bringing his mind back to answer. "I—I have been away nearly a month. We are a close family with firm faith in our Creator. My folks and my brother run our engineering company in Kansas City. I do a lot of outside sales for the company. I like it all right. I could never sit at a desk all day." he replied as his eyes rested amiably on Molly.

"No, she thought. "You are not the type for desk work; I can see that. And what do I see?" she asked herself. *Oh, God will You help me to be wise?* Molly pleaded in a silent prayer.

While Shadow slept, Molly and James easily conversed around the fire. There was a relaxed note in their conversation, as if they could confide in each other.

Molly soon learned that it was easy for James to talk about his family, but he evaded the things about him that she wanted to hear. When he spoke of others, she could tell he loved family and close friends deeply, because his concern was shown about them. His parents sounded like people she would like to meet. But why this desire occurred to her, she wondered.

"What about the trail out of here and back to the ranch?" he asked. She was staring at him, but did not reply.

"I mean is it a good trail for Shadow to ride back on, even though he is weak? James again questioned her, looking at Molly with a tilt to his head, trying to figure out why she was so quiet all of a sudden.

"Oh, yes, it is a good path—not dangerous." She quickly recovered and blushed over her dreaming.

"We do not have to leave real early, and it will give Shadow more time to rest," she said.

"Good, however, I will ride with him if I have to," James said with concern. Again concern for her injured friend was in James's voice as she smiled a shy smile to his reply and again felt her face blush.

"You sound like your company is quite successful. So what are you doing adventuring out here," she asked, changing the subject back to him.

"Other things mean more to me than gold," James replied to the pretty brunette sitting beside him.

"You know—peace of mind, heart, and soul." He now believed her hair was the color of sunshine sifting through pale brown leaves.

"And, if blessed enough, finding real love besides—you know," he added quietly, watching her dancing eyes. Molly looked up at him quickly, but did not know how to reply.

Chapter Five

Walk with me down to the large spring where I can get water for the tea, Molly? James asked. He had enjoyed talking with her into the late afternoon. To Molly, time seemed to pass so quickly here with James and Shadow.

"Tea? You surprise me, Mr. Russell," Molly smiled.

When he looked at her, he saw eyes that held the softness of spring flowers. He had never met anyone like this Molly.

"Molly," he repeated as he held out his hand to help her rise to her feet. She smiled at the way he said her name, accepting his kind help, and they began their hike to the spring.

Down the trail, he stumbled over a rock in the path. It was as if he couldn't concentrate. And where did he come up with the stuttering he seemed to be doing? There was this warm feeling inside of him, such as he had never had before. She laughed with a lilting sound and asked something playful about who would carry the water back from the spring.

As he glanced at her and thought about her tease, his smile turned into a wide grin. She liked his face. It held softness for her. They walked on.

The two were about half way there when a flock of wild ducks, frightened out of the water, flew up below them. Molly stopped quickly in amazement and James ran right into her, nearly knocking her over. He held out his arm and caught her around the waist.

"Sorry," was all he said, as his embrace lingered there. Molly smiled, turned her face toward him, and brushed her fingers on his arm, then up the side of his cheek, where she felt the soft beard touch the edge of his upper lip before she spoke.

"It's OK. I won't break." What happened next was as natural as the sunrise. The soft kiss he planted on her lips lingered there for a few moments. When he felt her hand in his hair, he drew her closer, kissed her hair, and breathed in her soft-summer scent. He held her for a moment longer, not wanting to ever let her go.

"I shouldn't have done that. I meant no disrespect to you all." When they parted, he added, "I must confess, though, that I wanted to do that from the first moment I saw you running towards me." He looked at her with a twinkle in his eye, eager for her response.

"Running towards *you?*" she argued. "I was trying to reach Shadow, if you will remember." He smiled and said, begrudgingly, "Thank you all for reminding me of that."

She turned to go on down to the water, filled her container, and waited while he filled his, too.

"What kind of tea are we going to have?" Molly asked, wanting to change the mood of things.

"It's Chokecherry tea," James said, smiling at her. "Yesterday Shadow told me to go pick them down near the warm, protected area of the spring. It is for healing and stamina, he said."

"Well, you do not need any more stamina," she replied and smiled as she passed by him. On the walk back, they talked about Shadow and how soon he would be able to ride. James admitted he did not really know the answer to that question.

"Shadow is a hard one to figure out, but his wound looks as if it is so much better and it had quit bleeding. We'll have to see in the morning."

Molly could see that he was a man of few words, as there was only the apology that he shouldn't have kissed her. She smiled at the incident, although she knew in her heart that she had encouraged it.

Supper was eaten with more quietness than Molly could visualize. She was glad she had time to think about her feelings. She was being foolish over a man who was a complete stranger to her, someone she had just met. Although they had talked and she had had a chance to find out why he was here and where he was from, what else did she know about him?

With a slight smile, she reasoned in her mind that she knew he was kind and decent. She had seen that and heard it in his action and conversation, and in his concern for Shadow. Then too, there was that apology to her concerning the kiss. What was he thinking right now? She glanced over toward him and could not believe that each on their separate paths had come together from more than a thousand miles apart.

James was aware that Molly was looking at him. He was thinking that he was pleased she had come into his life. He knew now in his heart that life was good and that today it left nothing else to be desired.

The early morning light caused a stir among the horses as their blows and stomps woke the two late risers that were huddled around the small smoking fire. When Molly moved, she realized she was snuggled up against James's chest. She looked up at him to see him smiling at her. He removed his arm from around her shoulder, and with a sparkle in his eye, teased her.

"If we keep this up, people will believe we are fond of each other." He rose and stretched himself to his full, six-feet-three-inch frame and felt the muscles ripple along his arms and shoulders.

He began to rebuild the smoldering fire. She watched him as he continued with long strides toward the horses. He hobbled them so they could graze, then went down to the big stream to get water for the morning tea.

Molly's attention was drawn to Shadow Runner because he had awakened and was trying to stand up. She reached him quickly and, when he leaned on her, he successfully stood. She could see that his side was still hurting, but he had more color in his face, and looked at her with clear eyes. She let him speak first.

"It is time to return to the warm haven that has bound us together, little Estelle," he said plainly.

"Yes, after tea and some biscuits I brought with me we will go home. God has been good to us, Shadow. He gave you back to us."

She spoke with tenderness, then helped him sit on a stump near the fire. He smiled at her, knowing they shared a common faith. When Shadow was young, he had met a missionary who was on his way to the Oregon Territory. The missionary had shared his faith in Christ with him, and led Shadow to the Lord.

The Whitman group spent several months in Fort Boise during the time that Shadow's father was trading there. As they became friends, it was also this preacher of the group who was influential in helping Shadow go to the agricultural school in New England. While Shadow was at this school, he learned more about his new Christian faith. He also became proficient in the breeding of cattle attending classes there.

After breakfast the horses were saddled for the trip home. As they helped Shadow mount Bourbon, the old Indian did not make a sound. His face was ashen and they knew he felt weak after days of high fever. It was agreed that on the first part of the return journey Molly would ride the roan and James would walk, leading Bourbon.

As they began the long walk back down the trail, a silence that comes with morning in a forest came upon them—a kind of silence that speaks. There were game scattered here and there, and a buck came out to scan the fresh hills with dubious approval, then turned, shouldering a path to more familiar levels.

The riders stopped to watch him, only glancing at each other with a smile. The sky was a deep, polished blue and the sun was beginning to stretch its rays over the mountaintops, warming the earth. Frequently as the morning sun shone on the trail, James saw the top of Molly's hair catch its glow—as if a halo was upon her hair.

He smiled at the illusion, but believed she did look like an angel to him. Then he recalled the evening before, when Molly and he had sat around the campfire talking until the early hours of the morning. The night had been unusually warm and the sky particularly clear. They were two mere humans that had been allowed the privilege of seeing the heavens showing the Northern Lights as the variations built, leaping toward God. Never before had he seen them so beautiful!

James knew also there was something building and leaping in their relationship with one another. He had found it hard to keep his eyes off Molly, and he touched her arm or hand every chance he got. She was more guarded than at first, when she had been down by the pond with him. He wondered if she had had second thoughts about him. Because of this, he hadn't been aggressive.

He knew very little about this Molly Newman, but he had a special attraction to her that he had never had to any other woman. He had seen her kindness to both himself and Shadow. He felt that she possessed the ability to be thoughtful at the right times.

When Molly looked him in the eyes, he felt his blood rise. When they touched, he wanted to hold her next to him and never let her go. Molly heard James behind her and wondered if he had caught any

40

sleep at all last night. She remembered his touch as they sat around the fire gazing at the heavens. She knew she needed to be careful. The memory of his kiss was still with her, and she could easily have given in to the longing for just one more, but was afraid it would not stop there.

Last night they had learned more about each other. Their backgrounds were very similar. Both came from a rich ranching heritage, with grandparents owning large ranches in the Midwest. She learned that he, too, had an older brother. His name was Luke, and the brothers were very close.

"He was with me during several childhood illnesses and always read to me," James said about him.

"Although I would rather have been out riding one of my grandfather's thoroughbred horses, many times Luke would take me for a buggy ride. We would go down to the river and watch the riverboats go by. We learned the names of the ferryboats and where they were going. I think it was there I learned to be curious about what made them run. Perhaps that is why I studied engineering at the University."

"Tell me, what Luke is like?" she coaxed. "Luke was a quiet boy. I'd say shy and reserved. He read a lot, and he made me inquisitive about what was in books. As I grew up, I spent more time reading good literature."

Molly enjoyed hearing of James's youth. It was a side of him she needed to know more about, and he already knew more about her than she knew about him. When he'd asked, she'd had told him about her uncle first seeing this country when he found silver in the mine that was near their property.

"This was where Dalton and I loved to go in our younger years, when we could," she had said. Molly also told James how she loved this valley and was planning on homesteading a place twenty miles east of here.

She remembered the surprised look on his face.

The morning wore on in a steady trek with no breaks until James said, "Let's rest here. I want to check Shadow's bandage."

"Good idea," Molly agreed, but she was feeling guilty about her riding and James walking—especially in those wet boots. She was glad for the time to stop and refresh themselves with some cool drinking water.

Shadow rested on the dry grass and drank from the stream. Molly and James sat on a log overlooking the silvery stream. Molly enjoyed watching James' admiring eyes upon her as he began to tell her why he was really in the Northwest.

"God challenges us with a golden opportunity many times, and I knew my life could stand improvement," he related. "I had no goals, and when I heard you all tell of the land you wish to homestead I was envious of you. My search for happiness and personal peace of mind didn't seem to be heading anywhere, but now I know that this day, like all other days, is a special gift of God, and it is because I have met you—Molly.

"Something has changed. Perhaps my destiny is in the balance, and right now I can only say to *you all* that I want to know more about you and your family. Perhaps I could spend some time at your ranch . . ."

He touched her hand as she let his fingers entwine with hers for several moments. She liked the way he made her feel, close and special.

Molly drew in a deep breath. She was taken by his earnest talk with her. She could feel her heart beating fast in her chest and knew it was excitement about James staying longer to be with her. When she was able, she answered him.

"James, I am sure we would welcome the one who saved Shadow's life."

"Oh Molly, let me hear you all say that *you* would like to get to know me," James asked with sincere pleading in his voice.

"Well, Mr. Russell, it is said one's worth is determined by his deeds, and I believe you worthy of my attention because of your deeds." She smiled at him, then got up and readied herself for the completion of the ride to her home. When it was time to remount the horse, Molly spoke again.

"James, this roan horse of yours is not even tired, and he is big enough for two to ride. Don't you think so?"

"Well Molly, I thought you all would never ask!" he scolded as he swung up behind her on the back of the saddle.

"Now, how do I hang on?" he teased, then remembered he must mind his manners and act like the Christian man his father raised him to be.

Molly ignored him. She trusted him to be a gentleman. With Bourbon leading the way carrying his burden, they began to make good time bound toward the ranch. James noticed Molly turning in the saddle, occasionally glancing at him as they talked. Then she turned away, but not before he saw a smile begin to appear on her slightly moist lips.

Oh, those lips! He remembered them well, and it was all he could do not to put his arms around her slim waist. "Maybe she does have feelings for me," he thought.

Molly could feel James' warm breath on her neck. It made her want to look at his handsome face, but she kept her head turned as much as she could for the rest of the journey. They conversed often about what had happened with Shadow and wondered where this evil person was who had done this to him. The hills fell away before them, revealing a wide, high plain. In the late afternoon light, the hills were like a softly spun shadow.

Molly loved to see the sight of her home from this high trail at this time of day. James thought the rugged new land seemed a far cry away from the warmth and flow of the place he knew as home. Molly could see smoke rising from the fireplace in the house and felt the warm welcome that she hoped would always be there for her.

Neither of them noticed what seemed like a vague breeze—there was a rustling of the willows near the creek. So when a large, shadowy, brown figure moved through the twigs, they were not aware of what was roaming the grounds of the Three Circle ranch. Riding along in silence, their heads looked up to the sharp whistle of a red-tailed hawk as they watched it soar high into the heavens above them.

Chapter Six

It was late afternoon when the three rode by the winter pas-tures, where contented cattle grazed and milled about on dry, fall grass. Golden sunlight lay upon part of the house just below them. Shadows in the lane were dark and pleasant, with trees that hung wide and protective over the large, log home.

More than a mile from the barn, the glacier-fed creek that runs through the pasture made a long, sweeping curve through a thick stand of Quaking Aspen before winding out on the flat land. There the silvery stream moved more slowly by the front porch of the house.

Dalton was nowhere in sight. Molly had left James and Shadow at the bunkhouse, but was looking for Price to help James lift Shadow off the horse and into his bedroom.

Molly could smell Lee Chi's bread baking as she reined her horse up to the front door. Lee came running out as she dismounted.

"Missy Molly," he whooped in his Chinese accent, "where you been all night? We worry about you and Price go look for you."

"I'm OK, Lee, see." She gave him a quick hug to reassure him. "Would you go help with Shadow? He is at the bunkhouse."

"Yes, Missy! I'm eager to see Shadow. I so glad you have brought him home. Is he all right?"

"Yes, we think he will be. There is a man with him whose name is James. He will help you. Go now!" She smiled at his concern. As she entered the house, she was moved that Shadow had refused to stay here in the house. He had insisted he would be more rested in his own surroundings. Perhaps he was feeling better. Just to be home should make him feel better, she believed.

Home—this house! She smiled as she entered the main room. She looked around and sighed. "Comfortable is what I am here," she said aloud. Molly knew it was a house built with love, a fine, strong, log house. It was not like the large stone one grandmother had in Kentucky, but it stood firmly at the center of their lives.

The walls of the house were huge pine logs about forty feet long, and were chinked with little poles and plaster. Hand-hewn log partitions divided it into three rooms on the main level. A large, open stairway partially divided the main room and the kitchen. The floors had been made by splitting smaller logs through the middle and laying them flush with each other. They were polished with linseed oil and were smooth enough to dance on.

Through the front windows she could see the large, covered porch—her favorite place. It was filled with many memories of the times she'd spent there with her grandfather. She went to the kitchen and prepared some coffee, knowing how James had missed it the last two days.

"James," she said aloud in a soft voice, smiling at herself for saying his name. Was she being silly? *At twenty-two, I should be more grown up,* she thought. And yet, she knew James was kind and considerate and that he had similar attributes as her father and grandfather. In the wash area off the kitchen she busied herself changing clothes and fixing her hair.

Reflecting in the small mirror there, she saw a well-tanned face with wide, blue eyes, long, light brown hair, a small nose, and a mouth with full-rounded lips.

"You have your mom's features," her Grandmother had said to her on the day she graduated from college. Through the window she watched James approach towards the house. This tall, midwestern stranger who had ridden into her life seemed to be just what she'd been waiting for. Yet they were so far apart in their future plans.

What will come of a romance like this? Molly asked herself this question as she said a quiet prayer for God's answer. Outside, James seemed to hesitate, studying the house and yard. Then he stopped before the house. He could see Molly through the window, and a tangled rush of emotions flooded his senses like leaves in an autumn gale. He felt like a drifter, and to him *just someplace* was no place at all. He had always drifted on, farther west.

Someone else could have taken this job at the firm and traveled to the great Northwest, but he was restless, never wanting to stay in one place. He had been doing this for the past five years since getting out of college. Now he envied these people. They had found their somewhere; it was here, and they were really living and enjoying it.

When James went into the house, he realized it had a sense of order that was not just simple, but rightness defined every room. He glanced over the room's furnishings—two horsehair couches, a large, round oak table with straight chairs, and other wooden, padded ones, as well. Continuing to examine more closely the old pictures, candle holders, and many family items, he knew it was a home full of the heartbreak and triumph that had shaped this family.

"I can see Molly here, and why she loves this home," he thought as he turned around looking at it. He felt there was a warm, everyday welcome here, and he liked it. He glanced up as Molly entered from the kitchen with two cups of hot coffee. He watched her set the cups on the table. She was wearing a long, flowing skirt that clung to her slim body in the right places. It made her even more charming than he had imagined.

When she turned toward him, he had not yet caught his breath and could barely speak. Molly saw the devotion in his eyes and stood quietly for a moment, enjoying his approval, letting him drink her in. Then she extended her hand toward his—and he softly grasped it, and then tenderly pulled her toward himself.

"Molly," was all he said, as their lips met in a desire they had both been holding back. There was no patience in this kiss. He took and she gave. She poured herself into the kiss. Until now, she had pretended that desire wasn't necessary as there was more than passion— *until now.*

The emotions that she showed nearly swallowed him. He was dazed in knowing that nothing would ever be simple again. It nearly frightened him, the desperation of the flame he felt when they came together. He wanted to reason while he could, but the taste of her only caused him to draw her closer. His hand tightened in her hair, though his mouth became gentle on her lips. Feeling a hesitation in his lovemaking, Molly pulled back first.

"Wait, this is too fast," she admitted, resting her head on his shoulder. "No, I've waited years for you." he said, unwilling to release her. She continued to protest, and managed to step away.

"I know that because of the way I responded to you it might seem"

"Molly dear, you cannot deny we have something very special." He held her by the shoulders and made her look directly at him. "Y . . . yes, maybe, but is that the most important thing in a relationship?" she asked, fighting the longing.

"Molly, we can work it out, talk it out. Time takes care of a lot of it," he replied.

"Oh, James, you know that before I met you I was lonely," she began. "I want you, but I don't—"

"Look, Molly, I wasn't trying to hurt you or take advantage of you. I wouldn't," James interrupted. "But I will confess I am glad you broke up that kiss," he said, with a grin on his appealing lips. Just then there was a commotion outside and through the window they saw Molly's brother dismount from his horse.

"Dalton is back!" Molly exclaimed.

After introducing Jim to Dalton and an explanation of what had happened the last three days, it was time to eat the supper Lee had prepared for them. Lee had taken Shadow out his food, then Price and he joined him so they, too, could hear of Shadow's unexpected adventure.

Molly, Dalton, and James enjoyed getting to know one another better while they ate the delicious meal. When they were finished, the two men went out to the barn to check on the mares. Molly was glad they were getting along so well. She did not know when she felt such happiness. It was a happiness she never knew was possible. She remembered James's arms around her and his lips pressed against hers. He was everything she'd dreamed of, so tender and understanding. She could not believe any man could have the effect on her that James did. Her thoughts enveloped her and swept over her.

"I am falling in love with him," she sighed softly and wondered how she could love him as she had only known him these few, short days.

Are my instincts to be trusted? Didn't mother tell me she knew father only a few short weeks before she knew he was the one for her? Is a certain time pattern required here to trust my adult emotions?

Just then James returned to the kitchen to find Molly seated at the table. He sat down beside her, looking at her closely.

"You seem flushed. Are you feeling all right?" he asked, touching her cheek.

"I'm fine," she answered, blushing when he ruffled her hair slightly. She studied his lean, Celtic face, and then asked him, "What can I do for you, Mister Russell?"

James, lowering his head, gave her a quick kiss and replied, "I came in to ask if y'all would take me up to the Willow Creek silver mine tomorrow. Dalton said Mr. Spencer was up there. He's the person I need to see about the machinery our firm sells."

Molly had not yet recovered from her earlier reflections, and James sitting here next to her in the dim evening light, did not help. She almost said, "Yes, yes, how could I ever say anything but yes to you—forever?" It was a moment before she could say *anything*.

"We'll need to leave early as it is a long day's ride up and back."

"Great!" he said, as he tenderly reached for her and pulled her closer to him. He took her face in his hands and kissed it several times, lovingly and gently, but the kiss that landed on her lips lingered with firmness.

It was in the sweet hush of early morning that they left for the mine. The dawn rose with bright crimson hues above the ragged mountains and spread its warmth across the dewy wetland.

Molly realized that James had been in a good-hearted mood at breakfast this morning, but she had not slept well, arguing half the night with herself about the differences James and she seemed to have.

She had a love for this western land but James talked of his eager return to the Midwest. She wished her mother were here. She would have some answers for her. The two riders rode on . . . through ever-changing vistas of timbered slopes and craggy peaks.

About a mile from the dig they saw a set of fresh horse tracks. When James saw them, there was a frown on his face and he questioned it to himself.

Who would be coming up the track, too? Was it another visitor to the mine, or was this the same person that caused us the difficulties we have been having? After what happened to Shadow, I should not have asked Molly to come. It may be this same murderer is still in the area. I must be watchful, there are lives here that I care about, he acknowledged.

The *glory hole* was complete, with its small lake and running stream. It was a beautiful place with an abundance of beautiful mountain scenery. James and Molly rode by the old cemetery that was down the road north of the mine. There were two remote graves near a lone pine tree that stood with intriguing grave markers to tell the tale of their deaths.

Molly remembered reading on one headstone that a man had been killed by Indians. She shivered as she recalled hearing the rest of the story. She was only ten- years-old, and although Dalton often accompanied her, it wasn't until she was older that she could visit those gravesides again.

Near the stream there were the old log buildings that served as living quarters for the miners. Molly remembered the summer days when she sometimes came here with her Uncle. There was a quiet solitude before the crews moved in. She enjoyed the springtime of mountain splendor—with the early wildflowers showing brightly in the fresh grass.

In the summer there was much bustle and the activity of busy miners pushing loaded ore carts from the tunnels mouth. In the woods, some men were busy falling trees for mine timbers and others began digging many miles of water ditches that were urgently needed. That had been an exciting time for her, and as these memories came bursting forth she told James of Idaho's bonanza years in the old camps and mills.

Molly talked of the turbulent and troubled lives of pioneer miners with such passion that James wanted to reach out and touch her. It gave him an insight into how much compassion Molly had, and he smiled at his pick of such a girl. He was beginning to think she was indeed just right for him.

When they arrived at the mine no one was around. There was not even an animal tied up near the entrance.

"Do you think we have missed him?" Molly asked. As James dismounted near a tied-up tree, an unseen rifle cracked sharply with an angry slap-kicking a four-inch splinter from the tree right next to his head with no damage. James yelled for Molly.

"Get down, and get over here!" James took his rifle from the saddle and ran for cover behind a large tree, trying to cover Molly's approach. Molly and Bourbon ducked around a tree, where she dismounted quickly and hurriedly tied up the horse. Then she ran toward James, keeping herself behind trees as she made he way toward him.

"We're sitting ducks out here. Follow me," James whispered as he grabbed her hand and pointed to the mine opening. Keeping their heads low, they dashed inside the mine. He kept between her and the gunman, thinking there would be more shooting, but none came.

Where was he? What was he after? Why were there no more attempts to shoot us? James wondered. When they got inside and out of gunshot, James turned to her.

"Are you all right?"

"Yes," she said in a low voice. He looked at her and cursed under his breath for bringing her here.

"I'll stand guard while you all look for a lantern," he said when he finally got his voice back. Shortly, she returned with the lantern, carrying a shovel, also.

"I thought this might come in handy before we get out of here," she remarked, lifting the shovel.

"What do you mean?" he questioned. "We need to find another way out of here," she answered, handing James the lantern.

"Hardly. We could get lost and starve to death. There may be fifteen miles of workings," he said, alarmed. She went to him.

"James, I am aware you are fearful for my safety, but I know this mine and I think I can find the uphill tunnel that exits to the top of this mountain ridge," said Molly. "Remember, I was here a lot when my uncle opened this mine."

"Maybe that *is* a good idea. We could be here till dark with him out there," James replied.

After he lit the lantern, they began their adventure deep into the mine. A drift took them into perpetual darkness except for the light they carried. Molly held James' hand and said, "It is good to have the light." *And you,* she was thinking.

"Yes," he replied, tightening his grip on her hand. "But where are the workers and Mr. Spencer?"

"Do you think they were shot?" Molly asked. James did not answer. His instincts told him to get Molly to safety and to her home as fast as possible. They walked up the incline of the shaft, climbing as quickly as they could in the dim light. There were many obstacles in the path, but James was glad they did not have to use the shovel before they saw a small light at the end of the shaft.

"There is the opening," Molly exclaimed, excitedly.

"This shaft house opening should be on top of the ridge, just below the summit we came up."

At the aperture the sunlight was very bright, and while they waited patiently for their eyes to adjust they listened for any sounds. James peered out cautiously, studying each area for any motion. There were trees all around them, and he saw a few birds—watched them some before he climbed out.

Still keeping his head low, he ran for the nearest tree, and then signaled for Molly to follow. He kept her covered, ready with the rifle as she ran towards him. He prayed. Nothing. No rifle shots. Not a sound, except for their breathing as he caught her and held her close for a long time.

Harris Davis watched the two riders ride by on their way to the mine. It was a good thing he had heard their voices or they would have caught up with him on his slow, tired horse. When they stopped their horses near the trees of the mine entrance, he raised his rifle and took aim.

It was the large roan horse he was after, so the rider would have to go. Slowly he began to squeeze the trigger.

An instant before he did, there was a movement to his right. His horse saw it, too, or was it the shrill cry of a hawk that made the horse jump?

"I missed," he uttered in disgust. Quickly getting off the jumping horse, he tried for another shot, but too late. The two riders were just ducking into the mine entrance toward safety. He cursed again. Then he saw that the roan horse was free and appeared to be moving his way.

"Easy prey!" he sneered. He kept his horse between himself and the fleeing riders as he slowly maneuvered his mount up to the big roan. He caught him easily and thought he may as well take the other horse, too.

Where was it? It was just here. He heard a noise behind him and realized his own horse, with what gear he had remaining, was trotting down the trail. Something had frightened him. Another sound made him turn quickly. He saw something. It was more than a frameless twitch of motion—it was a brown streak.

At first he thought it was the other horse, but it was nowhere in sight.

"What the—?" he said nervously. He could feel tension mounting everywhere. It seemed to be advancing like a slow, relentless flood. It was beginning to push at him. Harris felt a shiver run through his spine that he tried to shrug away. Shaking his head, he mounted the roan and pushed him into a fast gait. He rode into the trees and down the south trail, trying to catch his loose horse.

The evil that Harris Davis bore was as if he had diffused a black specter into the forest, leaving a dark gloom in his wake. It was darkness so dense that he never saw the dark shadow moving toward him in the trees.

Thirty minutes later, Molly and James cautiously and quietly climbed down from the ridge in view of the mine entrance. Molly touched James, then gestured toward her untied horse near a large tree.

They approached Bourbon and his head shot up. His large, brown eyes recognized her, but he made no sound. There was a quietness that she could not define.

Sometimes in these mountains there are things that are very hard to understand, Molly thought. James was looking at the ground, where he noticed many tracks. He picked up a shiny, empty shell cartridge.

An odd caliber, he thought as he put it in his shirt pocket. Molly came over to him and, leading Bourbon, tightened the cinch, then put the reins on his neck. After James mounted, she put her foot in the stirrup and swung up behind him.

When Molly put her arms around James chest, he heard her breathe a prayer, then seem to relax as she finished talking to her Maker. They made the only commotion James could hear in the forest as the horse nervously stomped the earth with his hooves, knowing he was going home.

A large-shouldered animal, fat and deceptively lazy-looking, was sauntering across the grass in the meadow near the south trail. He, of course, made no fuss at all, but the wind from the red-tailed hawk's broad wings cracked lightly through the green willows near the stream.

Chapter Seven

Molly and James arrived back at the ranch at about dark. The first thing Molly did was go find Dalton to tell him what a narrow escape they'd had. She learned he had gone to meet their parents at the stage station at Stanton Crossing.

It was a day's ride there. Accordingly, Dalton would not return until the next day. She was not sure if their parents would be on that stage or the one that was coming the following week. Molly wished her brother had been there because he would know what to do about the awful scare they'd just experienced.

Molly related to the others what had happened and their narrow escape from the bushwhacker at the mine. When James showed the empty cartridge to Shadow, he examined it, looking at Molly with savage eyes.

"He used my gun, I'm sure. There aren't many rifles that are that caliber in this area," he said angrily. "We all need to be more careful than I was."

James said, "When I think of the danger I put Molly in, I could—" He could say no more, but Molly put her hand on his arm to calm him. She smiled at him and answered his angry words.

"James, none of us gave the matter as much importance as we should have. Do not blame yourself. I go out by myself in those mountains all the time. In fact, I may have seen the devil that did this to us and Shadow."

She then told them about the encounter she'd had just three days ago when she saw the outsider on the trail.

"Why did he need another horse? He probably has Scout, Shadow's horse?" James asked. They all smiled and turned to Shadow for the answer.

"Ha! He couldn't ride Scout, no one can ride him but me—unless I tell Scout it's OK. No, he did not get anything when he tried to kill me!" Shadow shook his fist in the air.

"Maybe we have heard the last of him, as he got what he wanted this time," Price said.

"Be careful, I know he will be back. I know that kind," said the aged Indian. "The kind that takes and takes." Shadow's voice rose as he spoke. Molly glanced at him with concern.

"Now we have upset you, Shadow. You are still recovering, and you need not to be upset."

"Do not worry about me, my Estelle. I was well enough to go for a ride today. Price helped me saddle up the paint and we had a good outing," he said with a slight smile. Just then they heard a noise from the barn. Realizing it was a horse shrieking a loud whinny, Molly cried out.

"It's Mickey!" They got a lantern and, as fast as they could, answered the distress call. When Molly and James entered the dark barn, the glow of the lantern cast their shadows on the wall.

"I do not know why most foals are born at night, but most of them are." Molly stated.

"Yes, it was that way in Missouri too," James replied. The mare was lying on the earthen floor. Molly bent down to her and spoke soft voice commands to the mare. Under the gentle glow of the lamp, she placed her head down against the smooth, warm belly of the mare.

"The new life is in there and it is giving out a rebellious cry," she said to James. "This is Mickey's first and first things are not always easy."

"No, I guess not," replied James as he reached out to help her to her feet. Still holding her in his arms, he caught her chin to tilt her head for a kiss.

"Y'all are my first love, you know." His heart was leaping high in his chest as he held her eyes with his own.

He has a certain unrefined style that is strongly appealing to me, Molly thought as she gave herself to him in a kiss. The kiss deepened.

After a little sigh, Molly placed her arms around his neck. It was good to touch in a full embrace and to feel his tender caress.

He kissed her again, mesmerized by this young and beautiful frontier woman. Still holding her close, James sighed as he brushed his hand down her shining hair.

"You're lovely, Molly. Can I talk about how I feel about you when we get back to the house?"

Before she could answer, Shadow and Price came into the barn carrying the supplies they needed for the foaling.

"How is Mickey doing? Shadow asked. "Pretty soon we will know the answer to that," Molly replied. "For now, we must be patient."

"Yes, there is only room for patience and care at a time like this, and hope that is born is worthy and good!" Shadow exclaimed. The mare struggled for an hour more, and Molly became overwhelmed as she noticed Mickey was breathing in spasmodic jerks and that her groans were deep. It somehow made Molly feel suddenly tired—and a little frightened.

Shadow had begun a low chant as the difficulty Mickey was having worsened. James asked if he could examine the desperate animal. They nodded, and without a word James began to take over. Soon he realized that one leg of the foal was turned wrong, and that that was what was holding up the birthing process. He straightened the folded hoof, then waited.

"For now, that is all I can do," said James. Shadow agreed.

"The time is not yet. We cannot help. We must wait and watch."

With that, Shadow sat down cross-legged on the straw on the floor. While the lamp painted experiential pictures on the wall, Mickey's labor increased. It seemed to flow in methodical tides of torment. When they first got a glimpse of tiny hooves, Shadow was up over the mare. His talk was gentle to her. Then the sheath that the small newborn wears shined against the dim glow of the light.

The group leaned in wonderment.

"Is it all right?" asked James.

"I have the hooves in my hands, but must work gently." Shadow spoke softly, working to free the colt. Mickey strained with all she had, and gave one more hard muscle surge. Then Shadow gave a light pull on the hooves and the colt slipped out.

Silence! Everyone had been holding their breath. Then a sharp *crack* and the bag was broken, revealing a wobbly little head. For Molly, to see the soft nostrils suck at first taste of air made her gasp. Then together they slipped the whole bag away, cut the cord, and applied medicine.

"He is a strong horse colt, full of the tremor of life!" Shadow exclaimed. Molly turned to smile at James, who returned the smile.

"Oh, he is beautiful!" she said. "Yes, I remember that my grandfather enjoyed witnessing this scene of new life many times at his thoroughbred ranch in Missouri," James said, still smiling.

"He was a kind Christian man who was gentle, like Shadow." Shadow put his hand on James's shoulder.

"Aho wa . . . *thank you.*" Molly was delighted with the tiny animal. She rubbed him dry with a heavy cloth, handling him all she could, and talked to him in a soft voice as she helped him stand.

"I am going to call him *Uno Amour,*" she declared.

"One Love, that's new," James translated. He studied Molly's face for a minute. "Yes, we can have that," he said with love in his voice.

She smiled a shy smile to him, then Shadow spoke gravely.

"It is the mare I am worried about."

"Oh, no!" Molly cried. Through great, big tears she stared at him. James reached for her and held her as she seemed to him to be very weary.

"She is not strong enough to stand. Probably lost too much blood. It may have been the foot that injured her. Let's watch her and give her time to rest. Price, see if she will drink any water," Shadow instructed.

Price nodded, then spoke to the two weary onlookers.

"Go inside and clean up, both of you. We will watch her now. It has been a big day for you."

"It has been a day larger than a day. Yes, now go and see to it that Molly rests," Shadow instructed James.

"Goodnight and God bless." When they left the barn, a slant of light from the moon caught the two lovers as, arm in arm, they ventured out into the night. "Oh James, what else can go wrong now?" Molly lamented.

"Well, look at it this way, you have a beautiful colt, Mickey will make it, and we are safe. I would say it has been a pretty good day. Now, you need to get some rest."

He led her to her upstairs bedroom and after reassuring her that he would take his turn in the barn watching the horse, kissed her on the top of her head and said, "Good night, Molly dearest."

The dark gray dawn rose with a breath of frost from the high peaks above the valley floor. Winter was well on its way. The cold dawn created a mist that was rising from the stream beside the house. Its moisture coiled about the slick, dark trees that glistened and dripped with its beads.

It was the smell of breakfast that woke Molly. After dressing quickly, she came down to the kitchen to find James sitting at the table.

"Good morning . . . *coffee?*" James spoke with a smile as he poured her a cup of fresh, black java. She was attired in a matching sapphire skirt and blouse, which made her eyes the color of blue sky. She eyed him with his trim beard, and his blue eyes held hers. She could not believe any man affected her way James did, and this morning she enjoyed having him there beside her.

"Yes, thank you, James. I can't believe I slept all night. How is Mickey?"

"Mickey is better. She is standing now, and has allowed her colt to nurse," he replied. "Now, let's not keep you standing. Here, sit down and eat some of these fluffy biscuits and this thick bacon. I am so glad to see you looking more like yourself, Molly."

"Oh, I will be myself only when father and mother return," Molly replied as she sighed at the way he said her name.

"OK, I know something that will help," said James. Show me your valley. It looks like a beautiful day for a ride."

She looked at him quietly. There was that grin again, annoying and tantalizing. When she answered, she spoke with excitement in her voice.

"Yes, and maybe we can ride up the trail and meet Dalton and my parents as they return today."

This was the time of day that Molly loved most—daybreak. Today there was a red sun to ride into. There was warmth and life and a sweet scent from the night dew on the sagebrush that studded the edge of the valley.

Shadow had helped James pick out a new horse for him to ride today.

"I want you to ride Diablo, this paint stallion," Shadow told James. Stallions are more alert, more curious, and more easily excited. Notice how his head is up testing the wind. He will know at once if a strange horse or man might be approaching."

Shadow intently lectured James, and James then knew that Shadow was expecting him to watch out for Molly's safety. Molly herself was enjoying watching a friendship develop between the two men.

"He's a beauty," James said as he led him to the post in front of the tack house. James took a brush, and the friendship began as the big horse got acquainted in the best way a friend could, with a good brushing.

Shadow smiled. He could see a trusting bond would be established between man and beast. James completed the saddling and then mounted the big stallion. James's wiry, lean frame had the look of a man accustomed to setting the saddle.

"OK, it's you all and me, Diablo," he drawled as he patted the horse's neck. He took hold of the reins and they trotted out with Molly on Bourbon, traveling alongside.

"I like the way you ride," Molly said after awhile, smiling at him. His manner as he rode was completely relaxed. His slim frame was tight in the saddle as they trotted along.

"A fine horse can make any man look good. Yes, a fine horse that has a spring in his step as this one has is a pleasure to ride."

"And you are a pleasure to ride with, Miss Molly," he replied with his engaging smile. She blushed, as he knew she would, and he loved it.

The sweet fragrance from the cottonwoods that clustered along the banks of the river was strong. Along the river bank, they could take a trail that was known about only by the few families in the valley. Molly felt it would be safer, and she was sure Dalton would come back by that passage.

James looked at the wide valley with its scatter of cottonwoods and the murmur of the stream. He lifted his head to see the magnificent splendor of the mountains. The tops were gray and snow-streaked, glistening in the morning sun. He had never been in a place like this before—a valley where cattle grazed in belly-high grass that was now turning brown as fall approached.

An hour later, they climbed a ridge and he could see where settlements had sprung up. Molly showed James where the Bert Blazer ranch was and told him about Elizabeth being close friends with her and her brother. They spent the rest of the morning riding side by side, getting acquainted with family history.

At about noon they climbed to a summit, then stopped to rest the horses. James's horse nickered softly, and James reached for his gun as they moved quickly behind some trees. Soon two riders leading three extra horses came into view. With much relief, Molly could see it was

Dalton and Elizabeth. But where were her parents? She could not wait to ask him that question.

Dalton was as surprised to see them as they were to see him and Elizabeth.

"Hi, what are you doing here? Is everything all right at home?" he questioned first.

"Yes, we're all OK," she answered. "But where are father and mother? Did you hear from them? Why is Elizabeth with you?" She began a barrage of questions.

"Whoa," he said. "Let's get off these tired horses and you can read the letter I received from mother and dad at the Crossing."

They found a place away from the main trail where they could sit and see the high valley below.

"Good to see you James. Have you met Elizabeth?" Dalton asked, acknowledging the beautiful girl with dark, auburn hair that was standing next to him.

"No, but I've heard about her. It's nice to finally meet you," James smiled, extending his hand toward her. Elizabeth took his hand, smiling back at him.

"Hello, yes, finally."

"Here, let me tie up these horses while you all rest," James declared in his Southern drawl.

Anxious, Molly continued to ask him, "Dalton, tell me, will they be on the next train?"

"Here is the letter. Read it then you will know as much as I do," he said, handing his sister the letter. The four sat down under some tall pines, and she began to read the letter out loud.

Dear Dalton and Molly, with regards to all,

We pray you are all well. We miss you very much. We are quite well, now, but we will be delayed, perhaps four more weeks. Your mother is recovering from some surgery she had to have. She is fine, just weak, and needs to be here close to the doctor. Do not worry about her.

Instead, remember to pray for her and for our return trip. We will send word every week. It will be sent to Naples, where Charlie will bring it to the Crossing for you to retrieve.

Now for some news of the ranch. I have had successful business dealings. One of the most urgent items is that I have sold fifty head of our mixed breed yearling bulls. It is urgent that these bulls be put on the rail at Naples, where you will ship them to Denver. The name of the ranch where you'll take them is enclosed with the address of whom to telegram when you get them loaded.

The rancher must have the bulls before winter sets in. Please prepare to do this immediately. Good luck and I am counting on you.

We send our love,
Father and Mother

When Molly finished, she glanced at Dalton. He saw that she was near to tears and reached over to hug her till she could talk about the news.

"You know mother is all right or father would have told us."

"Yes, of course, you are right," said Molly, and with this reply she quit her sniffling.

"This letter is dated nearly a month ago. How are we going to get all this done now?" she asked.

"Yes, I noticed that, and that is why Elizabeth has come . . . so we can have extra help to get ready to leave the day after tomorrow. There is a lot to do to prepare for the cattle drive. We need to bring these bulls up and sort the bigger ones, as well as pack food and supplies for the trip," he replied.

Molly looked relieved, "You have already begun all of this in your mind, big brother, haven't you?" She smiled and gave him a hug. Dalton enjoyed the praise and clung to her for a moment. James could see that the two had great love and respect for each other.

Yes, they are close, he mused, and they have shared years learning tiny secrets about each other. They have such a good relationship. I can't wait to meet their parents. But will I still be here in this wilderness by then? He wondered about his future, thinking about his original plans.

"Come on, let's ride!" Molly suddenly announced with enthusiasm.

"Why don't we take the cutoff back? It is so beautiful, and James hasn't seen this mountain range from that side trail."

Down the trail, Dalton pointed to strange horse tracks in the soft soil. It showed a lone rider, probably pulling another horse with a light pack. The tracks turned off on a higher trail to the north.

James told Dalton about the trouble Molly and he had encountered at the mine. When he had finished, Dalton exclaimed, "My final conclusion is that no one should be out in the mountains alone and all must pack a gun."

The rest of the way to the ranch very little was said. There was a lot to think about. They came down off the mountain in view of the wide valley. James could see there were farms and ranches scattered like the builders of a new land, each hugging to himself all that spread from the door of this cabin to the horizon.

There were wide, green fields of pasture. The gray saber of the hills beyond and dark mountains above were now veiled in rose and purple with streaks of snow on top.

They came upon the sun-kissed hills where the cattle grazed. *A peaceful place,* James mused. *I would like to see this valley in the spring.* He smiled as he thought about the possibility.

Molly saw the snow on the mountaintops and felt that winter was in her head, but eternal springtime was in her heart.

And what will spring bring, I wonder? Will James be here? He was thinking about going home on the next eastbound train. Oh, can I imagine my life without him? We haven't had time to talk. Maybe tonight, even though there will be so much to do to get ready for the cattle drive, she concluded.

She glanced at James. Seeing a smile on his handsome face, she wondered what he was thinking. A mile from the ranch Molly was sure she heard gun fire.

"You hear that?" she shouted, as they stopped their horses to listen. The gunfire was happening near the ranch. They put the horses in a run and the anxious riders arrived at the scene just in time to see a stranger that was riding James's stolen roan horse. He was leading one of their ranch horses as he disappeared through the trees at the upper end of the pasture, traveling at a fast gallop and caring a smoking rifle.

When Shadow saw them approach he came running out of the barn, shouting in his native language and waving his rifle in the air. Barely able to understand him, Dalton asked, "Are you OK, Shadow?"

The angry-faced Indian replied, "Yes, but Price is shot in the arm! I think he will be OK. The bullet went through his flesh." Dalton thought for a minute, then spoke.

"It is too dangerous to go after that killer tonight. It will be dark soon. We need to see to Price right now."

He had hardly spoken when Molly, off her horse, handed the reins to James and went toward the barn.

"I may need your help to get Price inside the house where we can care for him," said Dalton to James, who was tying up the horses. An hour later, as things settled down and Price was laid comfortably in the kitchen, they began the evening meal Lee had prepared for them.

They were more quiet than usual, and Dalton felt concern for their safety. "As I see the problem, I think we'd better cancel trying to get those bulls to the railhead. There are not enough of us to do the job. We cannot leave the ranch unprotected."

"Maybe all that that intruder wanted was another horse and we will not see him again." Molly spoke to Dalton with concern.

"Even if Shadow and I could take those bulls out, I wouldn't leave you here now," was his reply.

"Why not? I can ride and shoot as good as anyone," she argued.

"It is out of the question. With the outside chores, the mares foaling, and the weather getting worse—too many odds," Dalton declared.

"But father is counting on us," Molly argued. The argument continued as James walked out onto the porch. There was turmoil going on inside of him, but why? It was because he knew she needed help.

Should I become mixed up in this, he wondered. "In a few days, I will be on my way home, and anyway Dalton should make the final decision here," he concluded.

Thoughts of the young woman inside came to him. He could hear the desperation in Molly's voice, and it disturbed him. He looked in through the window, where he could see Molly was now standing, shaking her head to Dalton. The light from the lamp spilled across her face. He turned away and spoke aloud.

"Such a pretty face, one I have come to—Oh, Molly, you are my whole life. Do you know what you have done for me? I'm in love with you!"

"James!" Molly called to him from the doorway. He turned around to see her standing there with her arms extended toward him slightly. Molly had a smile on her face that was just for him, and he knew she had heard his confession. His arms went around her, wanting her close to him always, and it was a question of who held who the tightest.

They stood that way in the dimming moonlight, then he kissed her with tenderness and with much passion. Through those first urgent waves of passion, she felt a quiet joy.

I know that I love him, and that I will go on any adventure he goes on, Molly confessed in her heart. When they parted, James spoke to her.

"Let's go inside. I have to talk to Dalton to tell him that I will go on the drive to get the bulls to their destination at the railhead.

"Oh, James, you are wonderful to want to help," Molly cried happily. When they told Dalton of their plans, Molly and James slipped back out to the moonlit porch.

Molly was still bouncing with joy and all the worry disappeared from her face. She was radiant in the evening light, wearing her shiny silk blouse, and the fancy leather riding skirt. She had worn her hair pulled up this evening, and a strand fell softly over her lovely face.

James wound his finger around the strand as he softly kissed her hair. Then with their arms around each other they stood watching the moon play *hide and seek* with the clouds that created long shadows through the tall pines. James turned to face her.

"Molly, I believe that the important, exciting changes in one's life take place at some crossroad where people meet and build, laugh, labor, and cling to their dream. This place is the other end of that dream, the attainable one."

"Yes," Molly agreed. "And the meeting of two people's hearts in this remote Idaho mountain range, such as when I saw you working over a task with hands that were kind and tender, is a God-given blessing. Yes, it was you, James. When I met you, my heart stopped. I can't go back to the way I was. If you want me, I'll go with you as your wife wherever you want to live."

Her voice was soft. She spoke without hesitation. The way she looked at him, James felt his heart leap in his chest. He knew now that there would be no turning back for him, either.

"But, Molly that is what I'm talking about. My dream is here, too. Not only with you, but here in these mountains," he said smiling and looking tenderly in her moonlit eyes. She stared in disbelief, but the look in his warm eyes told it all.

"This is what we shall do with the moment we are in now. Let's see, where did we end off?" As a smile caught the corner of his mouth, he drew her closer to him. Then in the fading light he began kissing her again. To the west of them, in deep silence, the leaden clouds moved slowly across the sky. Ready or not, the first storm of this fall season was on its way.

Chapter Eight

By the next day, preparation had begun for the cattle drive to Naples. It was decided Molly would take the lead. Dalton was to stay at the ranch as he was the strongest one to do the chores and help with the mares since Price was laid up for a few days. With the help of James and Shadow, they should make it to the railhead in four days.

The threat of the intruder was always on Dalton's mind. He had the feeling that he would meet up with the bushwhacker again. On the trail they would be short handed, but could get by.

Molly knew the first section of the trail well, and Shadow knew the mountains and the best places to go over the passes on the second and third days. Dalton said he had a lot of faith in James's ability to think fast and to help in any emergency.

The driving of the bulls would be hard work because these animals would need to be kept close. They were of the Durham type. That made them different from the leggy, light-muscled cattle that were generally kept on the high desert. Shadow was much improved and his job would be to stay in the back with the pack animals until the pass was reached. That would take two long days.

At the first sign of dawn the birds outside started up their usual clamor. The noise woke Molly, as it usually did. She could hear preparations for the trip being completed downstairs.

We are leaving tomorrow! She thought. *All this is on my shoulders. Can I do it?* All these thoughts ran through Molly's head. She knew she would rely a lot on Shadow. If anyone could get through those mountains at this time of year, he could. *Shadow?* Oh, she must talk to him, as he always gave her the confidence she needed.

Dressing quickly, Molly went downstairs. In the kitchen, she asked Lee where Shadow was.

"Mister Shadow out fetching the pack mules, Missy. Here, sit down to this cup of coffee," he said to her, attempting to get the worried look off her face, and then he continued.

"Dalton and James were up early sorting bulls down by the barn. Can you help Elizabeth and me with the food details?"

"OK, I'll help, but when Shadow comes up here, I need to talk to him," Molly replied. The morning went fast as the kitchen work proceeded with all helping out. Molly went up to pack her riding clothes and remembered she might need to get some spare clothes for James. She went out to the barn to find him so she could ask him about it.

A slow drizzle had begun to fall early that morning. The north winds whispered lightly among the tall pines beside the house. Molly had put on her rain jacket for the lengthy walk across the yard. A short distance from the barn, Molly gazed on James, who looked up and saw her coming.

It's the prettiest thing watching a woman walk when she knows you are watching, James was thinking with a smile on his lips. He went to meet her. Molly tossed her head as she watched him.

Returning the smile, she almost knew what he was thinking. She was a western woman that had found her song in the majesty of the land—a land graced with rugged beauty wherever the eye fell. It was an unspoiled country of tall trees and endless plains, nursed by mountains yielding clean, sweet-falling rainwater that was, at this moment, falling on her happy face.

James no longer felt like a stranger in a foreign land. In his mind, he was walking toward his future. He was taking pleasure viewing her wet face and hair and the vibrant young look it gave her. *She was beautiful!* A surge of desire ran through him as he arrived at her side. He touched her face then he rested his hand on her arm, holding her at arm's length.

"Molly, I need to hold you at a distance, or I will hug you right here for all that are watching to see . . . and I don't want to embarrass you," he said with a slow smile as he looked into her bright blue eyes.

"Oh James, thank you for caring about my character, but I will look foolish if I have to take *you* in my arms and wish you a good day," she teased back.

"Ma'am, I admire a woman who has the courage to show fondness for a man," he challenged, as he drew her closer to him. He could see the pulse at the base of her throat beating stronger.

Molly felt her heart throbbing. She felt if she looked into her lover's eyes she would have no strength—her knees weakened by his embrace. She felt a stir in her heart that was stronger than all, beyond resistance, an exquisite agony of tumultuous exultation of the woman who loves and knows love in return.

The two lovers hardly realized that the rain had quit falling as they continued to speak terms of sweet devotion to each other. The wind died down and the sun came out and began to dry everything. They turned to see the double rainbow gleaming in the west.

"A good sign of many blessings," Molly said as she stretched up on her toes to give James another kiss.

The morning brought an eerie mist not only along the Malad River, but in a ground fog that hung everywhere. This trail drive would have to begin by keeping the bulls close in line as it might be easy for one to slip away undetected.

Molly was not discouraged and did not think of the enormity of the task. There was a job to be done, and she had a lot of confidence in those who were helping her. James was especially friendly to her at breakfast, giving her the feeling that the very things about him that irritated her seemed to fan little flames inside her. She wondered about her ability to resist any unwanted advances—*or would they be unwanted?*

The men from the ranch had helped them come as far as the main fork of the river to get the cattle across the already-swollen river and away from their familiar surroundings. The river had risen sharply, Molly noted. This meant that there was bad weather ahead.

Before Dalton left her, he gave her the familiar wave they'd used as a signal when they played together as children. By then the rain was hitting noisily on her duster. She tried to chase away any fears but kept wondering. *Did they have a chance? Was it she that was in charge?*

Oh, why am I thinking this way now? Dalton believes in me. She breathed a prayer.

All day, Molly and James rode back and forth, pushing the bulls in line. Shadow, on his mare Chita, was keeping the reluctant pack mules moving as they continued the push from behind. By midday, the clouds were still resting low on hidden peaks and pressing down, but the rain had stopped.

The trail wound through a stand of stunted timber, allowing the wind to snap at Molly's face. The chill made her shiver as the bitter October cold crept around her. She pulled her gray, wool jacket tightly around herself.

At this altitude, before the storm turned to snow, they needed to get to the shelter called the Smokehouse cabin. It was built to withstand winter storms, as it seemed they were going to have this evening. They kept the pace up so they could make the distance to it the first planned stop.

The mountains had surrendered the granite grayness of full day to the encroaching blue of evening. With sunlight fading from the surrounding summits, darkness slowly came upon them.

The sight of the old cabin was a welcome one. The bulls were easy to drive into a large catch pen beside the cabin. They had enjoyed almost no rest or food along the way and here was a chance for both.

"I'll see to the horses and check on the pack mules. You go inside to get warm and dry," James told Molly. In a short time the cabin was snug and warm. Shadow already had a big fire going in the cook stove and was preparing the evening meal.

The warmth felt good to Molly. *What a day they had had!* Even with today's thoughts on her mind, her eyes watched the door for James to join them. James approached the cabin knowing Molly was inside waiting for him.

Today she was certainly full of fire, punching out orders, he thought. He honored her drive to deliver these bulls in the face of impossible odds and he believed he'd never known any woman like her.

I certainly admire her spirit and I am happy to be a part of her life, James mused. Over the past two days he had made all the excuses he could think of to see her. A new kind of love was building, a rather magic spot in time, like the first time his eyes caught hers and he knew they were meant to be together.

Today, they had not spent any close time together and he was looking forward to this evening. As he came inside the door, he felt her eyes upon him. He greeted her with a smile as he took off his coat and hat.

"There are a few stars appearing in among the clouds. With some luck tomorrow, it may clear," he said with hope in his voice. Then he went to her and, at once, they clung in an embrace.

He could smell her damp hair and enjoyed it. The desire to kiss her was strong, but he waited until he was sure she was agreeable. Then he felt her arms tighten around him. Unable to contain himself any longer, he rained soft kisses on her neck. Molly's skin trembled as he continued kissing her face.

Something about this man had her hooked. It was easy for her to be honest about her affection for him.

"James," she said softly, "you are my first love, too."

"I'm finding out more and more that I like about you, Molly," he replied. "Every day I am so elated that I can spend these days with you."

As a quick smile lit up his eyes, he added, "But I cannot live on love alone. Let's eat!"

They finished a hot meal of stew and biscuits. A second cup of hot coffee was in their hands as they sat around the table and began to ask about one other. James asked Shadow many questions about his family.

"I only remember my father. He was a great chief; he wore an eagle relic. And this made anyone who doubted him fear. He had great visions and not many were called to see such visions," he told James.

"Do you have visions?" James asked. Shadow smiled and nodded as he turned to his Estelle. She was smiling, but remained silent so that Shadow could recount the story.

"I was up near a rocky ledged overlook in the mountains above our ranch when I became aware that I needed to be listening for something—I knew not what. I had sat down near the stream and was looking at the cloud vision once again, this time with lightning. The cloud flashed and thunder roared through the range. Yet the cloud was not dark; it was bright and clear.

I looked to see the spirit and knew it was the good Old Man. And now the sun was behind the cloud, making a brightness I have not seen since. Like a vision from the heavens, a shadow was cast upon the earth. It was a shadow of a small girl. Beyond her was a beautiful, green land. I marveled at what this meant. I knew somehow that such a valley lay just below me, and that I must go there. When I did, I found little Estelle."

When he finished telling the story, Shadow began to sing the song of the Black Horse Riders. It was a beautiful chant. His voice was powerful and rang with music. Molly and James sat together near the warming stove, and as he put his arm around her, she leaned comfortably into his shoulder. He kissed the top of her head. They sat there looking into the dancing fire until the chant was over.

"Now, my son," Shadow began, "we must smoke together so that there may be only good between us."

Shadow believed that the lobelia plant contained a special medicine that helped him heal in his chest and that is why he used it in his pipe. He prepared the tobacco in the pipe, then said, "This pipe was handed down from Father to son, and since I cannot give it to Estelle, you must have it someday." He turned his head and looked directly in James's eyes, then lit the pipe and drew from it for a while. He then passed it to James.

"May we face the winds and walk the good road to the day of quiet Hetchetu aloh!" Then he looked upward and said, "And with your power only can I face the winds, good God above. Thank you."

With that prayer, Shadow put away the pipe, then rolled over on his bedroll and fell asleep.

When the morning dawned it was dreary and raining. There was no chance the storm would break away till mid-afternoon. Shadow could see snow on the mountain pass.

"If we're going to camp at the lake meadow tonight, where there is shelter for the bulls, we will need to make good time." They completed the packing of the mules and closed the cabin up in a short time. The brave, daring spirits working here in the early morning light gave James a glorious feeling to be a part of it.

Oh, I am more than glad I came, James thought. *Yet,* he questioned himself, *to cross these mountains with a storm approaching some would believe was either very brave or very crazy.*

He heard somewhere off in the whiteness what might have been a bull elk bugle an eerily high and mournful trumpeting that echoed across the hills. James saw Molly smile at Shadow as they heard this call of nature sound.

They really have something special, James noted. Sometimes it was just a look, sometimes it was a word, but there were special meanings to each signal they had to each other. *I have heard that there is a special bond between people when one has saved another's life. Shadow is more of a grandfather to Molly than anything else. They even think alike, as far as I can see.*

The air was sharp and frosty. The fragrance of wood smoke was still hanging in the meadow around the cabin as the riders herded the cattle out of their pen. The trail went along the beaver ponds where a beaver stuck it's sleek, dripping face up from the water, then dove out of sight. A cold wind came up and blocks of dark clouds began stacking above the western horizon. The temperature dropped.

"What we don't need is a storm before we get over the pass," James stated.

"No," Shadow replied. "If the bear is still with us, we will be guarded. Let us spend one day as deliberately as nature."

Molly smiled, then replied, "I will take the lead today. You two follow me." With a whoop, she broke her horse into a fast trot. They traveled like this all morning, with the weather steadily worsening.

At the bottom of the pass known as Timberline, high winds and driving sleet had made the pass dangerous. The sleet cut into the bulls' pinched faces. They lowered their heads and whipped their tails.

"We're an hour ahead of the main storm; let's see if we can reach that meadow where the lake is before we stop," Shadow shouted into the wind.

In the wildness of the storm, they started up the trail. The animals needed a lot of tending, for they were unwilling to stay out in the bad weather. Trees were scarce. There were a few bushes, but the landscape was mostly rocks. The ridge seemed to offer no relief and continued upwards in one unbroken sweep. Molly saw some tracks in the fresh snow. She was sure Rocky Mountain sheep ran here but, like nature, these were sheep with this climate in their blood.

Suddenly one of the larger Durham bulls darted for cover in some bushes. He ran out of sight into the fog that was limiting their range of vision. When Molly was able to get around the line of cattle she went after him.

The side of the mountain was steep and wet. Bourbon began to lunge upwards and not, as he was directed for safety, across the mountain.

"No, Bourbon," she shouted, but too late! Molly could feel that the rocks were not maintaining their positions. She saw the ground give way as Bourbon's hooves hammered along.

Molly flung herself off the horse onto the uphill side of the incline, hoping to give the horse better balance and the ability to recover. In spite of this help, Bourbon was slipping downhill, crashing through bushes and rocks. Trying to reach him quickly, she cut through to some large rocks near the ledge of the cliff. A low growl made her stop.

She turned and paid attention to the uphill cliff above her head. Molly had heard this sound before and was not too surprised to see, standing in a cave opening, eyeing her, an enormous cougar. Rays of light darted from the cougar's large eyes. It was a female that had her lair there in the rocks. She showed her teeth as she repeated the low growl. Her ears went back flat while she let out a snarl that seemed to be frozen on her face.

Molly froze. She knew not to run, but fear was gripping her senses. She watched the cat to see its next move. That was what caused Molly to scream, because the cat was crouching on her haunches ready to spring!

At that moment, James riding at a gallop came upon them.

"Yawl, yaw," he screamed! He was making all the noise he could, including yelling to divert the cat's attention to himself.

I must be fast on the trigger and accurate, because there will be no retreat for Molly, James feared. He leveled his rifle and blazed away, hoping that, even if he did not hit the animal, at least the noise would frighten it away.

When Molly saw James move in on the animal, and that its attention was diverted to him, she knew retreat was an option. She quickly backed downhill, moving toward her horse. The cougar sprang at James like a cannon!

James drew his hunting knife, thinking that if the bullet did not stop it this might be a close fight before it drew its last breath, *or his,* he thought. He felt a rush of wind and got a glance of a whirling ball of fur and a snarling face. The attacking cat hit him in the shoulder, thrusting him hard to the ground.

He cried out in alarm and also in pain. He rolled down the mountain, away from where the animal had landed. Molly reached Bourbon and, with shaking hands, pulled the rifle out of the scabbard, cocked it, and settled in, waiting for her next move.

James got up and went to retrieve his rifle. He looked over to where the cat had landed near some undergrowth. Then a flash of brown appeared between himself and the cougar. James put his hand up and wiped his sweaty brow because he could not believe what he saw!

Standing on its hind feet, swaying back and forth was the largest bear he had ever encountered. The bear let out a ferocious growl at the cougar, which refused to give ground but approached with caution. The movement the cat made was too slow. With one swing, the front paw of the huge bear caught the cougar with such ferocity that the animal did not have a chance.

He approached again as the cat whirled around, and with one more sweep of the paw, the bear rolled the cat again. She landed near the steep ledge. This time there was blood on her neck. She got up slowly, clawed her way up the steep bank, and did not look back until she had found the crest.

James picked up his hat and ran to Molly, who was staring as if in a trance.

"Let's get out of here," he said, taking hold of her arm to withdraw. The fog had rolled in, making visibility poor. It created a dim view of where the bear had stood. The only sound they heard was that of their flight to some cover near a fallen tree.

"This is a good place to make a stand," James said breathlessly. "We can see from here if the bear comes at us." Then he asked, looking around, "Where is Shadow? He has had time to secure the pack string and be here. He could hear from the gunfire that we were in trouble."

Molly shivered in reply as her large blue eyes saw for the first time that there was blood on James's ripped jacket.

"Oh James, you are injured," she cried. She found a cloth in the saddle bag to press against the bleeding wound.

"This is not important," he said. "You were in danger and I could not lose you." He lifted his face to the cleansing rain, letting it wash away all the fear and anger. Molly finished dressing the wound, and then she touched his wet cheek with a soft kiss.

In the dim light something wild and untamed disappeared in the fog. Molly noticed it was very quiet. It began to rain hard and the entire world was dark gray. The only noise she heard was the steady slap of the rain on her jacket.

"Time to get rolling," Shadow said as he came upon them suddenly.

"Where have you been?" James asked, startled by even the sound of his own voice.

"I was here," he replied. "You can always rediscover an old path, and wonder over it, but the best you can do is think—I know it, but even if you remember it, that unforgettable mountain no longer remembers you."

With that, he handed James the reins of Diablo and the three swung into their saddles to gather up the herd. Life had already stilled for the evening. Now the mist had turned into something between rain and snow, creating a clammy drizzle that clung to Molly's face. Within the hour the drizzle became large, wet flakes of snow, making it almost impossible for the horses to keep their footing.

When they reached the meadow near the summit, they were a tired bunch. As the clouds moved out, they saw the lake shimmering in the hidden light of a dying sun.

"Thank goodness!" was all Molly said. They camped a short distance away from the lake. The wind howled through the shrieking forests like troops of demons. The chilling air, already white with falling snowflakes, became dense with the drifting snow mounds.

Around the campfire, they huddled in a makeshift tent of boughs. Molly began to clean the claw-marked wound on James's shoulder. He watched her fingers as she worked and it was a pleasure to feel her touch on his skin.

"Molly, my love, you are cold and tired, and yet you labor over me." He planted a satisfying kiss to her lips. Then he rose with her in his arms. He placed her upon the sheltered bed and laid her within the warmth of the heavy wool blankets. She clung to his neck, pulling him down with her.

"If we are to stay warm tonight, I need you," she said, holding his face to hers. Wrapped in each other's arms, they did not care at the moment what transpired in the world beyond.

The early light shadows were creeping through the shivering pines. Shadow Runner enjoyed the silence and the profound solitude of the ever-present, endless blanket of snow. He had not slept well.

He had been keeping a fire going all night and continued to look at the flames and the dropping coals and embers. He thought of his Great God and was thankful that he could give his strength, his energy, and his love to the two sleeping near him. He uttered a silent prayer for more strength and safety for all, for this new day.

Shadow stepped out of the shelter and looked around at the giant cornices on the right and the steep rock slopes on the left. He viewed a narrow snow ridge running up to a snowy summit glowing clearly in the early morning light.

"Good morning, my Estelle," he greeted Molly as she emerged sleepily out of the shelter.

"Oh, Shadow, it is going to be a clear morning. I prayed for this," Molly exclaimed.

"Yes, my Estelle, so did I. Let me get the supplies for breakfast, and you and James can give the horses grain," he said as he nodded to James, who was now pulling on his jacket.

As they walked out to the animals, a snowshoe hare skimmed across the snow—its white winter coat catching the glittering of the sun. They both smiled as James reached for Molly's hand. Their boots crunched on the ice-crusted snow, causing the horses to look up as they approached. They fed and saddled the horses, then returned for some of Shadow's fresh- brewed coffee, which gave off a wonderful aroma in the fresh morning air.

Shadow pointed to the winter clouds that were beginning to assemble their hosts around the loftier crests on the far-off horizons.

"Every day the weather appears more threatening, showing angry heralds of the gathering storm," he remarked as he hurried them through the meal.

A heavy snow had fallen at the lake. There was a delicate interplay of sunlight on the water, creating a mirrored effect as they drove the herd by it. Molly smiled at James as he looked back at the haven they had enjoyed for the night.

"We'll have to come back here sometime," he said to Molly with a faint smile on his lips.

"Yes, I would like that," she breathed in reply. All morning they traveled through snow that had thawed and frozen again. The wind stayed to the northwest, causing it to be very cold. This cold dampness they felt even through their wool coats and heavy chaps.

On the summit the snow was three feet in depth. This spot above the tree line looked like a world new and barren, with the coldness of space. They struggled through the snow and in due time reached the foot of the precipitous cliffs. All the forces of nature seemed to combine for their downfall. It was becoming more and more important that they get off this ridge before the late afternoon storm blew in.

The ridge, now bathed in broken sunshine, narrowed to a knife's edge where the trail went down and around the mountain. The cliff fell away one thousand feet straight down to a naked bed rock below. All of a sudden there was a violent eruption of noise as the bulls took flight in the opposite direction.

With a loud burst of snorts and clicking heel bones, it was a head-long stampede! Something had spooked them. The cattle ran a good distance away from Molly and away from the edge, where they stopped and milled around nervously.

Molly remembered that just before this she had felt tenseness in her horse's movements. Then Diablo stopped suddenly when he caught a scent that had never met his nostrils before. He snorted loudly and became wide-eyed with his head up to catch the wind.

"Not another mountain lion," James prayed as his hand went to his gun. Quickly, Shadow came up to see why they had stopped in this manner. He tossed the pack animal's rope to James and said, "Wait, do not move!"

With caution Shadow edged ahead, then stopped and got off his horse. He picked up a large rock and threw it ahead of him on the trail. It disappeared in the snow. Then with a whoosh and a crashing sound, all of the ground under where the rock went in, gave way! That which was once trail was now air. It created a large void that was impassable.

Molly gasped! Chita backed away with a scramble, as the earth under the snow shook visibly near her.

"What the heck?" James cried! "The trail just vanished!" He had never seen such a near-disaster happen so quickly. Molly, on Bourbon, stood trembling beside him.

"I was about to proceed down that trail, and if they had not stopped," she cried out . . . "Oh, Shadow what will happen next?"

"I should have been in the lead, my Estelle, I am sorry you were frightened. I pray He shall cover thee with His feathers from fear and danger, and you will let it roll off your back like water off the protective covering of His wings."

Just then there was the sound of a sharp whistle from a bird towering above. They lifted up their heads to gaze at a red-tailed hawk soaring high in the heavens. A smile came to Shadow's lips at this sight, and then he spoke.

"Let us rest here while I check out another way off this summit." Molly and James dismounted and found a small alcove near a group of taller pines.

"A great place to wait for Shadow," James said as he put his arm around Molly, attempting to keep her warm. The sun mounted higher in the heavens as the heavy clouds moved east, allowing some of the rays of the sun to fall on them with friendly warmth.

"Yes, this bower is out of the wind and is a godsend. I was getting really cold. That is why I was not as alert as I should have been," she said, blaming herself for the delay.

"No, you should not blame yourself," said James. "Besides, nothing happened. In a few minutes we will be down off this frozen mountain," James's smile was reassuring as he held her close. She snuggled closer and, her chin resting on his arm, looked into his blue eyes.

"My dear, you have been a stronghold for me on this journey," she said. "I am grateful for you." James's heart beat faster in his chest as he returned her gaze and replied, "Molly, you are everything to me, and are all that I desire. I would go to the end of the earth for you."

Feeling a strong desire to kiss her, he lifted her chin, tilted his head, and placed a soft kiss on her round, red lips. A warm tingling between them grew strong as the kiss continued.

Moving quickly, Shadow reined Chita to retreat around the small rise on the uphill fraction of the trail.

If we can get around that damaged trail anywhere, it should be here, he thought. He went through heavier pine trees and when his horse held up, he brought up his rifle. He scanned the hillside, for what he knew not. He just knew that whatever had scared the herd was a worthy benison, as Molly and some of the cattle would have fallen to a sure death.

I must be careful, something is going on that I cannot explain, he realized. Shadow got off Chita in order to examine the fresh tracks in the snow.

"Someone else is up here," he exclaimed under his breath. "This one might be our explanation—if I can catch him."

It began to rain and Shadow knew that it chanced of more snow as the night approached. He pressed Chita to a faster pace as they rode to the very top of the ridge where they could see into the valley below. There they remained for a long while, looking at the drama being played out beneath them.

He was in a mean temper and as cross as a bear. Harris Davis had not succeeded in causing enough trouble with the riders that were driving the herd of bulls. All his work of destroying the narrow trail had not been of any significance. The weather had cooperated in covering all his tracks and helping him cover up the makeshift boughs he had put on that narrow passage.

He had been up half the night working on it and was caught in the storm, causing him to be wet inside and out.

I would not have done all this, but I need their horses and at least part of that herd for the train fare back east. I must get out of this country pronto, he thought. He camped down the mountain from them to be sure he had not left any tracks. He took a chance and built a small fire in an attempt to get himself dry. He was hunched over the fire cooking a cottontail on a green stick.

The camp he had hastily made lie snug against a rocky cliff and the ground sloped down to a big spring. Suddenly his horse blew a snort and pawed the ground, trying to get free from the short rope that held him. He was pulling at it with a lot of force.

"What the heck!" Davis began. Then something moved among the brush across the creek. The roan horse went crazy and managed to break free. He was desperate to get away from a scent he did not like, and when he realized he was free, he began backing up. Suddenly a red-tailed hawk made a noisy dive toward the earth. With a screech, it darted low over the trees near the horse. That was all the roan could manage. He whirled about with the remainder of Davis's gear and rifle and took off at a gallop down the trail.

"Whoa, whoa," Davis shouted after the frightened animal. But in vain, for fear gripped the horse and he was directed away from there. Davis returned to the fire, not conscious of what else to do. A person in this mountain range without a horse or a gun was a dead man.

He began feeling the same rush he had felt at the mine. He looked around to see what caused it. His eyes had the look of a wild animal in a trap. He felt sick and needed a drink of water. He picked up the water bag and walked down to the stream to fill it. There was a quick movement on the other side of the water. A flash of brown focused his attention.

A large brown bear silhouetted against the snow on the side of a low talus slope was advancing toward him. This was an animal that could smash open the skull of a moose with one blow. A light dust of snow whitened its silvery brown coat.

With winter coming, one could see that its body had layers of fat. Davis knew he could not outrun the savage animal. He turned around looking for a place to make his stand, but he found no place in sight.

A rolling slope behind the brush had cut off a view of the land beyond. He feared for his life.

He could smell the bear when it was about twenty feet away near a thicket. The animal had his snout raised and was panting the air. Then the attacking eight-hundred-pound bear gave a loud grumble, swinging his head in Davis's direction, and took two more steps toward him. In desperation the man pulled his knife from his belt, and faced the bear.

The cold October rain fell from the sky upon the forest. High on the ridge above this raging battle, a pair of eyes viewed the scene. As the bear closed in, the rider turned his prancing horse away and trotted down the trail to return to those who were waiting for him.

What had been a sky of blue became a ferment of clouds clotted before a driving wind. The riders departed off the summit with their vision blurred by curtains of rain. At their back, it looked like a trap. When Shadow returned to where Molly and James were waiting, he told them he had found a way down that would be steep, but short. He spoke to Molly.

"The shape of the Shadow has changed and it will change again." James looked at Molly to see if she understood. She nodded her head to the old Indian.

"Let's do it!" Handling the steepness of the mountain would have been difficult enough without the driving rain. Molly knew that to have stayed and been caught out on the mountain top with such a storm approaching, would have been "seppuku," as Lee would have called it. She tried to keep her spirits up for the rest of them.

It is only a day's trek across the final pass, but now with this detour—I don't know. She feared in her heart. The wind eased and the snow began to fall—big flakes spinning as they swirled down upon the high trail. Shadow rode alongside of Molly.

"If this keeps up we will have to make camp early at the Singing Cliffs. There is a good place for the cattle," he assured her.

"Sounds good. Lead on!" she acknowledged. They came upon a narrow passage and made the cattle move into single file. The snow continued as they wound their way above the timber line—ever so slowly upwards. It would have been a better journey if the tension within them were not there.

I need to talk to my love, Molly smiled at herself for the thought. She rode up alongside of James's horse. James turned and smiled a warm reassuring smile at her. This did help lift her spirits to see him looking so handsome in his buttoned-up sheepskin coat, his black hat pulled down tightly.

"Are your teeth chattering from the cold?" she teased. Then she looked into those dark blue eyes, waiting for an answer. With a grin, he answered.

"Yes Molly, you know you are the only warm thing in my life, and I haven't touched you all day." She blushed, and she knew he liked it when she did. She was rewarded with a big laugh, which produced the same gleam in his eyes that she'd had admired before.

"Perhaps we need to let go of what might happen and enjoy the moment," James said as he leaned over the side of the horse nearest her. Molly answered him.

"How do you know I am worried, Mr. James? Shadow does not seem as worried as he was yesterday. Maybe something happened that he knows about and chose not to tell us. I will have to ask him," she announced.

James planted a kiss on her cheek, then she rode away to get back into the lead. As they came across the summit, another high valley lay below them, but they knew it would not be as difficult as this one was to climb out of. They could see the trail, visible in many open areas below them. Across the valley a coyote answered another one with a yipping howl. Sounds were magnified ten times in a cold, gray world that had become colorless around them. The snow had stopped and the clouds were moving east. Shadow rode up alongside of Molly.

"It was only a snow squall. We will be dry by the time we reach the cliffs." He smiled at her. She nodded and smiled back.

He always seemed to know my thoughts, Molly remembered. An hour later as they dropped lower off the high mountain, the sun began to melt the snow. Glistening patches of snow fell from the pines. Soon they were riding on dry ground. The sun, a liquid red globe, touched the cliffs just beyond this canyon.

"The dropping of day's curtain is happening, my Estelle, and as we approach the Singing Cliffs, you will hear the moans of lost spirits as the wind blows through the trees," Shadow told Molly.

The forests were darkening and it was a little spooky at twilight. Molly and James rode side by side along the high cliffs. The cattle moved at a slow walk in front of them while they grazed on the tall fall grass that was plentiful near the thinning trees.

"This is where we will camp," Shadow announced. "The bulls will graze here, and we can hobble the horses so they can get plenty to eat."

"It is a beautiful spot. Are these alpine lakes named?" Molly asked as she got off her horse.

"Not that I have known," Shadow replied. "I guess I will name them then," Molly said as she watched James hobble Bourbon for her. They pulled the saddles off, laid them near a fallen tree, and put the blankets over them to dry. James reached for her, drawing her close. When she put her arms around his neck, his lips found hers, as they had many times before.

The kiss was tender, as if they had no secrets or shadows. It was a kiss of cloudless love.

"Oh," Molly sighed when they finally parted, "what was that for?"

"A promise that we will come back here sometime," he replied, still holding her close. "Yes, in the springtime . . . the flowers are everywhere in this range," she said with bright eyes.

"OK, spring it is," he agreed. Under an orange sky they set up camp.

"I am going to get some fresh meat for supper," Shadow announced as he walked toward the lake carrying his gun.

"Yes, that would be good," Molly smiled at him. "We'll finish here." James took Molly's hand and spoke to her.

"Let us go sit at the overlook. I want to ask you something." They sat on a trunk of a fallen tree with their arms around each other, silhouetted against the skyline. The darkness crept in beside the two lovers on this western horizon at evensong.

"This is the place for us, Molly, a place for beginning and ending. Beginning my life with you and ending my lonesome life. I have found my place. It's with you. I love you, Molly. Will you marry me? I know I need to ask your father, and I intend to, but . . ."

Molly held her hand gently over his mouth to stop his talking. "You've said enough. Oh, James, do I need to kiss you to get you to be quiet?"

He looked at her deep blue eyes and knew her answer. Her waiting lips were there for him and he kissed her with wanton passion. She kissed him back with a lingering kiss, also wanting more. James suddenly knew that kissing Molly had become too much . . . yet not enough. He drew her away so he could talk to her.

"Molly, I fear we're getting into dangerous ground. Let us get married when we get to Naples so you can come back East with me for a few months. We could have that time together on the train. Say you will," he pleaded.

She saw the solemn expression on his face, but managed to answer. "James, I can't get married without my family there. My mother has so many dreams about my wedding day. You know, women's dreams—a white dress, flowers, and all that." She looked pleadingly at James, tilted her head, and sighed softly. She knew he did not understand.

"Are we going to have our first argument?" she asked. It was a minute before he replied.

"Molly, I can't deny you anything, especially your plea to me like this. But what if we telegraphed our parents and asked them all to meet us in Kansas City for the ceremony?" He touched her face gently, waiting for her reply.

"Oh, do you think we could?" she said excitedly, embracing him.

"Yes, we will be two days in Naples before the eastbound train arrives, and that will give us time to make the arrangements."

His arms encircled her waist, drawing her closer. Her head rested gently on his shoulder as she thought what wonderful plans they had made! Her confidence was soaring, although her eyes were blurring with tears of joy. Molly felt a thundering of her heart and was wildly happy in his arms. He lowered his head to kiss her ear, and began whispering to her between kisses. She sighed with pleasure as his lips began their journey down her neck.

Suddenly a dark thunderhead of living animals appeared, hitting against them in the darkness.

"*Bats!*" James yelled, trying to shield them from being hit as the invaders flew by. He knelt with her on the ground, then her hands were up in her hair fighting the intruders.

"Oh, my," she moaned. "Help me!" It was a swirling black vortex of noisy darting creatures that came right at her. Quickly, James pulled off his jacket and placed it over her head to protect her. He soothed her, hoping she would quit her sobs.

"Molly, they are insect-eaters and I'm sure we're only in their path as they are on their way to slurp up water and catch bugs over at the lake," he tried to reassure her. He thought, *I will protect you, be your protector, and always be there for you.*

A lump came to his throat because it was then that he realized the true responsibility of what a marriage would hold for him. The bats had gone as quickly as they came. He removed the coat and spoke softly to her, still holding her closely.

"Molly, are you all right? I will protect you," he repeated. For the first time since the attack, she opened her eyes. His face was the first thing she saw. Fear left her and she replied with softness, "Yes, thank you."

She reached out for him like a drowning soul, pulled him down to her. They kissed with a fierce urgency, and the touch of his lips on hers made her catch her breath.

One hour before dawn loud yelps and growls woke James

"Wolves!" he yelled, jumping out of his bedroll. It was then that he realized Shadow was up and already pulling on his coat.

"No, my son, its coyotes; there are no wolves this far south. But there is trouble out there. Sometimes the coyote has an uncanny way of causing trouble. Do hurry and saddle up. We may have a chase as I hear the bulls running from the noise.

"Molly, you stay here and secure the other horses. Come on James, let's head off the cattle," Shadow roused. Going out in the dim light and saddling up in the dark was taking too long.

"Cinch tight," Shadow instructed. "They have a head start on us and it will be riding by the seat of your britches out there before the light is good."

"Do you have a plan?" James asked.

"Yes, you go straight down the trail; it leads to the lakes. I will have to break off if I see some tracks going towards the cliffs. Try to keep them from any steep hillsides. That pack may try to run one or two over a cliff. Good luck, and fire two shots if you need any help."

With that said, Shadow gave a war hoop, spurred his mare into a fast pace, and disappeared into the breaking dawn.

Where had Shadow gone? There was a turn in the trail—maybe he went that way? Forest enclosed both sides of the trail. James could only hear the gallop of his horse. The wind rushed around him and the brush whipped his chaps. Caught up in the excitement, he held his reins loosely forward. The stallion responded.

The big horse settled into a pace that dazed James. He could hardly see the trail he was thundering down. Nearly being brushed off on a low-hanging pine branch, he slowed. Traveling that fast, he realized the danger as he did not know the way. James could hear the sounds of the howling and yapping coyotes, but no thundering herd. He hoped Shadow got them rounded up as he hurried down to the lakes.

Molly could not wait any longer, so she quickly saddled the strawberry mare and swung up on her. At a lope, she soon reached the overlook. Listening, she could hear coyotes howling. It sounded like a warning to her. The sound came from the alpine lakes into a world of dark pine and rock. When a streak of light showed over the canyon's rim, Molly spoke to the horse.

"Come on. Shadow needs our help." She kicked her steed into a fast trot down the winding switchbacks toward the lakes. She entered the big meadow and went down to the first lake where the savage sounds were coming from. When she was near the lake, she heard Shadow yell.

"Shoot!" Molly moved forward out of a grove of trees. She gasped when she saw Shadow beside a big tree fighting off a snarling coyote with a stick.

"Get clear!" James yelled to her, "You're in my line of fire." "Shadow, look out!" she yelled, fearing greatly for him. The largest of the angry pack, a male coyote, was snapping at Shadow.

The mad beast growled and then went into mad ravings. When he snapped and barely missed him, Shadow began to climb the nearest tree. Molly could see that Shadow's free arm was hanging irregularly and there was blood running from a wound in his hand. Just then James fired. The animal whined in protest, but the bullet did not take him down.

"They are crazy; it's the smell of blood and nothing else matters," James yelled.

"No," Molly yelled back as she dismounted. "It's rabies! Shoot to kill!" At that instant they both began firing at the attacking animals. Many fell back dead as others limped away.

James became aware that the stallion was acting up behind him. Remembering what Shadow had told him, James turned to pay attention to the fuss Diablo was making. He froze at the sight. Slipping on velvet-padded feet, two crazed coyotes were creeping closer and closer toward Molly's back. He could not shoot as she was directly in his line of fire, so he yelled.

"Molly, look out!" Molly whirled around, but the rising sun was full in her face, blinding her. She put her hand up to shade her eyes. She could hear the snarling killers and feared they were nearly at her feet. Then she realized they had turned back and were creeping away.

There was a hullabaloo and Molly was sure that there was something else there scaring them away. She tried to make it out but, blinded by the sun, she could only see a tall, shadowy figure close by.

It was near the entrance, which was heavily wooded. With the sun behind it, all she could see was a dark form. She darted around the trees, and then ran quickly to where James was standing. He had his rifle up and ready to cover her escape!

Run faster, she thought, and prayed as she fled toward him. Again James was there for her. He held out his free arm and caught her as she ran into his arms. She was trembling so badly she could hardly stand.

No time for weakness, she reminded herself. They heard a ferocious growl and turned to see brown fury raging down on the coyotes like a dark cloud in a whirlwind. The battle was going on, mostly hidden in the grove of trees. For a while, neither spoke. Diablo became edgy. James moved over to still the gallant animal.

Within a few minutes the forest became very still. Not another coyote was in sight. "Shadow! We must go to him right now," she said when she could finally speak. When they came out of the shadows of the tall pines, they found Shadow sitting on the ground under a tree. Molly ran to him.

"Are you really all right?" she began. He grasped her hand in answer.

"Yes, my Estelle, except for a cut I got riding through the trees. The Great Spirit has again given me mercy and protection." Molly took his other hand to see if she could help with the wound.

"What was that?" James asked, meaning the rescue they had witnessed in the trees. Shadow was always the same quiet individual, easy and lovable—the same one whose grandfather had guided the Lewis and Clark expedition over these mountains. He sighed, then answered.

"This time of year, when the bears have been feeding upon berries, they are always around this lake meadow." Knowing that was all the answer he would get, James replied, "Yesterday I thought I saw a large brown one, but it left before I could be sure."

"Yes, I saw him too. Let us catch my horse, and begin our day," was Shadow's only reply.

Chapter Nine

My plan is to follow the Wood River all morning using the old Ulgatcho Indian trail. Then we'll swing south to the Trading Post. This will put us near the Ice Caves and within camping distance of the meeting place of the waters called Tatah. There is much grass there for the young bulls to eat. It will prepare them for the long trip to Denver.

Shadow was showing the wear of these early morning encounters and as Molly listened to him, she made a mental note for him to have a long rest when they got these bulls to the railhead at Naples. As they packed, Molly said to James, "I' m rather sorry to leave the cliffs and the beautiful view it affords us."

"Yes, and the beautiful life we have promised each other here. This place will hold many memories," he added as he leaned over and planted a kiss on her cheek. Molly smiled as she watched the cattle move together.

"I am so thankful that after the encounter with the crazed coyotes we are all safe. And the cattle, they acted so sensibly as they followed Shadow's mare to a safe place near the lakes. The tension has gone out of me. I pray we will have a good ride to the valley below," she confessed to them.

"The Good Book has said to have faith and we can raise mountains," Shadow proudly stated.

"Well, we've done that! And you, Shadow . . . how was your faith when you were running from that mad coyote?" James teased.

"I thank you again for the help, James, but the Good Spirit would have provided," he said in reply.

"I still can't believe you were ready to sacrifice yourself for a bunch of cattle, Shadow. You know how much you mean to me," Molly said.

"All would have gone well, except for my rifle jamming," Shadow said. "I still cannot figure that out. You keep that gun so clean, and baby it so," Molly said as she studied her Indian friend.

When Shadow did not answer, they knew the discussion was over. He did not like to go over past events. How many times had Shadow scolded Molly for crying over spilled milk?

They continued off the mountain. The trail down was steep and rough in spots, but they knew a wide, high valley lay beneath. Soon they would view it all with the many streams flowing into the Big Wood River. The soft morning breeze came rolling down from those rugged Sawtooth Mountains, setting everything in motion. It carried the clean smell of melting snow as the sun continued to beat down.

They entered a valley that was lightly wooded with cottonwoods along silver streams that were running full from their beginning. The soft, misty morning light had the brightness of a summer's day.

"Unusually warm for the first of October," Shadow remarked, and Molly wondered if there was more meaning there.

"I love this time of year," she stated as she motioned her hand to the colorful landscape. Now the light was affording them a full panorama of the hills that lay before them. Applied here and there were scraps of fall colors that were broken by familiar gray brush slopes.

"Yes, here life can be wild and free. There are plenty of elk, antelope, and deer. I have seen their tracks. They are beginning their migrating for the winter months."

Shadow smiled. A dove uttered its soft notes—a murmuring not so much of sadness, but more a morning greeting to the intruders. The drive continued with no break as the trail was easy for them to follow. Late in the day they drove the cattle out onto the range of belly-deep grass that rippled in sun-kissed waves, on and on into the shadow of the higher canyons.

"Our stop should be early in order for the bulls to get their fill on this feed." As Shadow spoke of the bulls you could tell their care was a priority to him. He had become a great cattle rancher in the twenty years he had been with them. The encampment was made on the river bank in a level, fertile bottom land. The water of the river was clear, even though many of the tributaries had become swollen and muddy during the late afternoon.

After camp was set up and the cattle were grazing nearby, James and Shadow declared that they were going hunting.

"We'll bring back the meat for the evening meal," James said as he gave Molly a wave and a wink. They scattered a gaggle of geese downriver. James took careful aim and brought down a fat gander.

"Good shooting! I guess I can entrust you to always protect Estelle," Shadow teased. James smiled.

"I thought she was always your Estelle?"

"We will have to powwow over that," he laughed. Together they stripped the goose and ran a green willow through it for roasting. Then James put it securely in his pack, and they started back to camp.

Molly had gone upstream to take a bath. She had seen an outlet that was screened with trees and she couldn't wait to get in the water. The water was cold, but it served her well. She returned to camp, built up the fire, and began to prepare the evening meal.

When James and Shadow returned they made a table of logs and stumps for sitting around the fire. The warmth was welcome to them in the chilly night air. James gazed at Molly in the glow of the firelight. She was wearing a light blue blouse and her shining damp hair was pulled back with a white scarf. James approached her. He reached out to stroke her hair, then lifted her chin up towards himself.

"You look beautiful, my Estelle." She blushed at his touch, then took his hand and kissed it and returned his smile.

"I'm glad you're here with me." They enjoyed the hearty meal of roast goose and hot biscuits. Shadow was very talkative. Molly and James listened to the soft chant he sang in his native language.

James knew that when he was finished he would want to share the smoking his pipe. The melody was melancholy. When he finished, James asked, "While you prepare the pipe, I wonder—would you tell me about the song."

"My son, I speak of the trouble that came to our people in those days when the buffalo hunt was alive. Their spirit still walks in the old lands and dwells on the beloved Smoky Mountains where we loved to hunt and fought the Snake people and Wasichu.

"I was a grandson of Shoshone and I sang his song because we never lost the magic. Even after the Indian wars, we had a proud spirit that remains powerful and undying." A sigh that was deep within him came out like a wind that springs up cool when it's hot under the sun. He paused as he puffed on the pipe.

"Yes, once a great warrior, but I have no family—no one to mourn for me." He handed the pipe to James, and then continued.

"Who's to say his spirit is not stronger than any other—and does not run faster than his shadow?" Then Molly knew he was talking about himself. She went over to him, gave him a hug and spoke.

"Sun Runner you are, and to me you will always be a great warrior." The two men smiled with admiration at Molly. She looked lovely with the glow of the fire on her face. The reflection of the light gave her an angelic appearance. She was young and vibrant, and in James's eyes most desirable.

Shadow was so proud of her. Molly saw him smile a smile she had never before seen spread over his wrinkled face. He puffed another puff on the pipe, then got up, put the pipe away, and said, "Hetchetu aloh." Then he lay down on his bedroll and immediately fell asleep.

When James came to Molly beside the dying fire, she reached up to him as he approached her. He liked the way she openly showed her affection. He took her in his arms, where she always seemed to fit. The kiss they gave each other was lingering and began a desire the young lovers grasped until the night grew late.

The glow of the flames moonlighting on the rushing water reflected a window of gold. The only other sound was the crickets beginning their evening concert.

The morning dawned cloudy with a sharp wind out of the west. Shadow was awakened by the noise of the river. He saw that the water was high and felt the river's raw power. This concerned him greatly.

"Time to see the rising sun . . . and face the morning," he announced to the two still in their bedrolls near the cold fire bed.

"What's your hurry?" a pretty sleepyhead asked.

"The warm weather we are having has concerned me," he replied.

"Yes, I noticed the snow melt signs were very heavy," James said as he pulled on his boots.

"Oh, Shadow, how will that affect us?" Molly busied herself with her hair fixing and got up slowly, still looking to her Indian friend for his answer.

"Where we cross the river it is narrow, deep, and swift. If it is at flood stage, it will be dangerous.

"Why can't we cross here? It is not dangerous yet," she inquired. Being patient with Molly, he answered her kindly.

"We must take the cattle downriver at least twenty miles to get around the lava flow between ourselves and Naples. There is not a good trail for cattle in this crater area. A person on horseback might try it, but cattle running into one of those crevices, or getting a leg caught in those formations, could be done for."

"If time is of the essence, let's get on with the drive," James coaxed Molly. "Right, no coffee time for you," she smiled back at him, pulling on her coat.

"I'll pack your saddle," was Shadows reply, then he added, "No time to waste." They turned east as they drove the herd through the broken plain lying north of the rail town and traveled hard all morning. The gray clouds moved north and the sky was empty, allowing the sun to come to life and blaze down on the valley.

The river gorge looked as if it had nothing but time on its side. Years of erosion had done much damage. Sometimes the river was wild, and sometimes it looked peaceful. The steepness of the gorge varied, often exposing the muddy river in dark forms. Their moods grew more somber as they rode along it. About noon, they stopped to rest the horses and refresh themselves by some lacy ferns of willow shade that seemed to give off some peace and contentment.

When Molly sighed deeply with anxiety, Jim heard her. He went to her side and spoke gently.

"My dear, do not worry so. Please relax. It will not help to stew."

"You sound like Shadow, but this trip has been nothing but using our wits against the forces of the wild," she replied in low defeated tones so as Shadow would not hear. She continued.

"Maybe it was the tired look Shadow had that frightened me. I am not sure of his age. He could be nearly eighty-years-old."

"Molly, think of the long road behind us and how we've come safely this far," he encouraged. "Now we have ahead of us the last day's ride up the Big Wood and to our destination. *What a trip!*"

Molly went to him, put her arms around his neck, and said, "Thank you." Then they kissed as he held her an extra-long time and did not release her until he felt her relax against him.

When Shadow gathered the pack horses, he mounted Chita and announced, "We need to get across that river now!" Then he turned downriver and began to drive to the crossing. They journeyed most of the afternoon and passed scant growth of mahogany and cottonwoods that blended with the sage. Molly hardly noticed the beauty in the fall scenery. Following the dark, congested river was becoming more terrifying as the last of the small creeks ran full into the nearly flooded river.

She tried not to look at it, but she had to. It was an infernal thing. It boiled and beat and shifted from one channel to another and from the center, then to one shore or the other. The angry water spread, hissing, running like a mill race. Shadow stopped and announced his observation cautiously.

"The banks here are less steep. We have to get across here—and now.

"Can't we wait a few days? I don't feel friendly with this river today." Molly could not repress a shudder at the thought of crossing above that noisy rapid.

"Estelle, you do not realize the waters' true significance; you must appreciate it. Water is the greatest thing on earth. I have dug for water in the desert, watched it seep through the sand and fill up so I could sip it. I've felt it moisten my parched mouth and give my body life."

He hesitated as he saw Molly's fears to move on in life begin to ebb away. We will go in above the constricted rapids. Now prepare yourself for a swim," he instructed as they dismounted to get ready.

"You have done this before, my Estelle, just take care." James nodded and spoke to her.

"When I get these boots and coat off, I will lead as I have been and you get the bulls in right after me."

James quickly mounted up again, then turned and winked at Molly before he rode over the steep bank and slid down into the water. The stallion went right in at his command. He was up to his belly as he entered. In two more steps, James slipped out of the saddle upstream from the horse. With his grip on a saddle strap, he kept close contact with the horse and the two of them began to swim across as the current picked them up.

Molly and Shadow were busy keeping the bulls in close and the pack horses were next. They followed James, swimming against the dangerous current. The Big Wood slid by with a menacing roar. The water whirled and bulged against them, taking them down toward the rapid. Above them, it was wider and shallow enough for the horses and cattle to get their feet under them again. James's horse stumbled for footing above the rapids just as he remounted him.

"Easy boy," he encouraged as he calmed the horse from panic. Diablo continued across to an eddy where the embankment up was not as steep. The horse hit solid ground and plunged onto the shore. He moved him around some scrambling cattle and whooped for them to move on. Then James turned to look back at the rest of them.

Molly was swimming beside Bourbon in the swift current. They found the shallow rapids at about the right place. Then he saw Shadow in the deep water allow his horse to go at a greater distance downstream. What was he doing going that far?

"Shadow!" he yelled, and motioned in alarm. Molly knew Shadow was in trouble when she heard James yell at him. However, Shadow acted as if he did not hear the warning. *It must be the noise of the cattle,* she thought.

The water churned like thunder near the break of the rapids. Then Shadow's mare went under the water. It was frigid and turbulent and very deep there. She could only see the top of Shadow's head. Molly screamed in alarm! Just then Bourbon hit the bank with a grunt. Drawn to Molly's attention was a pack horse having trouble getting up the steep bank.

"You are blocking our way," she said out loud. She reached down and caught the lead rope, tied it to the saddle horn, and proceeded to drag the animal up the bank. By the time she looked up again, she could not see Shadow or his horse anywhere downstream.

She *could* see James, and realized he had gone to the rescue of Shadow. James was riding Diablo at breakneck speed down the river to where the horse was last seen. He stopped quickly, dismounted, then dove in the turbulent waters. Molly gasped.

"Oh God, help them, I'll never do this again, I promise," She wailed. "What if I lose them both? No, no!" Her heart sank as she watched with fear. She knew that in that raging water was the man who truly loved her. *I must act,* she thought, as she spurred Bourbon down to the pack animal.

She took a long rope from the panniers, then rode immediately down the river bank, until Bourbon became even with the swimmer. When she got off the horse, she tripped as she slipped down the wet, steep bank with the rope in her hand. She got up and waded out as far as she could without the current catching her. In two big waves, she circled the rope above her head and let fly the loop on to her target.

James seized the rope, although he had floated about half way out in the dark water with Shadow's dead weight dragging him along.

Quickly he wrapped the rope around his chest. Then he signaled for Molly to pull them out.

Molly could see he was about finished. James had a grasp on Shadow that he would never have given up. They both might drown unless she helped them. Molly pulled on the rope, climbed up the bank, and ran up to Bourbon, where she tied the rope around the saddle horn. Hurriedly she led the horse farther up the bank, pulling the rope tightly behind them. She only stopped when the men were safely to shore.

Frantically, she ran back to the nearly drowned men. As she approached James, he was laying face down in the mud. She laid her hand on his back and felt him shudder and cough.

"Oh James, I thought I was going to have to dig two graves out here on the bank of this angry river," she moaned to him. Then she put her arms around him to help him sit up.

"I'm okay," he uttered. "Go see to Shadow."

Chapter Ten

She looked at Shadow and remembered the things he had said to her about water giving life.

Look at you now, she thought as her faith was shaken. *Do you still feel the same? Well, I don't.* He lay there near his precious water, and Molly saw the mud on his face and in his hair. The stillness of his wet body frightened her. He had never opened his eyes, and when Molly felt for his pulse, she felt a very weak one.

"Oh Shadow, this river has beaten you!" Then his eyelids fluttered open. He reached for her hand. His breathing became slow. He strained forward with a gurgling sound in his chest. Then he fell back against the bank.

"My heart," he whispered, and then became unconscious again. *"Shadow!"* she cried with desperation in her voice. Her eyes blazed as she stared at him. Then gradually they softened and she gave a long sigh and turned to James.

James knelt beside them, feeling a lot better than he was. He looked for a sign of recovery in Shadow.

"He is so weak. Can we get to Naples tonight?"

"Yes, we could make it before dark," she replied, studying his face. He reached out to touch her, and then spoke.

"You get my horse, and I will carry Shadow over to that stand of cottonwood. We will make a stretcher, so bring the small pack horse too, as it has the tools on it that I need to work with."

They worked the next hour beside the warm fire, getting themselves dry and making the frame for the litter. Then they prepared the pack animal to pull it. The other animal carried the things that were necessary for their trip to Naples.

"We will leave the bulls here. I will find someone to come out here and tend them," he said.

"The important thing is getting Shadow to a doctor when we can," said Molly. They left the herd, the extra horses, and some camping supplies there in the meadow near the river. Shadow's horse was never recovered.

Within the hour they swung into their saddles. Now, riding beside James, Molly had time to tell him what was on her mind.

"James that was an irrational thing you did going in after Shadow. I will never ask anyone to do such dangerous acts again."

"Molly, love is the only rational act. But remember, no one exists alone. I did what I had to do, for all of us, and would do this again, if needed." He reached over to touch her hand, and held it until she looked at him.

"James, I love you," was all she said. It was enough for him. He gave her a faint smile. It was all he could gather up. His worry for Shadow was wearing on him.

"A heart attack is what I think Shadow has had. It made sense by the way it all happened at the river." From the river, they turned south to Naples and traveled for the rest of the afternoon. They could see the tops of many buildings over the rise in the sagebrush flats that ran to the hills. As they brought Shadow through town on a makeshift stretcher, many eyes watched with interest.

Trudging down the dusty street, Molly could hear the ring of the blacksmith's hammer. She watched the bustle-skirted women pausing at the shops as they strolled down the wooden main street. There were gamblers, miners, cowboys, and sheepherders crowded along in front of the many saloons and gambling houses. Molly saw one person looking as if he were going to come up to them. She called to him.

"Mister, please, where is the doctor's office?"

"Follow me, and I'll show you," he waved. They went down the main street near the end of town to a large building with two signs hanging out front. One read: "Naples Infirmary." The other read: "L. L. Neher, M.D"

By the time they got to the front steps, there were several men there to help take the sick man inside. Molly thanked them and her warm smile seemed to be enough as they acknowledged her and quickly left. Some time later, Molly and James walked out into the street.

"Dr. Neher seemed real kind. I think he will do his best for Shadow." James knew Molly was reluctant to leave the office, as the doctor had insisted. He continued.

"We have made him real comfortable and it may be hours before he regains consciousness." Molly was not listening to James, as he directed her down the street to the Grand Mc Fall Hotel.

"This is a very nice place, a beautiful lobby. You will like it. He led her up to the entrance.

"I will go in and get us rooms, then you go up and rest, I will have the things you brought sent up to your room. I will be right next door, Molly, please listen," he said as he took hold of her.

She looked at him with a frown on her brow that was always there when things were at their worst.

"OK, Molly?" He asked as he shook her slightly, then hugged her, holding her against him for several minutes. Then he turned and went inside to register them for their rooms for the night. The honky tonk piano at Diamond Bell's rang out loudly and a big burly coal-fired steam engine sounded a chug up from a start, hissing steam.

Molly heard none of this. She stood on the boardwalk and only acknowledged with a nod as James left her for a moment. Her eyes were still on the building where they had left Shadow. Even though the doctor was very nice, she felt that Shadow still needed her. She felt like crying, but realized that the doctor was right; Shadow may need time.

She quickly went inside. Before James went to his room, he ordered a bath to be sent up for Molly and asked for a housekeeper to attend her. The hotel manager introduced him to Mary Bowen and assured him that she was the best girl for the job.

"Hello, Miss Bowen," James politely said. "Do you know where Molly can get clothes for a trip back East?" he asked the pretty, dark-eyed young woman.

"Yes," she replied, then continued, "but call me Mary. My sister can make her anything she cannot buy here."

"That will be so helpful. Now I am off to the mercantile store to get her the items I know she will need. Later we will talk of the clothes I wish to be made for her. When I knock, please get the things at the door from me, for I know that will be more proper," he smiled.

He left her a good payment of money, and said to her, "Take good care of my love, Mary."

Oh, how good it feels to be clean again! Molly spent nearly an hour soaking in the warm bath to take away the aches and tenseness she felt. She thought about this day and knew, like everyone else, that the river had marked her. James and she had seen a side of it that they would never forget.

She smiled as she thought about James making her have this time to herself. *James, my love!* She believed life was going to be good with him spoiling her. At she thought of James's love for her, her heart leaped—and desire was indeed a part of her love for him.

Mary went up to Molly's room and knocked on the door. She explained who she was as she knew Molly was not expecting anyone. When she heard the plan, Molly gladly welcomed her in.

"I need to talk to another woman," she said. "It has been a long time since I have had the chance for girl talk. You know what I mean?" She smiled at Mary.

"I am here for you, Molly. First I have brought you some cream for your skin, for when you finally get out of there," Mary teased. The two young women were about the same age and already were enjoying getting to know one another. Molly asked Mary to tell her about herself.

Mary had come to Naples with her family when she was very young. Her father was a supervisor for the railroad. They lived in Missouri when he first came to manage the new railroad depot here at Naples. They had a large house built for them upon their arrival. Except for a finishing school term, Mary had always lived in this valley. She enjoyed the work at the exclusive hotel meeting most of the visiting guests.

"If you have the time, I would like to invite you out to our house for an evening," Mary said.

"I'd love to," was Molly's reply.

"Give me time to see about Shadow. He is so ill that I'm afraid for his life."

"You were so fortunate to have made it at all the way across the flooded river. It has claimed several lives in the last few years," Mary told her. Molly replied with a sigh.

"We were certainly blessed with safety on our drive here, but the doctor said Shadow suffered a heart attack before he went into the river. I remember how he was so insistent that we get these cattle to the railhead. It was as if he was driven. I should have seen it coming and didn't."

"Oh no, you can't always know about old people. Sometimes my uncle was just bossy, and sometimes he was concerned," Mary added. "He was someone I greatly admired and we had such fun together, but before he died, he was different. Sometimes I think God allowed him to see into the future."

Just then a knock at the door interrupted the girl talk. Molly was just finishing dressing. They both answered.

"Who is it?" They laughed.

"James," was the impatient reply. Again, a giggle.

"Your love calls." Mary bowed."

"No, do not let him in," Molly motioned. "OK, I'll save you, but he sure sounds impatient," she remarked with a smile.

"I am sorry, but Molly is indisposed," Mary said through the door and could hardly keep from laughing.

"That's fine. I just wondered where Molly wants to eat dinner," was his cool, deep-voiced response. Feeling sorry for him, Molly came to the door, opened it a crack to talk through, and said, "Hi James, could we eat here? It may be faster. I want to see Shadow again tonight before it gets too late."

"Then we will meet downstairs in the mezzanine when you are ready," he replied. He went downstairs and out into the street, where he walked down to the telegraph office. He sent three messages, then went to keep his date with Molly.

In the evening after dinner, Molly and James sat on a bench near the edge of town. It was a beautiful moonlit night and James's arm was around her shoulder.

"Molly, you look stunning in a real dress," James smiled. His eyes sparked a hint of a tease. She was wearing a pale-colored silk frock that was so stunning on her he hadn't been able to take his eyes off her all through dinner.

"Thank you, some admirer sent it up to my room. I do not know how he or she knew my exact size or this short style I like to wear." As she spoke, a turned-up corner of her lip revealed the joy. He touched the corner of her mouth.

I love the way you tease back, he thought. Her eyes were on him, and she was thinking. *James, you look like you are about to kiss me. This awareness of each other and this special attraction we have has not changed since we first met.*

The moonlight caught her eyes. She was so lovely, this western woman that James loved and admired.

"I have fulfilled part of my destiny in finding the woman of my dreams," he said. The desire toward her rose in him as he took her completely in his arms. He kissed her neck, and then his lips met her wanting lips with a kiss that swept him up and away. He then began a series of kisses on her face that made her sigh. She had her arms around his neck. In this teeming embrace, Molly could feel the beating of his heart.

"James," she began, as she pulled away with consideration. "We were talking about my dress, and I wish to thank you for it." James felt her hesitancy.

"Well, I had some help picking it out, and it is just made for you, my dear." Molly blushed, "The dinner was very nice, also, and to be here—just the two of us. It was what I needed to face the doctor and his report about Shadow."

James knew Molly had heard the words that Shadow was going to die, but they had no validity at the time and she needed to talk about it.

"He is a compassionate doctor, but does he hold in his hand the knowledge of life and death, like God? Oh, what is the matter with me? He is a kind man with the desire to help ease pain . . . even mine," Molly said as she moved into his arms for comfort.

"Somewhere there's a door I can open so the light can flow in to show me the future without Shadow." She gasped a cry, holding back so much emotion. Holding her tight, James spoke softly.

"Molly, go ahead and cry. You need to, but remember this . . . Shadow will not be gone, be will always be with us. He will be with us when we ride the mountains in the spring and fall. He'll be there when we collect cattle, when the foals are born. He'll always be there." Molly then began to sob inconsolably. After awhile the sobbing was only a shudder.

James turned her face to him and said, "Molly, you are a strong woman of the western frontier. You know of life and death. Shadow is an old man. Perhaps he wants you to let him go. You must think of him." He touched a tear falling on her cheek with his finger, and then lifted her chin. Molly looked at the man that possessed the special tenderness she remembered, the kindness that had attracted her to him. She was reminded of what transpired between them in his care for Shadow.

"I love you." was all she said. Then they walked back to the hotel. In her room, Molly could not sleep, so she began a prayer.

"Oh, Lord, we were so happy. Do we need forgiveness for being happy? Was it selfish? One is suffering; please show me a sign of what is right. What is right to do?"

With that prayer on her lips, she fell into peaceful sleep. A brief downpour of the storm the night before had left the fragrance of the sage, pure and agreeable. The late morning sun was warming the earth and the rolling foothills throughout the wide valley. The black horse pulling the buggy blew his nose as the tension in him released. He trotted out to the open prairie.

The three of them were seated together on the buggy's padded bench, drinking in the scenes of the morning. Just three days ago Molly had confessed to James that she knew in her heart concerning Shadow's passing.

"Know what, my love?" she asked. "Now I know Shadow is going to die. We have been close for almost a quarter of a century. I am sure my life without his presence would have been but a black whirling void which I dare not look at, but for you, James."

"You must have knowledge that Shadow was a blessing that God loaned to you, and now He is asking that you put this gift behind you, Molly. You cannot prevent it."

"We see day by day Shadow getting weaker and the far away look in his eye," she cried. This Sunday morning, Shadow showed signs of more strength. The good doctor suggested that James and Molly take his patient out for a ride in his horse-drawn carriage. On this beautiful October day the dry grass in the meadow was lust and long, brushing the wheels as they sped along. They rode up and down shady, wooded, gentle slopes and through sunny meadows.

When they reached the river, they saw that a small lake had been formed at its flood stage. It was blue and tranquil, shining in the afternoon sun. They drove to the far end and stopped beside a big cottonwood that had outlived its time and had given way to the winds that sometimes howled up this valley.

James helped Shadow down from the wagon so he could sit with his back against a stump. When Molly sat close to him, she said, "A good place for our picnic."

"Yes, a place of chicory," he said softly, lifting his hand at the abundance of birds. "And deer wander through these dense cottonwood groves." He pointed to the sharp, pointed tracks in the soft dirt. Molly could tell he was pleased with the place.

They finished their picnic and Shadow began to talk.

"Once my people and others like me possessed this whole, vast land to call home." He motioned toward the land around them, then continued.

"We were happy here, but we had our sorrows, also. Molly, nature to a saint is sacred. If we are children of God, we have a tremendous treasure in nature. In every wind that blows, in every night and day, in every sign in the sky, and in every blooming and every withering of the earth. The test is to bring this into subjection, and we can have power to face difficulties. There is a coming of His Spirit if we simply use our starved imagination."

He paused. His eyes held Molly's, then he said, "Devote to God the sunrises, the sunsets, the sun, the stars, the changing seasons. Associate your ideas worthy of God with all that happens in nature and your hope will be particularly bright. His glory covers the heavens and His praise fills the earth—His splendor is like the sunrise and rays flash from His hand, where His power is hidden. This the Good Book tells us we can have. These things I have known for many a year." He raised his hand into the sky, but did not continue. Then he leaned back against the tree as he reached for her hand.

Molly remembered the first time Shadow had shared his faith with her. Although she was a young girl at the time, it was his words that influenced her to live her life for God. Shadow had said, "My faith is a foundation that guides my choices and gives me the hope, the purpose, and that peace that comes from understanding how much God loves me."

Then Shadow spoke again. He said, "Surely one could have peace of mind and heart here. It's a beautiful place, my Estelle. Remember, every instant of our time together with our loved ones is precious. Thank you for bringing me here."

Molly searched Shadow's white face and saw the tired eyes that sought hers. "Yes, every moment—I will never forget you," she replied. On the ride back to town, Shadow, leaning his head against James's shoulder, fell asleep. Molly and James smiled when they looked up in the blue sky to see a dark dot moving in a floating motion far above them. They forded the creek where the trees and shrubs surrounded its crossing.

A noise through the trees brought their attention to a large brown bear that stood upon his hind legs and swayed back and forth with the motion of waves. The horses did not shy and Molly and James felt no danger as they passed by the big animal. They continued their journey back to Naples with more strength to face the days ahead.

"Molly, Molly!" Mary's voice was low but intense as she tapped on the door of Molly's room.

"Molly, where are you?" She got no answer, so she hurried to James Russell's room and knocked loudly. James opened the door and, with a surprised look, asked, "What is it, Mary?"

"Do you know where Molly is? The doctor wants her to come to the infirmary immediately!"

"Oh, it's Shadow," he cried, quickly getting his coat. "Thank you, but no, I do not know where she is. I will try to find her."

"Oh, I hope it is not bad news," Mary said as she walked with him down the stairs. James replied, "I am afraid it might be, and today we were going out to bring in the bulls to pen up so we can ship tomorrow. She was really looking forward to getting out again, but was afraid to leave Shadow. She has been with him almost every hour of the day this week."

"Oh, poor Molly, she needs her family here. When did you say they might arrive?" Mary asked.

"Tomorrow," he answered, brightening up his response. "And if you can keep a secret, my folks might be here then, too. I also sent for her brother at the ranch when I knew Shadow was ill."

"It sounds like there are important plans in the making," she smiled. "Yes, good plans, but I'm afraid the sad ending with Shadow's illness might need to be taken care of first."

"Let me know how I or my family can help you and Molly," she said, adding a goodbye as he left the hotel. Down the street, Doctor Neher found Molly in the small chapel of the infirmary.

"Miss," he said as he touched her arm. "I have been looking for you. It is not good news."

"Yes, I know, I was with Shadow all morning. We said our goodbyes—for now." She spoke with a choke in her voice. The kindly doctor took her hand and offered his sympathies, then left her there. Molly was thankful that she'd had these last three days with Shadow and for the talks they had had.

Shadow's words that morning were still on her mind. He had said, "Two things you think are important right now in your life, dear Estelle:

desire and ability. You can lose one and then you will find out the other is not as important."

She was not sure she understood him at her young age. She knew they would have more meaning as she continued in prayer with her God. In addition, he had told her upon his death that he wished to be cremated. She agreed, for this James and she could easily promise.

"James," she said aloud, then smiled at herself for saying his name. Maybe I will always have this warm feeling when I think of him. Oh yes, I hope I always feel this way, she thought.

"Molly," a deep voice called. She turned and moved right into his arms. She clung to James and wept. He let her weep away her grief. For like showers, her tears would bring a new springtime to her and a new hope in time.

James had already told the nurse attending Shadow that the service for him would be tomorrow after the train from the East arrived. Then he had gone to the chapel, knowing he would find Molly there.

"Do you still wish to go with me to bring in the bulls?" he asked Molly when she had recovered from sobbing.

"Yes, I know it will help my sadness, and Shadow and I already talked about it today. It will give us time to mourn Shadow without any real sharpness of pain," she said sadly.

"I have made arrangements for Gill to go with us out to the river, where Blackie is holding the bulls. With their help, we should be back in town before dark," he replied, still holding her tight.

"Good. I will go change, and then meet you at the stable."

"I will have the horses ready to go, and oh, please pick us up some grub and water to take," James asked. When Molly left the chapel, she saw Mary at the cafe.

"Molly!" Mary said quietly, as the two embraced, "I am sorry about Shadow." I know he was like family to you all."

"Thank you. We will have a service tomorrow out by the lake. If you wish to, come at three."

"Yes, I will be there. Well, here is your order, I will see you later." She started out, but turned to add. "Molly, wait, this may be important. There was a stranger here that was asking about Shadow. He was a rough-looking man with a scarred face, and he held his left arm as if it had no use. "Did anyone tell him where to find Shadow?"

"Not that I know of, but it is a small town. Just take care." "Yes, and I will tell James, and if you see the sheriff, would you tell him what you know?" Mary nodded in reply, and with a wave and a smile to each other, the two went their separate ways. When Molly got to the stable, she told James about the inquiring man. James strapped on his gun belt, checked his rifle, and handed extra cartridges to Molly.

"Best to be prepared," he said with a hint of a frown on his brow. "Now young lady, you do look terrific in that red, roan leather vest," he sparked, pulling her into his arms. She smiled at him, remembering how electrifying it felt to be held and admired by him.

"Oh, this, I just picked it up the other day," she said as she modeled it proudly.

"Well, what a pick! Hmm, you smell good, too," he said as he reached for her again. Then he kissed her on her neck. Molly was so proud: the vest had been extravagant with its hand-loomed wool trim and the big wooden buttons. It fit over the contours of her body with the two detailed pockets in the front.

"You are worth the extravagance. Besides the way you look, I like the way you kiss. Let's do it again," he teased.

Instantly her lips were on his and there was fire in them. He returned the passionate kiss, feeling loved and desired. After awhile the young lovers parted. He helped her tie her supplies on the saddle. Bourbon nudged her slightly in greeting. Then James put the rest in his saddle bags on his horse, Diablo, who danced with excitement and the anticipation of the ride.

They loped up the track toward the river. Gill had already gone ahead. James wondered if that was a good idea now that he knew about the inquiring stranger. Soon he relaxed and was enjoying himself.

I love life out in the open, he thought, *and the mountains draw me, in fact Idaho has claimed me.* Riding across a grassy knoll, he felt the wind in his face. He enjoyed the feel of riding Diablo, knowing he was ready to expand all his energy any time.

James had really missed being out on this Idaho range. He glanced at Molly.

"I have fallen in love with your countryside," was all he said to her, as she was not talking much. James sensed Molly needed some quiet time and this was the perfect place to get it. She smiled and nodded to him in acknowledgment.

I wonder what James is really expecting out here, Molly thought as she glanced over at him. However, the frown disappeared from his face as he strapped on his gun belt. Yet she remembered, *Shadow had said to always be ready when you are out in the wild. Shadow—What a beautiful fall day you picked to leave me!*

107

A tear fell from her eye. She brushed it aside with her gloved hand. *I see you, Shadow, in the gold-lined trees of the creek, in the sparkling yellow leaves that fall along the road, and in the dot I know is a hawk that soars above my head.*

The fall colors increased the closer they got to the main river. They began to enjoy the ride, and most certainly the horses did as they picked up the pace. They were hard to hold up as they came upon the ridge overlooking the meadow near the Big Wood.

"Easy boy," James called out. Diablo obeyed with a tossing of his head. It was too quiet and there was not a living thing in sight.

"Where are Gill and the livestock?" Molly asked with alarm. "Maybe over the next draw," James answered with hope. "But we should be hearing them if they were that close," she spoke with dismay in her voice. They rode to the north, away from the river, where they found two of the bulls in a thicket. These bulls seemed frightened of them.

"It looks as if they have been run, and just recently," James said. He studied the many cattle and horse tracks, trying to determine what had happened. The trampled grass looked as if there had been a stampede.

"What will we do?" Molly asked.

"Follow the tracks. Gill may need our help even more than ever," he replied as he turned his horse toward the canyons to the North.

They followed the tracks up a wide canyon that divided in two. Tracks went in both directions. James and Molly stopped to decide what to do. "We need to stay together," James announced, looking at Molly's face.

"No, you are just saying that to protect me. We won't be that far apart, we will be able to signal if we need help. I will go up this narrow canyon riding along the stream at a walk. We can stay parallel to each other. James, I just know it will work out."

Her mind was set. James could tell by her voice. "OK, if you stick to that," he agreed. They entered the narrow canyon at a fast walk. Soon the canyon nearly closed, showing the cattle tracks single-file on the earth. The hillside was climbable, so Molly and the horse began to side hill at an angle to reach the top of the ridge.

Her idea was to not walk into any trap. She remembered the story. Shadow had told about the evil spirits in a deep, river-cut canyon less than twenty feet wide. A flash flood had nearly wiped out all the hunting braves in their tribe. She reasoned this was not possible on such a bright, cloudless day as today. However, she shivered from the thought.

She buttoned her heavy, gray coat, expecting it would make the eerie emotion she had about this place go away. The light changed on the face of the rock from reds to purple when she rode beside some old volcanic formations.

Most of the time she could see into the canyon bottom, but not all the time. Noisy squirrels and a slow porcupine were all that moved in front of Molly and her horse. Further down, along the skyline, Molly could examine uplifts and faults that created forms of limestone pinnacles. They were about to reach the first one when Bourbon stopped with his ears alert. Molly got off, led the horse behind the largest one, ground-tied him, and pulled her rifle out. Then she quietly peered out from the rock hiding place.

A bullet zipped by her face, followed by the sound of a sharp rifle crack. Frightened and dazed by the noise and attack, she fell on her knees to the ground, where she sat with her back against the rock. The horse jumped but did not move away. Molly reached for the rope and pulled him closer into the protection of the large rock fortress.

What should she do next? She and her brother had been shot at only once. What did they do then? She remembered that they needed to know who their enemy was in order to fight him. And to gain time so that help would come. She knew James would come.

Chapter Eleven

James followed the stream for a mile up the wide can-yon. He listened intently for any sound. The only inter-ruption that was disturbing the quiet was a crow that cawed as it flew overhead.

"I shouldn't have let Molly go by herself," he mumbled. The big horse moved his ears back as if he heard the worry in his master's voice.

They reached the main stream fed by the snow melt. Before crossing, Diablo snorted, as if catching another scent. The stream had been at high water level yesterday and left dark, wet earth where tracks were easy to see. James could figure that besides the cattle there were a number of horses that had forded the brook.

Most of the shod horses were bearing riders. He saw the pack mule's smaller tracks. Then he realized there were two riders' tracks just ahead of him—maybe an hour or less, he guessed. Being careful not to be ambushed, James left the broad trail. He cut far across the wide hill, traveling up to the high ridge.

"I should be able to see Molly when I top out," he thought. He kept himself hidden in the small Juniper tree groves as much as he could, hoping not to be spotted by the enemy.

"The enemy—who are they? Where are those two drovers I hired?" He questioned in his mind, knowing he should be able to put this mystery together. "Mary said there was a man in town that was questioning Shadow's whereabouts. Could he be responsible for all of this?

111

And what does he want besides the cattle? There is more to this than we know.

If Shadow were here, he could see through this in a minute. *Boy, I miss his help.* James pushed Diablo to travel faster up to the summit. He saw tangled branches and brush dressed in an autumn russet hue at the green, gray cliff. The cliff above sheered out with many crooks and seams in its weather-beaten front. Suddenly, they both heard the sounds at the same time.

Diablo snorted and tossed his head. James got off the horse and ground-tied him near the rock outlay. He crept out on one of the overhangs and peered into the canyon below. A dust cloud was rising up from in the bottom, about two hundred yards down the ravine. The lost bulls were moving round and round and began their bawling, nervous sounds.

There were two riders; only one looked familiar. It looked like they were trying to settle the bulls down and keep them from stampeding back down the canyon. Suddenly a shot rang out, followed by another.

"Bang! Bang!" The shots echoed in the canyon, but James realized they were not shots close to him. The shooting came from the top of the ridge to his right.

Two shots meant Molly was in trouble, he remembered with fear. *Where is she?* Then he saw a movement behind a large rock formation.

"These eerie formations can take on haunting appearances," he noted, shading his eyes from the dirt coming up at him. First he thought he saw a huge brown shadow beside a freestanding monolith. There were clouds moving in, shading the earth from the sun, which created many shadows. Still searching, he saw Bourbon move out in the sunlight near another formation as its brightness caught his red color fully.

The horse was standing behind a dome-shaped rock. A movement in front of the horse, in the shadow of the rock, had to be Molly.

"Yes, that is her gray wool jacket. Thank God she is all right," he whispered. Then the sharp crack of another rifle shot came from that ridge! He saw Bourbon shy sideways as the bullet hit near him.

"They are being shot at!" he gasped. "I must get there to help her." The dust cloud was beginning to obstruct his view across the canyon.

"The shooting must have upset the cattle," he thought. "If I am to get across before they stampede, I should be riding. A stampede with those bulls' strong bodies in such a rush and with their horns clashing is not what I need to be near!"

At this stage they exist only for flight and are just mindless, charging beasts." Quickly he checked the cinch, tied up the rope, then swung into the saddle . . . then at a fast trot traversed down the slope. He crossed the stream before the running herd got there.

It wasn't until he crossed the slow, quiet stream at the bottom that he knew what he was going to do. James was pretty sure he knew where the shooting was coming from. He had seen a small whiff of smoke rise from a spent rifle. He would circle behind the spirals of rock and come in behind the shooter.

An element of surprise always gave one an advantage. James and the big horse were about to the top when a lot of shooting began again. This time the loud battle was coming from the bottom of the canyon where the cattle were. Then there was the noise of the stampede, and the swirling dirt became worse.

Spurring Diablo on, he felt he must hurry to get in position. The firing of that rifle began again at the top of the ridge. This was alarming to James because he could not see what was happening.

One, two, three shots. Molly, are you all right? He cried out silently. Molly sat frozen to the rock she was hiding behind, her thoughts racing.

"Should I fire my gun back at them, or wait to do a surprise attack?" Then Molly wondered, *What would Shadow do? I am afraid if I show myself any more I might be hit, especially if the killer is a good shot. I must keep alert, watch Bourbon for signs, and listen closely. I just hope I can see clearly as this wind seems to carry a lot of dirt.*

She shivered again, not knowing if from fright or from the cold that seemed to be increasing. This waiting was getting to her. Harris Davis felt the air become suddenly colder. All around him he could see what he thought was a ground dust storm creeping in.

Slowly, it came pouring low over the hill, relentless, like some huge, crawling creature. He pulled his jacket closer to himself and cursed.

"If this keeps up I won't be able to see my captives and they might escape." He realized his shooting at them did not scare them.

"Hey you, give yourself up—come out from behind that rock right now," he yelled, his deep, cold voice rang out with hatred. He stepped out, away from the rock that was protecting him. Like a crazy person, he had his rifle in his good hand and was waving it in the air, moving toward where Molly was waiting.

Just then, James stepped out behind him and, with his gun leveled on the killer, commanded, "Stop there. Drop your gun and turn around!"

Startled by the voice, Davis stopped. He turned, and when he opened his mouth, strange wordless sounds came out of it. His voice rang with hatred. A quick flash of madness shown in his eyes, and all reasoning was swept aside by his evil nature.

James knew this corrupt person's next step would be to level his gun at him. Before this happened, James aimed, and got a shot off at Davis's rifle. "Bang! Crack!" The bullet made a sharp sound as Davis's rifle split into several pieces. The impact knocked Davis back upon the ground. James commanded again to the fallen man: "Get your hands up!"

This only enraged the outlaw. When Davis rose, the bellow he gave out was more chilling than the mist that was moving in. Like the crazed person he was, Davis gave out a shout as he ran at James. James stepped aside, causing him to run by him. When the evil man missed grabbing James, he realized his mistake too late. Davis had gone too far out on the edge of the cliff.

The mixture of mist and dirt swirled everywhere as the wind picked up. He stared into it. Staring into empty space, he saw it take shape, and Davis darkened as he saw a figure loom before him. It was dark and immense and moving in a sway as it moved closer and closer, now just a step away from him.

Davis screamed, "No, help me!" As he backed up one more step, he fell into space. With a loud cry, he tumbled to the rocks below, and to his violent death.

After this frightful scene, Molly ran to James and he grasped her in his arms, with the rifle at his side. They breathed words of endearment to each other. Then Bourbon nickered, and James whirled around, pushing Molly behind him.

Coming up the slope was a rider, his hat first visible before he emerged into full view. "It's Dalton!" Molly exclaimed. She began to run toward him.

Dalton had a big smile on his face as he dismounted and held out his arms for his sister to run into. Their embrace was long and happy as they danced around talking to each other. Then Dalton held her away and said, "You, Molly, soften my heart like the beauty of autumn."

She replied, "You Dalton, warm my heart like the tang of old wine." Dalton hugged her again. Then, with a twinkle in his eyes, he asked her, "What is there about you, little sis? I think you have changed. What is that glow you have? Are you that glad to see me, or is it this ornery young man here with you that have caused you to look so?"

Dalton then held out his hand to James. As they greeted each other, their eyes met. Both men's eyes sparkled with the secret they held together.

"How did you know to come here to this place? I do not think it was a coincidence. Dalton, tell me," she demanded.

"Well, I guess James had better fess up," he teased in reply. "Not now," James answered. "Let us join Gill in the bottom of the canyon and get those bulls on their way to that railhead."

They helped Molly catch Bourbon and the three of them began their ride off the ridge.

"You're still in trouble, James. You sent for Dalton, didn't you?" Molly began speaking as she rode alongside of him. She was still amazed that to just look at him made her want to touch him and to always be by his side.

"Yes, don't you think it was a good thing?" he asked, trying not to let Molly ask any more questions.

"Oh yes, and the sheriff showing up to arrest those rustlers was a good idea, too, don't you think?" Molly bragged with a smile.

"I suppose that was your idea? Well, it was a good one, my dear," James confessed, still not telling Molly why he sent for Dalton to come to Naples. He looked at her there in her felt riding hat with strands of light brown hair falling in her face. She was so young and adorable.

"Oh, Molly you are my life. Before I met you, I was just a wandering, lost soul. I should do a better job of protecting you."

These thoughts were filling his head as he remembered the danger she had just faced. "What caused that wanted murderer to jump?" Dalton questioned them from out of the blue. "There are a lot of loose ends here, I think."

He turned to James for an answer, who kept looking down the trail and did not reply. There was no answer from Molly either, and that was unusual, as Dalton had learned. Soon they came to the herd of bulls that were grazing near the brook; Gill galloped his horse up to James, nodded, and spoke.

"I didn't know I would get into such excitement. Blackie and I will have a great story to tell when we get to town. Also, I am glad we met Dalton on his way to town as we needed his leadership back there. I' m not sure we would have had such an easy time if he hadn't been here.

"Yes, that was luck, and I'm glad no one was hurt that we hired," Dalton said. "Thank you for all you did. You put yourselves in the line of fire defending our property and you gained a friend here. You will be rewarded as I want you to apply for the award for bringing in Davis," he added.

"Thank you, it will be appreciated," Gill said as he and Blackie rode off to gather the cattle. The cowhands took over and the cattle moved at a steady pace along the Big Wood River in the direction of town. Dalton, James, and Molly took the lead, enjoying their time together.

It was a time to communicate about Shadow and his last week here with them. When she told the last of the story to Dalton, he said to Molly, "The one thing I remember Shadow taught me was to not let our lives dwell on details. Make a decision and stick to it. I think that is   pretty   good   advice."
Then, with a twinkle in his eye, he winked at James and Molly, pushed his horse into a faster gait, and rode on ahead of them, leaving them to ride alone.

"What was that all about?" Molly looked with suspicion at James for the answer. James said nothing, but reached for Molly's hand. Then he pulled off her glove and placed a diamond ring on her finger.

"I love you, Molly." He kissed her hand before he released it to her. She gasped a happy sigh, looking at the ring.

"I love it; it's beautiful. Thank you, James, my love." The gold band glistened in the sun, but the large diamond was radiant, just like her eyes. Molly leaned over and planted a kiss on his lips. James had never been happier. They rode hand in hand the rest of the passage.

Shadows flooded the earth like slow-moving water with the grass whispering in the half-spent breath of the wind. There was a feeling of calmness, the first they'd enjoyed in a long time. As Gill and Blackie pushed the cattle into Naples, the town folks stood and stared at all those young bulls trailing down Main Street. Those that recognized Dalton in the lead with them began to follow on to the railroad corral. Unnoticed, James and Molly turned off the street to the Mc Fall Hotel just as the sun was sliding into a layer of clouds that banked along the western sky.

"Winter is in the air," Molly said as she gathered her long, wool coat around her tightly. The night wind had picked up in their long walk to the edge of the Little Wood River. Hand in hand in silent communication, they walked wind-blown along the starlit path. They could still see the lights of town. She sat on the bench and James took her hand kissed it, then sat beside her. He pulled her close to him and held her tightly to still her shivering form.

Soon the gleam of the moon on the water gave a glow that made it feel as if this was the end of space and that they were the only ones on earth. As far as they were concerned, they *were* here tonight at their favorite place.

"Molly dear," James began, "I have built castles in the air, and now I must put foundations under them." He touched her hair that flowed softly along her face, then reached for her hand, held it in a most tender way as if it might break.

"God has answered my prayer in His own way, in His own time," he began. "Was it only a chance meeting between you and me? I don't believe it. I found you to love you, and I want to marry you this week so we can go back East together. We could call it our honeymoon trip."

She began to say something in reply but he stilled her with his fingers over her lips. "It is time to construct our castle, my Estelle. You're everything I've ever wanted or ever thought I'd have," he smiled.

"You're everything I wanted," she repeated, "Yes, I'll marry you. I love you. Thank you for coming along on this drive with us and for often thinking of my safety. You have done so much for me, my love."

They embraced with a sweetness in their touch. "That is why you sent for Dalton and our parents, isn't it, so we could get married? This is the secret you had with Dalton," she stated when they parted.

"Yes, I have been planning this ever since we got into town. Then with Shadow getting sick and everything that happened, I had my doubts how it would work out. Oh Molly, you make me so happy. This is the beginning of our dreams."

"Yes," she replied, as the corners of her lips curved upward. "Great dreams I know you hold secretly in your heart for us."

There it is, she thought, *a whole new life for the taking. We will achieve grand dreams, one day at a time.*

He held her eyes with his, then gently drew her closer to himself. She sighed.

"Tell me more." His mouth met hers—so soft, so sweet. After the kiss, they sat there looking at the sky. The heavens, with the moon's luminous light, were bright enough to see by. To the North was the Great Bear constellation, sparkling its approval over the two lovers. The night drew late about them as, arm in arm, they walked back to the hotel to tell the others of their plans.

The next day dawned quietly. The rising sun caught the mountains and their tops shone pure white against the blue sky. In the west there were storm clouds piling up.

In the gray light of morning, James went down for coffee to the hotel cafe. There he found Mary serving coffee and just helping out.

"Hello," she greeted him.

"Good morning, just coffee please," he replied.

"Yes, I saw you coming. Will your brother be joining you also?" she asked, pouring the steaming brew.

"Sure will. Both of us are early risers. Luke should be here any minute. You two seemed to hit it off real well at the party the other night at the Grand Hotel ballroom," he teased.

She blushed, and replied, smiling back, "It was such a fine time. You were plenty attentive to Molly. I'm surprised you noticed anyone else there."

"Well, for my brother to pay attention to a girl was a surprise to me. He is normally quite shy. You are very good for him. Thank you for filling in at such short notice, Mary," He said sincerely.

"I had a nice time and I do not always get a chance to wear my good dresses, except to church," she added.

They looked up to see a tall man in a dark blue suit standing just inside the cafe door, looking lost.

"I'll fetch him," Mary said as she quickly turned on her heels and went toward where Luke was waiting. James watched them as they lingered at the entrance and talked effortlessly to each other.

"Hmm," he mused, *could love at first sight be running in the family?* The two walked together over to his table, where Luke seated himself. Mary filled a cup with coffee and handed it to Luke. Again their eyes met and stayed on each other until Luke spoke.

"Mary believes this blue suit is acceptable for the services today. She has agreed to ride out to the lake with me. Where can I get a horse-drawn carriage for us, little brother?"

"Mr. Baer has arranged many such carriages for us to use," James replied. "Well then, we're all set. Mary, I'll see you at two."

Luke continued to gaze at Mary with a star-struck look in his eyes. James smiled. He had only seen that look in the eyes of a man that was smitten by the love bug.

"Oh, my," he thought, "It looks like Luke will be here in the West for a long visit." The brothers talked at length that morning. Luke asked about Shadow and James told him of his past and of his belief in God. He did not refer to the brown bear incidents. Only Molly and he had understood the close connections surrounding Shadow and the large brown animal and his companion, the red-tailed hawk.

Today is the day of Shadow's memorial service, she thought as she lay lazily in her bed at the hotel. She had been reflecting on the events of the week and on the journey across the mountain trail to here.

"Maybe I hadn't ever been sure in my heart that I could have completed it on my own. And I know I didn't' because when everything was at its most hopeless point I said a prayer, and God graciously helped me. I am so glad I had Shadow and James to support me, also. Oh, I am so blessed," she rejoiced.

Molly finished her morning bath and dressed in the new dark suit dress her mother had brought her especially for this day. It was a new fashion worn in Kansas City. It had an ankle length full fitted skirt. The jacket was tight-fitting and sported a short flair at her waist. The cream-colored blouse next to her tanned face was very flattering.

Molly wore her hair up, with several dark combs holding it. She was just applying the last of her powder and make-up when there was a knock on her room door.

"Molly?" a voice called. "Mother, come in," Molly commanded softly. "I'm so relieved that you and father are here to help me see this day through," she said as she hugged her mother. "With your and Dalton's support I know we'll give Shadow the service due him. James was so thoughtful to wire that telegram for you to come as soon as possible."

"Yes, James is very nice. We will be blessed to have him in the family. We have also enjoyed getting to know his parents and brother on our trip here. In fact, it made a much more enjoyable time, even though it was also a time of sorrow," she replied with a little sadness. "Well, when you marry it will be our day of joy?"

"Oh mom, we have so much to be joyful about. For one thing I have never seen you look so healthy. Tell me, are you are as well as you seem?"

A smile appeared on her mother's lips as she put her arm around her daughter, then replied, "You have always been a compassionate daughter, Molly. Yes, I am fine, "as good as new," the doctor said. The trip here gave me time to gain some weight and strength. I am ready to be the mother of the bride," she added with pride. They hugged each other a long while before gathering up their coats to go out to join the men in their lives for Shadow's memorial service.

The procession that afternoon to the lake was long even in this small town. Many went who did not know the Newmans very well. There were a lot of onlookers, as Mary called them.

The donkey that carried Shadow's body was a curious thing to many, but Molly thanked James for finding such a beautiful animal. The donkey, well-marked with a dark line down his back, gave out the distinctive outline of the cross. It was not hidden by the burden he carried. Mr. Baer had done such a good job grooming him and placing the carrier he bore. It was a perfect donkey that depicted the belief that Shadow had about these animals being revered.

"If one carried Jesus, this was the one I pick to carry my body on my funeral day," he had requested. The casket was of polished pinewood. The carrier poles would be used to raise it up above the earth for the cremation that would follow with more wood added to the base of the structure. The sun cast long, thin shadows that deepened, and then shortened, as the low clouds floated across the meadows. The day had turned gray, leaving threatening clouds this afternoon from the west.

Molly and her mother were in the back seat of the carriage with Dalton. They had a heavy wool blanket over their lap. James was in the driver's seat with Elizabeth's father. There were two horses tied on the back, and one was Bourbon, saddled with a side-saddle. The other horse had a lead rope around her neck, which was made with braided horse hair. They proceeded on the road, parallel along the wild and tumbling Big Wood River. There were cottonwoods along its edge and junipers scattered over the hills above it.

They crossed the stream where Molly and James had seen the brown bear on the day they had taken Shadow on the picnic. James glanced at Molly and she returned his smile at his remembrance. The rustle in the bushes today was a small brown squirrel.

When they arrived at the lakeside, the pastor was already sitting in his carriage in the middle of the big meadow. The procession circled the pastor's carriage and when the last one was in place, he began the service by welcoming everyone. Then he continued with this story.

"There were three stone cutters. All day long they cut rock. One was asked what he was doing. He replied, 'I am cutting rock to make a living.' The other, when asked, said, 'I am cutting stone so I can provide food for my family.' And the third replied, 'I am building a lighthouse to stand in dark and stormy nights for those who need light.' The pastor looked up to the listeners.

"Have you found meaning in your existence?" he asked. "What is your story? I pray you will engage your heart and soul and not only your intelligence in writing the story of your life.

There are artistic touches left by the people of the Shoshone Indians that inhabited this region. We see them in the petroglyphs, their story of where they communed with the earth, their spirit-world, and with people who came after. We are here to honor a person who was a gentle shadow in our lives. Here is an individual who did control his own destiny from the instant he became a child of God.

"It was his choosing. Do not get me wrong. No person can choose the *where and when* either of his coming or of his going, whether he is in a teepee or the president's house. But he can choose whether or not to claim his great heritage as a son of God. This great miracle of becoming a person who is the son of Almighty God is his. He can choose these values that are timeless—immortal. This is the peace that passes all understanding. This person, Shadow Runner, had that. I pray that you who have lost this loved one will find some comfort in these words. Now, anyone wishing to say something may do so."

The pastor turned and looked at Molly, then gave her a nod. Just then, a storm picked up as the wind howled through the trees. The rain began falling across the lake. Lightening flashed from a cloud and it thundered as the sound of it roared through the valley and hills. The distant howl of a coyote drifted to their ears. Then the sound came again, causing a shiver down the spine of all who watched.

Then the wind slackened and the drenching rain held off from coming in their direction. It was then that Molly stood up in her carriage. The crowd, which was about ready to go for protection from the rain, stopped to listen to the pretty young girl that had loved the old Indian like a grandfather.

Molly said, "It wasn't that difficult to hear Shadow's voice out here on the prairie with the animals he knew and loved. He taught me considerably much, and I loved him."

The noise from the screech of a hawk down by the lake interrupted Molly and made the people glimpse in that direction. Also, through the mist of the lightly falling rain they could see a large brown bear silhouetted on the skyline past the lake. He looked very grizzled at this time of year. His long coat waved as he traveled at a walk, flat on the soles of his feet.

He stopped, then stood upright, swaying with his nose in the air. He made a deep-throated tone as he hesitated there. The red-tailed hawk made a swoop over him and whistled a sharp pitch. Then the bear looked up at the hook-beaked bird of prey that made another dive closer to the bear. Its long claws and broad wings were easy to see as it almost stopped in mid-air, like a salute. Then the bear and the hawk turned east to begin their journey into the wilderness. They soon disappeared with the storm.

The people sat motionless as they watched. After a while, Molly said to them, "Friends, now I will release Shadow's horse to run free." James helped her down from the carriage and on to her waiting horse. Sitting side saddle, she rode toward the lake, ponying behind her the extra horse. When she got a good distance away, she removed the hair bridle from the young mare and released her. She cried in a loud voice, "Hetchetu aloh—it is finished."

She waved her hand and the young horse took off at a gallop. Molly sat there, quietly watching the horse run. The clouds had moved away and had given the sun all of the evening sky. The sunset, painted splendid gold tints, outlined the red blood explosion of color on the distant, high peaks. It was as if the whole western sky were on fire. Molly drew the cool crisp mountain air into her lungs. In this deep breath she felt the life of it creep in to renew her. She could feel the challenge of the mountains and gave out her salute. It was the same salute Dalton and she had learned from Shadow when they were young. With a smile on her face, she reined her horse around to return to those who loved her.

Chapter Twelve

I am to be married, Miss, and I want you to create my wedding gown. Molly said to the pretty sister of Mary.

"Here are some ideas." She gave her a leather case that inside held the necklace with matching earrings that her mother had brought her from the collection her grandmother kept in Kentucky.

"These I wish to wear." She showed her the dark, red rubies. "I desire to have a gown designed to complement these jewels." The young girl starred at the sparkling gems. Her lips formed an *"Oooh"* sound.

"There is only one wedding gown design to make that will go with these, Miss," said the seamstress. "May I suggest the ivory white silk velvet material with overlaid Galway laces?"

"You sound as if you could do it!" she spoke with delight. "And call me Molly."

"Hello, Molly, please, my name is Lydia." They smiled at each other. Then Molly asked, "When can you get started? Be sure to hire extra needle women if you wish."

They continued with the details of getting the measurements and when they finished, Molly asked when she would need to see her next.

"I am so eager to see this come together," said Molly.

"Yes, I will need you for the first fitting tomorrow, please." Molly smiled at Lydia, shook her hand, and said, "Oh that will be wonderful. I'll be here in the morning."

As Molly left the house, she was thinking of the appointments she needed to make. One with the shoe maker; one for the personal items she needed to acquire, and one with a hairdresser. It would be fun, too, now that her mother was here to help and to be with her. Yes, she needed support.

Was she getting jittery about this marriage? Remembering the night before, when James stood before her at the riverside park, the scene was beautiful. Over the prairie slanted the first dark shadow of night, and the dark shadows from the trees made a romantic scene that danced upon the water.

James had said to her, "It's a lot making someone happy, but I will try with all my heart and soul." Then he kissed her, and when the kisses grew too urgent, James pulled away. He felt her shudder, and was shocked at the depth of her response.

He buried his lips in her long, flowing hair, and sighed, "My Estelle, I love you so." The memory of that evening, gave Molly courage and new commitment. With a smile on her lips, Molly hurried down the street to find those who loved her.

Three days later Molly was dressing for the ceremony when a strong chill of doubt again rushed over her. But her mother and Elizabeth were there to carry her through.

"I suppose most brides go through the same experience," she asked her mother. "Yes, but I have one question for you, Molly. Are you sure you want to marry James?"

"Oh, yes!" she replied.

"Then let us say a prayer to calm you, Molly."

"That is what I need," she replied. So she began, "We are told to wait on You, Lord. Give me the strength and courage I ask for, the understanding and the love that's needed. I ask for Your blessings—today, and for the rest of our lives. Amen."

When Molly finished, she and her mother hugged each other, and said words of encouragement that helped. They finished dressing just as they heard the piano strings begin the strains of the familiar old march. It was such a beautiful setting at the large home of Mary's parents.

When Mary asked if Molly would like to get married in her home, she had said she would be delighted. It was so exciting to see all of their plans come together. At the head of the stairs, her beautiful attendant, Elizabeth, began her walk down the stairway to join the rest of the wedding party. Molly reached for her dad's arm. He was waiting to escort her down the stairs.

The big smile on his face gave her courage, and she remembered how much she loved him and had been loved by her parents in return. "You are beautiful, Molly. We are so proud of you," he said as he took her arm.

As they took one stair at a time, Molly began to view the guests. Her mother smiled at her with approval and love. Elizabeth gave her a nod and an adoring smile. Then her gaze turned to Dalton, who was so handsome in his best suit, standing beside James. He lifted his hand just enough to give her their secret brother/sister wave. She smiled at him, then at James.

Molly's eyes caught his gaze and desire bloomed in her as they were transfixed there for what seemed like eternity. She could tell his eyes were approving, and she almost knew what he was thinking. James realized he was staring, but the beauty of the one he loved was so overwhelming that he had to catch his breath and stir slightly to get back into the present.

Molly's face was radiant. The bridal veil outlined the delicate beauty of her face and she looked happier than he had ever seen her. The light from the window caught her light hair, and he was reminded of the adventure they had together on the mountain on the day they brought Shadow back to the ranch.

I loved her then, too, James reflected. When she came down the stairs to join James, he watched the beautiful, white, long, flowing gown move with her. He thought her body appeared so slim and it was then that he had a glimpse of her delicate grace. The dark richness of the rubies against her alabaster skin on her neckline made her even more engaging. James took a deep sigh as she approached him. He reached for her hand and vowed in his heart that he would never let her go. It was the promise of a grand and everlasting love in their journey of beginning their new life.

It was springtime—a year from that wonderful day.

"It is good to be out by ourselves again," Molly exclaimed. Molly and James were strolling to the end of the main street in Naples. They heard the cheerful lilt of piano notes ascend across the silence from town as they walked toward the river. She was wearing a bright blue jumper with a full button front. It was so pretty on her, with a high-necked sweater that matched her sparkling blue eyes.

James was holding her hand as they arrived at the bench that they knew as their special place by the river's edge.

"Oh I want you to hold me while I just cry," Molly sobbed.

"Cry?" James exclaimed. "Yes, tears of joy and good memories," she replied. "Well come here, you. I'm always ready for your warm self to fit into my arms," he teased. She came to him with her arms out too and knew she would gain the strength from him that she needed.

Is marriage an unsolved mystery? Do things really change? I do feel more complete. Molly reflected with wonder as a praise left her lips. *This is the way it always will be,* she declared inwardly. *My husband and me!*

When the sobbing was over, they determined to go for an early evening ride. Springtime was the best time to ride, with the sunsets so colorful and the earth so fresh.

Dalton had brought their own horses to Naples for them to ride back to the ranch. They found them in the stable, and with a lot of nickering and loving and petting, James at last got them saddled.

"This is a wonderful ride!" Molly beamed a broad smile at James as, side by side, they rode along the well-worn track. They had a wind following, and the world was as bright to her as if it were a new world, never touched. It had been an unbelievable, wonderful time back East, and time moved on, overcoming many things it met on the way.

Time, she thought, *Had it really been four months since their wedding here in Idaho?* They loped up the track toward the stream. She heard only the rhythmic creek of her saddle and the soft hoof beat on the short new grass.

Oh, how I have missed this, she spoke with joy. They smelled the blooming bushes of Syringa, with its white blossoms gleaming in the twilight evening. Then they climbed the grassy hills as they sped on toward the horizon. She remembered that Shadow had said *no horizon is so far that you cannot get above it or beyond it.*

They rode west like that for several miles—like they were trying to break into the falling sun. When the two happy riders stopped at the crest of a high ridge to rest the horses, Diablo became edgy. He tossed his mane, raised his tail, and pounded the earth with his hooves. Bourbon also picked up his head and his ears were alert. He turned his head and shrieked a loud whinny. There was a sound only horses could know to alert them.

James's and Molly's eyes followed their gaze, and then they saw it, too. It was only a small speck on the horizon now, but it looked like a lone horse was coming toward them at a dead run. They dismounted, and then let the horses graze as they waited. Soon up ahead a horse jumped and snorted, then darted sideways, but it was still coming for them. Close over the hill the intruder poked up its head, and then they recognized her.

"It's Chita!" Molly yelled in delight. The horses whinnied to each other. The mare came forward with no hesitation. Molly caught her easily. Chita nickered softly as Molly rubbed her nose. She seemed glad to find familiar ground.

James remarked to Molly that the mare was heavy with a foal. Molly showed her delight by hugging Chita's neck. While the horses grazed behind them, they watched the decline of the sun. Molly's light hair glowed in the slanting light of sunset. She was quiet beside James. When she looked into his eyes, she saw in them the reflection of the western sky. She looked at his face and spoke to him.

"Just you and me—our future is just over the horizon. When I looked out in the valley before I met you, I knew I would continue to search for a man who was cut out to live here with me . . . to love me and to build a home here in these Idaho mountains."

She reached for his hand, lifted it to her lips, and kissed his fingers. Still looking at him, she said, "James, my husband, I am so blessed that I married you. I love you."

She pressed her lips against his. He deepened the kiss and drew her closer and she could feel his heart beating strong and fast against hers. When they parted, she snuggled in the circle of his arms and sighed a contented sigh.

"More than anything, more than life, Molly, I love you back," he said with a catch in his voice. They sat there for a long time watching the changing colors of the sunset. She could feel Shadow close, almost hovering, like she imagined the angels did.

Thank you, Shadow, for always encouraging me to keep myself for someone God would send . . . like James, and now she knew why. The sky was aflame. Brilliant salmon pinks and crimsons were splashed in enormous strokes with the sun a blinding sphere of blood red. Molly looked around her and smiled. The country was warm and alive and with the marvel of spring.

In the delightful sundown, they talked of their dreams. They would build here in this rural area. In her mind, Molly could see it all—the

home, the children, the mountains, the horses, and well-bred cattle—
a dream that had in time become his, too.

"What a special gift Chita has given us," Molly said as her arms
went around James' neck. "I want to raise lots of colts," she announced.
"Ah, yes," he said with a twinkle in his eye, "but I think we will have
enough to do taking care of some mavericks of our own."

The corner of her mouth turned up. "Hmm, maybe so," she
laughed as she looked at the radiant sky and felt the new warmth
within her.

Part II:

The Lost Journey

Chapter One

Spring had graced the grounds of the valley floor with an abundance of wildflowers. Foothills dotted with clumps of gray brush and green trees created a beautiful scene. Added to this were visitor's lodges pitched near the large lake.

The lake was an ideal setting for a village with old cottonwoods shading its edges, while crowding around them were the shining leaves of willow bushes. The pale, white poles and faded skins of the teepees of the visiting people gleamed in the sun.

The visitors' small herd of colorful horses was grazing in the lush, spring grass beside the water. Clumps of blue flags of Camas lilies waved their welcome in the gentle breeze.

These plants were the reason the Indian tribe was here. Even time moved slowly as it basked in this lovely moment of the warm noon sun.

Elizabeth stopped her young mare so she could sit and enjoy the portrait the scene created. She knew this was history in the making, but how long would this natural beauty be here as the white man changed it daily?

Elizabeth had enjoyed hearing the history of the West when her teacher at the university made those early times and the people who'd lived them seem so real to her. She remembered how these stories of western places made her feel strangely homesick. They'd discussed the Indian wars and how badly handled they were by the government.

Sometimes warring bands using more modern weapons killed off a whole tribe. This left little chance for the defenseless tribes to protect themselves.

"How much we owe these people," she thought, as many of those natives helped the explorers to survive and map out this country.

"Our nation was built on the homeland of these people and we reduced most of the tribesmen to the condition of wanderers and fugitives. History tells us that because those wars were so devastating to all of the Indian tribes, these may be the last of this Kamiah band.

They were of the Nez Perce Nation, but called themselves *Nimipa*. They made their homes along the northern part of the Koos-koo-kee River valley. They were a valiant and honest tribe. They had sat in council with the American government and agreed to live in peace.

"When their word was given it was never broken, except in defense of the lives of their families and themselves," she recalled.

"This country gave you birth and suckled you—it was *your* country first," she had said to one of the young girls last week. Today she looked for the children she had taught in her class last week, but she knew most of the older children, who were expected to help with the harvest of the bulbs, would not be present.

"I will get a chance to talk to them after supper," she hoped there would be time to be with all of them in the small school she had started. Granted, there was much to do before the tribe left here. They had to dig up the edible root called *kouse,* and dry it in the sun. It could be pounded into powder for future use, or eaten in a stew with other vegetables.

From the lake they caught fish in traps and cured some of the meat into a food called *pemmican* for use in travel. They were good at these tasks since most of this tribe came from the large rivers of the Columbia basin.

Molly had been with her when she was here last week. Today she came alone, but as she thought of Molly, her heart ached. With Molly's new baby on the way, there was less and less time they had to spend together. They both had wanted to become acquainted with the different tribes that stopped in this small valley. Elizabeth realized Dalton had been right—this would not be without personal risk to themselves.

What was happening to Molly had frightened her. It was not only the complications of the pregnancy that Molly was experiencing, but the realization that marriage required commitment. She did not know how else to describe how she felt—unless it was that she was just not ready for this idea of commitment.

The discussion she had had with Dalton last night was still on her heart and mind. It was the first time they had disagreed so strongly.

"I do not want you to venture out alone, and I do not understand why you need to," Dalton had said loudly, visibly upset. She had replied with just as much disagreement in her voice.

"You do not even try to understand me. For as long as I can remember, I've been interested in what lay around the next corner. I love to get out and see things and meet other people."

Looking into his eyes, she knew he demanded an exclamation, so she continued.

"God has given me the desire to help these people, even in a small way, and they are only going to be here this month. I need to go."

"Liz," he replied, "you think you haven't discovered your place in the world yet, and it is in your own backyard."

"Maybe," she snapped, not willing to give in. "But I'm going tomorrow if it's nice weather."

"Please don't be a stranger to me," he spoke with a pleading in his voice. "I want to reach out," he said, touching her hair with his fingertips "It seems I don't know how."

His tenderness touched her and drew him to her at this moment. Theirs was a quiet togetherness, and she wished to be centered in this lovely moment, but she too did not know how to respond.

"The mountains were blue this evening," she said softly as she looked at the mountain splendor of the fading sunset.

"Yes, I saw them," was his gentle reply as he drew her nearer to him. Her long, auburn hair was glowing in the moonlight and the dimness gave her eyes a dark flash, but he remembered her beautiful, emerald eyes.

Elizabeth melted into his arms, where he held her quietly. It was not the first time they had embraced after an argument. He was always gentle and kind to her and that was what attracted him to her. When at length he kissed her full lips, she clung to him, returning the touch of his lips with a long kiss of her own. When she drew away, her hand was still on his arm. They watched the dimming light fall over the mountaintops and the shadows crept around them. Staring at this awesome beauty before them, they talked about their lives and the friendship they had long had with each other.

"I have been so fortunate to have spent this part of my life with someone as wonderful as you, Dalton," she stated.

"I have been the lucky one, Liz. Yes, we enjoy each other's company very much and we are so happy now," he insisted, reaching for her other hand. "Yet I know love lies unspoken, and my heart cannot lend itself to words. I am waiting for your answer on when we can have a future together. I have spoken my part, and I will wait until you give your answer, Liz, no matter how long it takes."

Dalton turned and left the porch. He mounted his waiting horse to begin the long ride back to his ranch. She remembered he did not look back.

She had felt restless this beginning of summer. This engagement Dalton was asking for she knew was vital to their relationship. He was three years older than she and ready for commitments. It seemed there was something—*why was she holding back?*

"My true value rests not in being Dalton's wife, but in my heart. Lord, why do I feel like I do not need to work on me? Since returning from college, I have not been as close to your guidance as I was, relying on your Spirit to guide me. I need to make right choices in order to influence others you put in my life."

She sighed deeply. These thoughts were like a force that kept opening spaces in her life. The noise of the children coming up from behind them startled her young horse, Princess. This brought Elizabeth back to today as she quieted the beautiful, red-coated animal she rode.

She searched for the pretty face of the girl named Star Dancer that she had visited with last week They had a good rapport with this young girl. It was not only because she could speak some English, but because she wanted to teach Molly her tribal language.

Molly had been impressed with her and remarked that she thought the girl was half white. Elizabeth remembered her wide smile and sparkling, dark eyes. She was disappointed that she did not see her among the inquisitive children today.

Elizabeth dismounted and walked the rest of the way to the village with them. In this beginning of warm days the wildflowers had felt the fervor of summer, dotting the land with much color. The cardinal red monkey flowers nodded their heads near Camas Lake as they shone brightly against the glistening water, making the scene so peaceful.

Elizabeth removed her large-brimmed riding hat. She took the scarf from around her neck and used it to tie back her long hair. She was glad she had chosen a light-colored blouse to wear with her riding skirt, as a day in the sun could get hot near the lodges.

As they approached the center lodge, Elizabeth again met with a friendly greeting from the spokeswoman, who raised her hand as she spoke the same words as before. They meant she was welcome to stay at her lodge and the spokeswoman asked, "Wy-a-kin?"

It was inquiry about her long journey here. Elizabeth's answer was that it was a beautiful ride and she was glad she had come. She saw that the tent Molly and she had put up last month still stood in the place of protection near the "boss" grandmother's teepee. This woman was heavyset and showed her age, with deep lines in her face and streaks of gray in her hair.

"Hello," Elizabeth replied as she raised her arm and opened her hand in the welcome gesture. She then smiled a big smile and waited for other responses. The woman spoke a word and a girl came forward with a drink to offer their guest.

Elizabeth took the vessel and, with a thank you, drank all of the water the container held, then returned it to her. This sign was the beginning of a trade venture. Establishing trade with them was as important as sharing her teaching since, to the native Americans, they went hand in hand.

Elizabeth went over to the pack she had brought and unloaded it from the horse. A young boy came forward and extended his hand for the rope of Princess, so she gave it to him. He carried a small bow and a quiver of arrows. She noted they were not as sharp as those used by the men, but she could tell he was proud of them and they looked almost new.

"Thank you, Aho wa," she repeated. He smiled at her and gave the horse a tug to follow as he went to tie her up. She spread out the contents of the pack on the warm summer grass. She had brought bright fabric mixed with warm, earth colors.

"I will be real busy at the spinning wheel this winter replacing these wool pieces," she had said to her mother as she was packing them. But not once did she regret her decision to share these pieces with them. Elizabeth looked around again, hoping to see the Indian girl, Star Dancer. They had such a good time learning together.

There was something about her that seemed different from the other girls. *I will ask about her as I have brought her a metal needle and some cotton to give to her,* she told herself.

The Indian women examined the material in awe, and Elizabeth could tell they were soon wondering how they could purchase such nice merchandise. She knew the men had left them no pelts for trading. With many shrugs and shakes of the head, it was obvious they thought they desired these items in vain. Now it was up to Elizabeth to offer a trade for this trip to be successful.

These people were too proud to receive it as a gift. She knew these goods she brought would not supply them for the winter, but it would help until they moved into the lower Snake River canyons for the colder months. The message she desired to bring these people was one of hope and love. She also wanted to teach them enough of the English language to help them trade and work with the white people—especially the numbers for counting money.

These were the things that excited Elizabeth. She believed she would have been a good teacher. That is what she studied in college.

"For now, God has given me these people in this place to be friends with, to share my faith with, and to help as much as possible in the brief time we have," she had told her mother this morning when she left the ranch house. She began to bargain with them over the many items they offered her.

She observed carefully what they desired from among the things that she had brought. For Elizabeth, the things she could choose from were the usual beads, opal bracelets, and some beautiful pottery pieces—all of which she liked very much. Then she noticed a buckskin cape with lovely beadwork on it.

"Oh," she sighed as she fingered it. She knew that she wanted it and wondered how it looked on her. The women who had made it, stopped to watch her as she gently touched the soft piece of leather. The same young girl that had given her the water picked up the cape and gently placed it around Elizabeth's shoulders. She nodded in approval, and with a smile tapped Elizabeth on the chest bone with a finger, then swept her hand out in a sign that it was agreed upon.

"Yes, I give you these things for this and the pieces I have already chosen," she signed to them. "I do want it all," she also replied and nodded her head. A smile lit up the young Indian girl's face. She turned to communicate to the woman next to her what had transpired between them. Noisily they agreed as they smiled among themselves and completed the trade.

Elizabeth picked up the beautiful pots and beaded items. She wrapped the soft leather cape around her shoulder, fingered it, then began thanking them each,

"Aho-wa," she said. Then she put the beautiful treasures in her tent. She could not wait to show them to her mother when she returned tomorrow.

Tomorrow? Yes, she answered her own question. She was staying another day here with these people. She wanted to share her faith and tell them about her heritage.

"No laws will help without true faith in God, who would give them His love, she believed. Elizabeth began her friendship with the older people as they celebrated the successful trading day. They sat in a circle together, drinking an herb tea sweetened with honey that she had brought.

Elizabeth could tell they enjoyed it, and as they asked questions of her, she took the opportunity to talk about her living God and what Jesus had done for her, giving her life eternal. After an hour of this session, the children came up and drew her away with them. They played some of the games she had taught them. There was a lot of laughter and they all watched and cheered. Then she gave them sweet treats of chocolate because she knew they would be looking forward to this same candy she had given them the last time they were together.

Chapter Two

The late afternoon was warm and sunny as these were the longest days of the year. Every season holds its own delights, as did these summer days. New blooming wildflowers were everywhere, and they seemed to jump in the sun's long glow of energy.

It was nice to take a ride before the evening meal. This was just what Elizabeth and Princess needed for their homesickness, which seemed to always be worse the first night away from home.

"I have noticed you are nervous, little Princess, and I know you have a lot of energy, but something else seems to have upset you," she said to the prancing horse. She knew the young filly possessed a temperament that required nurturing. She was as beautiful as her name!

Elizabeth rode with a steady hand and knee, and unlike riding her older trail horse, she watched, looking down to encourage the unskilled movement of the novice animal. She didn't' want any pitfalls on the trail and hoped to reassure this filly that she was there for her—always encouraging with soft guidance.

These horses needed some comfort and renewing of their friendship each time she rode them to build trust in their budding association, unlike the long-time relationship she had with her gelding at the ranch. Elizabeth took pleasure from the pace of this filly, which was smooth and easy to sit. Her senses were liberated and she enjoyed the rhythmic beat of hooves striking the hard ground near the washed shore of the lake. They made muted sounds when they reached the soft earth by the trees.

Here was an everlasting peace, she mused in her mind. The horse's ears flopped with the comfort of the movement. Sometimes when she rode she felt she could hear the whispers of God.

"My Lord, may I keep my heart loyal to you as you continue to bless me!" she whispered, in a prayer all her own.

"I am wealthy because being on a horse like this gives me peace," she said aloud, quoting the Indian, Shadow.

I can see why women are drawn to the power of horses, she thought as she felt the unreleased power of her mount pulsing through her veins, causing her to fill with a sense of freedom.

I know that I love riding because it fulfills my need for adventure, and I love to feel the wind in my face. To be on top of a horse with the reins in my hand, guiding this filly as she arches her neck and prances around, this exudes an excitement that I love!

Elizabeth smiled at this thought grateful that she had been able to ride horses most of her life. Realizing the need to rest the horse, she reined to a stop in the trees near the end of the lake. She unsaddled, then wiped the sweat from the horse with one of the saddle blankets and laid it over the riding gear to dry in the sun.

With tilted ears and bold, clear eyes, Princess pawed the ground and lowered her head to nudge her master's shoulder. She was coaxing her gently to go back the way they'd come. Elizabeth patted her horse's nose and spoke to her.

"We will soon ride back to the others, you big baby. Now settle down." Elizabeth wanted to wade in the water as she often did too cool and wash her feet. She pulled off her boots and socks, then rolled up her sleeves. She waded in the clear, cool water and began splashing it on her face and arms. This was such an exhilarating feeling, but she seemed to be alarming Princess, or *something* was.

The young horse was moving around wide-eyed, pawing the ground fiercely, and rejoicing in her strength as she tugged at the rope.

"Whoa! Easy, Princess. What's wrong?" She spoke softly to the filly as she approached. Her nearness calmed the young horse, so she sat near her on some rocks and began to dry her feet. Just as she finished pulling on her boots the aromatic and musty scent of horses reached her. Just as suddenly she heard the rhythm of hooves falling on the bare earth. Then she saw him coming toward her.

A black stallion was racing as if against the wind. His nostrils flared and his eyes were ablaze. His mane was long and shaggy and his tail looked brittle and broken. This wild horse lifted his head high and came through the narrow passage between them and the lake, splashing the edge of the water and making a deep grunting sound as a stallion does when he's calling a mare.

Elizabeth stared in disbelief at the stomping horse, and then spoke out loud, in hopes that her voice would soothe the mare.

"This horse is very familiar. Years ago I knew this dark, flashing horse. When I was young, I found a runaway horse near the Big Smoky Mountains."

She continued to tell the story to Princess, trying to quiet her.

"I was filled with bliss as I watched him gallop up and down along the river where we finally lassoed him. One of my very own horses, I imagined. I named him Raven, but later when the wild horse broke away from the main herd, my dad told me he was a dark, devil horse and needed to be free. It was later I learned that he had taken several nice mares with him. When he left, he also took away my youthful dream.

"In my youth, I imagined we had taken flight together, but this horse stole my youth." Tears ran down her cheeks as Elizabeth told of that unhappy time in her life. She had cried then also and her father told her to "grow up and face facts." They were gone.

He was angry over the loss of the mares. It seemed not to matter to him that she had lost the dark stallion. In a cloud of dust, the rest of the band came running through the narrow opening—their eyes wide and full of fright.

With tails tossed high they were only taking orders from one, and he ran among them riling them to a fever. Elizabeth noticed that many of the mares were heavy with colts. Yet this herd of thirty or more seemed to be at peace with the band they had built.

"There must be contentment in the heart that binds us," Elizabeth quoted as she remembered her mother telling her this wisdom. Elizabeth was transfixed there in an odd stillness of the moment. Too late, she realized the herd driven by the dark stallion was circling and running toward her and Princess. She moved quickly to get to a safe place, but her foot snagged on a root and she fell.

Get up! Get up! Oh, Lord, help me, she prayed, scrambling to her feet. Frightened by the sound of the horse's hooves coming closer, she screamed. Princess, already upset, was jumping and pulling at her rope. The scream was the final signal to Princess. She broke loose.

The spooked mare pushed against Elizabeth, who reached for her but lost her grip on the runaway horse as she tumbled onto the rocks.

Elizabeth toppled head first to the ground and the sound of her head hitting a rock made a sharp crack. The blood in Elizabeth's head throbbed, then became a roar, before she mercifully passed out.

The dark devil horse ran away across the meadow. His band and his new captive, with the broken rope dangling from her bridle, came running after him. The stallion's ears lifted sharply as he tossed his head defiantly. In a final goodbye, he sounded an earsplitting whinny that rippled the lake like wind. The stallion never paused but galloped off into the wilderness. Grayness was growing like a weight all around the fallen body, leaving only the whisper of the wind.

Chapter Three

The sun broke out through the thin white clouds, bring-ing a pleasant warmth to the afternoon. There were dark shadows on the path from the branches of the trees where she followed the trail. She had trotted steadily all that day, stopping only to refresh herself briefly at the stream.

She pushed her way through the undergrowth and lifted her head, searching for the scent of something to eat. Home was in the opposite direction and her instincts told her where it was.

That was where her litter of pups came into her life. It had been a difficult pregnancy, but she had slowly weaned the pups. The freedom she felt in her spirit sent her on a trek across the country. She had such a lure for unknown things. She did not know if it was the memory of a time when the wolf in her that was convincing her to go forward. She just slipped away from the kennel one morning and never looked back.

This was a new, raw country—a land of remote desert peaks and rugged, forested mountains. Perhaps the young bitch dog had come to this part of the land with a drive for life, even she did not understand. She was learning that in this area of clear, swift streams and deep valleys surrounded by high rock-strewn peaks there was very little rodent life to satisfy her hunger. She had eaten only once since she left home, and found she was not welcome at that homestead. She may have looked silver-gray in the evening light and, with black lines on

143

her face, may have given the impression that she was more wolf than she was dog.

The gray and yellow dog had spent a strange and foggy night after what seemed like a lifetime of comfort at the man's place, who had called her *Tigerus*. Now she slept, unconscious of the aching body or the hunger she'd felt earlier. On this second day, Tigerus stopped to nibble at stalks of grass and used her tongue to lap in a few berries, although most were yet green.

On this newfound trail there were scents of other animals that had recently been on this path. She hesitated, listening for any rustle as hunger began to rule her. This day was a tiring trek across the long valley, but to run with the season of the early summer was the longing she had to follow. She would not stop now for she had hopes of finding an easy kill in the bright twilight.

Panting heavily, she trotted steadily on. In the gray light of nightfall, Tigerus ran over the high crest, then down to the welcome lake at the far end of the valley. Wading far out into the lake, she drank long and deeply. Lifting her head, she listened and waited, with hope of finding food for the first time today.

Yes, she heard the rustle again near a fallen tree. Leaving the water, she crept quietly along the soft mud toward the log. A small head appeared around the end, but she saw the dog too late. In one leap the animal was held firmly in the mouth of its captor.

Tigerus spent the night near the lake, peaceful at last after the long journey. She curled up for warmth under the spreading branches of an old pine tree and fell asleep.

She woke only once to throw her head back and howled a long, lonesome sound. Long before the dawn broke, she rose and trotted along the water, reluctant to leave after finding food there. She hunted all day, finding more mice, ate her fill, and lay down in the shade, where she again fell asleep.

Tigerus was awakened by the sound of hoof beats. The clamor of them carried across the lake in heavy echoes. Going to a high spot, she could see a lone rider traveling along the lake on a dark red horse making a noisy display.

The dog was not afraid of humans unless they showed anger toward her. Her first instinct was to run to join the fun this horse and rider seemed to be having. But wait—a twist of the head and she was off—chasing her supper with the other forgotten for now.

Tigerus retreated into the bushes, her mouth carrying the dangling prey. She sat down to devour her kill. When she finished she felt an instinct to sleep but rose, stretching as if to declare the hunt over. Instantly, she leaped away to find the trail again.

She loped along the lake, looking for a sign, and picked up the scent and tracks of the horse and human. Suddenly, Tigerus froze as a new scent came into her raising the hair on the back of her neck.

Out from the bushes came a wailing shriek—like the scream of a terrified woman. Crouching low, Tigerus moved forward cautiously. She had experienced a wild cat when she was allowed to run with the hounds. She knew it was dangerous.

The dog, now two years older, had learned not to barge ahead, especially by herself. She passed a pile of driftwood, sniffed, then continued along the fresh scent. Suddenly Tigerus growled, then lowered her head, knowing she was close to the feline. Immediately, like a black storm, the feline jumped out on the trail in front of Tigerus.

The dog leaped back just in time to avoid the slashing of claws. Then the dog advanced snapping, showing her teeth, and boldly faced the cat square on. It backed away with its eyes glinting, but not before it gave out another loud outcry.

Tigerus held her ground, barked once, and flung herself across the distance toward the fallen body lying on the ground. This was the prey the hungry cat was after to take back to its den in the nearby rock cliff. The snarling dog faithfully guarded the unconscious human, but advanced with caution.

The dog was twice the size of the young, attacking cat. At the grown-up age of three, Tigerus' finely chiseled head was a large, erect bone with wide and strong jaws housing large, sharp fangs. Her long and muscular body was rigid, ready for an attack. The dog revealed, at first glance, all the qualities a larger ranch dog could possess.

Tigerus had a shining, silky coat. It was of a gray color, muted with yellow. Black streaks ran through the length of her long and thick fur. Her tail sloped gently down, curling near the ground. She was capable of swift speed, with her feet measuring six inches across the dark, hard pads.

The cat was surprised by the move and position the huge dog took. Tigerus watched as slowly her enemy backed away. Then quickly the wild cat retreated into the trees where the shadows of the forest swallowed it up.

Chapter Four

The dog, Tigerus never relaxed. This was her adopted family. She sat upright many times during the night—her ears pricked, listening. Her new friend stirred in uneasy sleep, waking the dog often.

When dawn came, the dog was reluctant to go to the edge of the lake and drink. Finally she went. She waded out belly-deep and drank her fill, still keeping her eyes on the quiet form on the ground near the trees. Tigerus returned to the motionless body and lay down next to her.

The coat of the dog was wet and touched the face of Elizabeth. Drops of water fell upon her lips, and the feel caused her mouth to open. She was faintly aware that something was near her and was trying to wake up. When Elizabeth stirred, the pain in her head caused her to moan. I'll just open my eyes, she thought, and maybe I will not have this agony.

Streams of light from the morning sun were too much for her so she closed her eyes again. After another rest, the dog stirred just enough to waken Elizabeth. She moved her hand and it rested on the dog's fur, now dry and warm. She forced her eyes open and saw what she knew to be a dog next to her.

Moving to sit up she was racked with suffering and nearly lost consciousness again. The noise that came from Elizabeth's lips startled Tigerus. She got up and moved in full view of Elizabeth's gaze. There she stood watching patiently as she whipped her tail like a leash against her legs.

When Elizabeth could focus on the object in front of her, she was not afraid. Somehow she knew this animal had been there with her through the night. The yellow dog lay down within reach of her hand and she reached forward as the dog lay, nose on paws, brown eyes open and watchful. Her fingers touched the broad and noble head and the deep and gentle mouth. They sat there like that for a long time while she petted the dog's head.

The hot sun burned down out of a blue sky. Elizabeth was thirsty. She noticed a water container just on the other side of the saddle and blanket she was lying on. She tried to rise, but weakened legs would not support her. To sit up made her head ache even worse than lying still. Nearly passing out, she fell back, and although it was summer she shivered as a cold chill ran through her. Then there was darkness and silence.

A whine escaped Tigerus' throat. She was feeling the need to help, but as evening was approaching, believed it a good time to hunt for food. The sweet sound of birds in the treetops encouraged her even more to find her fill. The big dog leaped to her feet and bounded away without looking back. The urgency was to go, then return as soon as possible.

Nothing was changed when she returned. She stretched herself down near the sleeping body and soon fell asleep. She was wakeful most of the remaining night. The faithful dog did not move from Elizabeth's sleeping side.

The sun came up over the ridge and filled the valley. A sound awakened Tigerus. Facing the trail, she began barking wildly. After a long time of this she could see someone on a horse coming toward them.

The yellow dog stood happily, swinging her tail. Her brown eyes alighted and with expression. Slowly they came to her, friendly people who would help.

For the next few days Elizabeth could only remember bits and pieces of her life. There was a trip on a gurney with someone leading the horse, and she remembered the face of the old grandmother who gave her liquids to swallow.

There was the crossing of a large stream that Elizabeth was carried across. She felt the water splash on her and enjoyed the coolness of it. Her recovery days at the big camp in the North Country were so much nicer. Perhaps the reason was that she needed less and less medication for her headaches and she was much more alert. Soon she was able to do her own bathing and personal care. She became aware that she did not remember how she acquired the yellow dog, she now called *Tigue*. Nor did she know what happened to her horse, or even where her home was.

The Indian girl, Star Dancer, told her that time would heal almost everything. Fox, the medicine man, would be visiting her again with healing herbs for her head. Eizi, as she was named by Star, smiled at Star's concern, and it was as though the wise one in medicine was going to give her all the answers about her past.

As the hot summer days came on, Eizi and Star were together all the time. The walks they took with Tigue, who was sometimes following and often running ahead, were helping Eizi gain back her health. Star was acquiring more knowledge of the English language that allowed them to talk together of things they both enjoyed.

Star shared her memories of living with her mother and father, and told of her faith in God. Her father had taught them about Jesus, God's Son.

"I then knelt and asked forgiveness of my sins and became a child of His right then, and it was marvelous!" Star related to her. Eizi became teary-eyed over the story, and shared her joy, too.

That evening, lying in her bed, Eizi was able to recall a young girl that looked like her, in a church on her knees, praying just like Star had related.

Am I remembering my youth, she wondered, and became very excited about this. Perhaps the important events will come back a little at a time, as Star had said. The next day when she told Star about her dream, Star exclaimed, "Oh Eizi, yes . . . *yes!*"

She danced all around her with joy. When Eizi could get her stopped, she questioned her.

"Star, you know more about me and this accident. Now tell me . . ."

Star bowed her head as if she had done something wrong and replied, "I have been holding back a lot. The medicine man suggested we not rush you, and now that you are better, I can tell you all that I know since we have met." Star began to relate to her the first time they met at the blue lake, the trading they did, and the lessons she gave—most of all the talks they had had about the one living God.

"It was as though you came just to talk about Him and his Son Jesus."

"Why do you say that Star?" she asked.

"Because you were so full of this talk, I remember it gave me so much joy to hear about your personal life. It was just like mine," Star said with sparkling eyes.

"Tell me more about you knowing Jesus," Eizi coaxed. Star settled down beside her near the clear pond formed by the waterfall that came down from the cliff. This was their favorite place to visit and to be by themselves. She began her story.

"My father was white. He was a trader of furs. He and my mother lived in a small cabin in the Clearwater range. That was where I was born and lived the first five years of my life. When my mother got sick and died, my father brought me here to live with my grandmother. I was happy with her and the other children of the tribe. After that we traveled a lot, and on one of those journeys, I remember seeing you for the first time at the blue lake." Star said.

"This blue lake, is it far from here?" Eizi asked.

"Yes, at least four days journey to the south and east of here."

"So, do you think when I am better I could go back there?" Eizi asked.

"No, not by yourself. I do not like the idea of it." She frowned as she replied. Eizi could not tell if she was unhappy at the idea of her leaving or if there were other reasons why she would not want her to go, then she changed the subject. There would be more days to inquire about that event. Star held the key to her mysterious past, of this she was certain.

Chapter Five

The stars were already showing in the soft, violet darkness that shaded off to a pale yellow above the peaks of the Sawtooth Mountains. The mountains were highly visible in this city of West Bannock that was built up again five years ago after a fire had nearly destroyed it.

The Orchard Hotel, with its iron shutters and pretty wide verandah, housed most of the town's visitors. Jesse Gannon had gained much information from Mr. Crafts, who ran the *Idaho World* newspaper. Jesse had left a notice to be posted, asking for any information leading to the whereabouts of his brother. The editor said he had a run on missing persons, but the inquirer last week was looking for a young woman.

He walked out on the dusty street, smelled the cooking from the café, and headed toward it. He'd had no luck either, either, asking the flannel-clad cowhands in the saloon if they had seen anyone matching the description of his brother.

Of course, four years was a long time to wait to pick up the trail of a missing person. Jesse entered the brightly lit cafe and was glad to find it full of ranchers, miners, and merchants. Maybe someone here will remember the fur trader from St. Louis who looked a great deal like himself.

He seated himself at a small table near the door and waited. Hardly anyone noticed him as he blended in with the other dozen men in

151

western traveling attire. He gave his order to the smiling waitress, re-fraining from asking her questions. She seemed bothered by the de-mands of so many people and from trying to keep up with her job.

As the evening wore on and many began to leave, Jesse looked directly at each person as they passed his table. He was watching for anyone to even faintly recognize him. This was the town that Ross had traded in as he made the rounds to and from other trading posts.

If Jesse got some information tonight he would be leaving early in the morning. Otherwise he needed to stay until the mercantile store was open tomorrow. Tomorrow and another tomorrow . . . *How many would he have before he gave up on this adventure and went home?* He longed for a good bed and though he loved this beautiful country, he had friends back in St. Louis that he missed.

Since the death of his ailing father, Jesse was able to go and enjoy other company for the first time in several years. As the cafe emptied, Helen had time to reflect on the patrons. Eating quietly at a table near the door was the tall, dark, handsome stranger she had just poured a last cup of coffee for. He looked like he had been going to ask her something as she got a good look at him.

"He sure looks familiar," she mused to herself. "Not one of the regulars though. If I *have* seen him, it was a while back. I think I will go ask him now that I am off work," she reflected. Helen started across the room, just as Jesse got up to leave. Helen hesitated and watched as his long, dark hair brushed the collar of his coat.

The stranger then turned and realized she was looking at him. He gave her a lopsided grin and nodded his head as he put his hat on to leave. Perhaps it was the grin or the way he nodded his head to her that she remembered. She boldly stepped forward with her coat in her hand, then she too started for the door. He held the door open for her.

"Thank you," she said. "Nice evening."

"Yes, it cools out here," he replied, eyeing her in a new light. Her manner was warm. In the pretty, blue coat she held a style of beauty that attracted him. The moonlight was shining on her light hair, and he noticed for the first time that her eyes were a violet blue. He knew he must not stare, but she appeared to also keep her gaze on his face. When she spoke again he nearly gasped. Had he heard her right? Had she asked, "Don't I know you?"

Finally he answered, "No, I don't think we have ever met before tonight. Do I look familiar?" He seemed to wait an eternity for her answer as she took her time to reply.

"Yes, I thought you were a man I met several years back, when I first came to this town. But if you do not know me, I'm sorry." She turned to go down the street.

"Wait!" he almost shouted to her, "I must talk to you."

"Please forgive me if I startled you, Miss, but can you give me one more minute of your time?" Jesse asked. Helen's face softened at his request as she replied, "Yes go ahead."

He reached inside his coat pocket and came out with a picture that he held out for her to see.

"Have you ever seen this man?" He waited for her answer, again it seemed like ages before she responded. "I believe so," she finally said, after studying the picture, "and I was thinking earlier that if I knew you it was several years ago when I first started to work here."

"Oh, you think he came in where you work? And it has been years since you saw him?" he questioned.

"If he is the man I am thinking of, he came in with a woman he said was his wife," she related.

"Wife?" he questioned, in alarm.

"Yes, when the manager did not want to serve her, he declared she was his wife," was her reply.

"Why did he not want to serve her? Did she cause trouble or something else?" Jesse asked."

"No, she was very nice and quiet. She even asked your brother if they could leave. She was dressed just like I dress, except for her shoes, and they were moccasins. The reason he did not want to serve her was because she was an Indian," Helen concluded, watching his face.

The shock on his face told her all. After a moment he asked her to tell him all that she could remember.

"I believe she called him Louis. She was very pretty, and young. Her hair was done in the same beads the local Indians wear." Jesse spoke next.

"Louis is Ross' middle name and he often spoke well of the Indians out here and gave them very fair prices for their furs. So I believe we are talking about the same man. *Miss?*"

He hesitated, looking at her pretty face.

"Helen Smith from Springfield," was her reply as she held out her hand to him. He stepped nearer, took her small, soft hand, and for a moment was lost in her smile before she tried to pull away.

He realized he still held her hand, then, embarrassed about the gesture, released it immediately.

"Nice to meet you Miss Smith," he smiled and backed away step. Helen replied with a small laugh, and nodded.

"The same," she said softly, "but I do not know your name," "Jesse Gannon, and I'm from St. Louis. We have a shipping firm there. I say *we* 'cause my brother and I used to run it. My name is spelled 'JESSE,' but pronounced *Jess*. I was named after my grandfather, Jesse H. Gannon, who was Territorial Governor of the Missouri territory." He saw her look up the street and realized she must desire to get to her home.

"I apologize for talking so much and standing here this way. You must be tired after working. Can I walk you to your room? I know it is late and I apologize for this interruption of your long day," Jesse said kindly to her.

"Yes, it is up this way to a log building with sleeping rooms on the second floor. My landlady will be worried about me. I have the same schedule I have had since I moved here. Sounds boring, doesn't it? Especially with the traveling life you have been living?"

She looked up at his weary face, and although he was good- looking, she saw that he was younger than she'd guessed earlier. When he replied, he seemed to let out a breath of air, like a sigh.

"It has been a long search, and I am tired from it. Can I see you tomorrow, and maybe we can talk some more?" They reached the boarding house and he took her arm to help her take the first step up to the porch.

"Yes, you can call for me anytime after the breakfast hour," she replied. Goodnight, Mr. Gannon."

Helen went inside, still feeling the warmth on her arm where he had held her for a moment.

It has been a long time since I have been attracted to a man like Jesse Gannon, she thought. His manners toward her were very good and she felt his touches lingering, and his gaze—those eyes—were like twilight when the blue sky begins to shade toward indigo. That was how she described them in her mind.

I am really looking forward to tomorrow and to seeing him again, she dreamed. *There is more I would like to know about this stranger.*

She smiled at herself and realized that if she did not stop, he *would* be in her dreams. Jesse went out in the warm summer night, walking slowly toward the hotel. The town seemed quiet for a mining town. The immediate area around the city had been extensively mined. Along

Morris Creek, many of the buildings were upon pilings. This created many steps going up into the buildings and many more down to the old stage roadways.

A funny-looking town, the stranger from the Midwest thought. *Out of seeing nearly a hundred people in three days, the only one who could help me was a young lady who works in a cafe.*

He thought about Helen, and wondered if she knew more than she was telling.

I guess I'll find out tomorrow, he pondered, remembering her smile that had caught him unaware. *Of all the people he had talked to she was certainly the prettiest,* he concluded with a smile.

He stepped upon the verandah of his hotel and seated himself near the railing. Sleep would not come easy tonight with all he had on his mind as he stared out at the bright stars over Idaho. He considered the freedom that he felt here and was glad he had come, hoping to heal his mental sickness and perhaps to feel better physically. The need to sleep all night and not be awakened by someone needing help, or by those frequent nightmares he often had, was weighing heavy on him.

His brother had told him about the Great Northwest and these mountains. He'd planned to come out here for years, until his father became ill. Jesse got up and stared into the heavens, wondering if Ross was looking at the stars tonight. He cried out to himself, *I need you, Ross! Oh, let me find you.* Then he went inside to his room.

The next morning, before Jesse met with Helen, he went to the mercantile store to buy more camping supplies for the journey. This time he came out with more information on the Nez Perce tribes in the area. They said he was about two days' ride from the first village.

Later, Jesse met Helen in front of her boarding house. The soft morning breeze of the early summer was refreshing, just as seeing her again was. Taking her arm, he led her outside and assisted her with the steep climb to the cafe for late morning coffee. As they sat and talked in a quiet place, Jesse looked at Helen in a new light. Later in the day Jesse reflected on their talk. He was glad they had had that private time together because she had been helpful in every way.

Jesse realized she was very observant of people, and he felt it may have been because of her faith. She had told him she was raised in a Christian home and had attended a faith-based college. It was plain that her desire was to follow her Lord wherever He would lead. She had come out west to teach school, or to open a business, but had not found the right town to settle down in. He learned she had no family ties since the death of her parents, except for an aunt and uncle living in San Francisco. She talked of visiting them when a suitable way to travel became available.

He could tell she was touched by his desire to find his only brother, but she left him with some advice that he asked her for.

"Accept life and its circumstances and be patient in your quest," she had said. "You are not dealt problems; you are dealt choices. You have the choice to focus on solutions instead of challenges. Let loose and let God lead. He is the One who gives us instructions. Your effort will be rewarded with faith. I know you will get peace of mind as you turn loose and look to Him."

He could almost hear her sincere voice and see her bright eyes when he recalled the talk they'd had. It had started when he mentioned he was leaving in the morning. She was surprised because tomorrow was Sunday, a day of worship, and a day when most people rested. Then again, he had told her he never rested. The days became long, and he was impatient concerning his quest.

Her faith was a lot bigger than his, and why? As a young man he'd never missed a worship service after he had given his life to Christ. Every Sunday his mother and brother and he happily attended their church. It was the beginning of wonderful family outings.

What had happened in less than ten years? he asked himself. That evening when Helen looked into the heavens, she thought about Jesse and the pleasant visit they had had that morning. Helen had seen the lines in Jesse's tired face and she could sense his loneliness. She felt compassion for him that he only had his brother in his life. She talked to him as if she might never see him again, even though he assured her that he would come back to this city in the mountains.

I wonder, Lord, as I pray for his quest . . . will I ever see him again?

On the trail to the Payette River the wagon track was wide, but when the trail forked and he crossed through a low pass in the mountains it was no more than a single trail. Jesse saw a broad basin ringed by more mountains and cut by two rivers.

The track that followed the bank of the north fork went down along a spacious valley. On top of a high ridge he could see out in the spacious meadow several hundred yards from the nearest trees. The village spread before him. Here, sheltered from the wind, there were several hundred teepees with white tops showing in the fading evening light and smoke rising from a dozen fires.

The sun had slipped behind the mountains, creating a dim hue through which to view them. He remembered reading about the Nez Perce tribe when the people numbered thousands and seeing them now saddened him.

As he rode closer, he was amazed at the many ponies grazing on the outskirts of the village. He pushed through them and rode straight for the center of the community. Most of the old men dressed in hides from neck to toes, glanced up at him, as they sat beside their dwellings. Some were smoking, others were whittling with a knife, and after he passed they again looked down at their tasks.

The women backed shyly into their tented homes. There were no young men in sight. The younger women and children were sitting around the fires, quietly eating. Jesse greeted them with a smile and a hand sign hello, but kept his horse walking until he saw a friendly sign in return.

Near the center he saw a man rise and approach him. Jesse reined his horse in and began his questions. Late that night as the fire dimmed, Jesse had learned enough about where his brother might be to be encouraged. His talk with the *wise men* gave him satisfaction that they had known of Ross. He said his goodbyes and rose from the group to go back to his own camp.

Jesse felt bone-tired and thirsty after a day in the saddle, but it was still a good feeling. He was confident that tomorrow he would find the Kimiah tribe and that would be the day he would greet his brother and the family that Ross had acquired. An owl called out with a long, lonesome sound nearby, as Jesse snuggled into his bedroll. He breathed a deep sigh, feeling lonesome, and soon fell asleep.

Chapter Six

A dense white fog rose from the river but soon the mist was breaking and rolling away. The Little Payette River was running full from the runoff, and beyond the big lake was Little Payette Lake. From there he was to continue north, to the encampment of the Kimiah.

"They should be just this side of the Salmon in a big meadow where there is a lot of sunshine," the Chief had said.

Jesse smiled at the description the men had given him of the destination and the valley he was looking for. With their help and that of the map, he would find the band's summer home. The trail he was on gave vista to a range of sharp, rugged peaks piercing the now clear-blue sky.

As he beheld it, he exclaimed, "It is such beauty! Anyone would be content here. No wonder Ross was reluctant to come home." His horse turned and looked at him. Jesse smiled and again spoke aloud.

"Come on, Skipper. Let's get down the trail so you can have your fill of this tall grass when we make camp."

About midday they surprised a herd of mule deer that ran in high graceful bounces into the pine trees near the lake. Skipper only turned his head at them. Then the deer stopped, turned about, and stood wide-eyed, with their heads held high, watching horse and rider pass. Jesse could tell they had never been hunted by the way they hung close. He intended to camp early tonight, so he could ride into the tribe's camp at early evening.

Jesse knew they were friendly to strangers, but if the young men were out hunting during the day, they would have had time to return by evening. He thought of what it would be like to see Ross again. Jesse urged his big horse, Skipper, into a faster gait as the rocks gave way to soft grass underfoot. He had a sense of expectation of something about to happen any day, and Skipper would just have to put up with him.

The days grew longer, giving Elizabeth ample time to heal. Lately she was anxious as something had been bothering her. She wondered about the fine edge upon which we live.

Waiting to recover, to be herself again physically, but in the waiting there was the longing for something or someone that seemed to be beyond her comprehension. For months there was little more to do but wait.

She measured the passage of time against the growth of different grasses—the flight of birds, the angle of light, the wind—until gradually these things were pulled inside of her and a barrier dissolved. The distance was covered.

In this passage of time she had gradually realized that we humans were two things at once; creatures of nature and creatures estranged from nature. There was nothing to do but dream. Elizabeth patiently waited out the full time of summer and this thought had come to her only later upon reflection. This quiet interlude in her life imposed on her a greater sense of some expectation about to happen any day. She questioned if it was the Spirit of God telling her to be content and wait.

The westering sun bathed her slopes, passed over her peak, then began to sink slowly beyond what Elizabeth knew would be a soon-darkening sky. She sat in silence watching this beautiful end of the day event.

She often came here to talk to her God. First she thanked Him for her healing and for the people in her life that had a hand in restoring her health. She learned that the Indians thought that disease was a fact of life and often beyond their power to cure—especially when an illness came on suddenly in a strange land far from home.

Most of the time all they did was make signs to wish the ill person well and to say goodbye so far as life in this world was concerned. So when Star found her and realized she could not be well in a short time, Elizabeth knew that it was a miracle they did not leave her there to die. She owed her life to Star and her grandmother.

Elizabeth realized another miracle had taken place when the young dog had come into her life at just at the right time. Tigue was a constant companion and was so protective of her mistress. She displayed good manners and obviously had had good care, as revealed by the glossy coat she wore. She also knew how to give much affection.

Where did she come from? She seemed to answer well to Tigue and this made Elizabeth wonder if this name was close to the one her former owner had given her. *Should I question these things?*

Star tells me to just to look forward to what God wants in my life. All these years have passed since Star had lived with her Christian father, and yet she still had strong faith.

I owe her so much. I am thankful that we have become closer each day, Elizabeth was reflecting. *And the language barrier is closing as Star always wants an English lesson.*

She felt Tigue jump as her sharp ears heard something. Instantly, her hand was on her neck, and when Elizabeth released her, the big yellow dog jumped up and ran down the trail. *What had disturbed her now? She never chased after wild animals unless she got permission to . . . .*

As the rushing sound of water filled Jesse's ears, he knew he was at a destination given to him by the men of the tribe. He looked up to view the shimmering silk of the cascading waterfall as it showered down the rocks. It was a wondrous display of swirling, glittering, diamond droplets.

The late afternoon sunlight sparkled full upon the rushing water as it fell into an alluring pond below. *What a great place to water Skipper and fill his canteen,* he thought.

With this in mind, it startled him when Skipper stopped so quickly, his ears at point. *What was in the trail ahead—a dog?* They stood there and stared at the large yellow dog that blocked their way. She did not seem hostile, yet did not yield an inch. Not wanting to start a confrontation, Jesse got off the horse in a gesture of friendship. Just as he started to speak to the dog, he heard a call; the dog turned quickly and bounded away toward the pond.

Taking a few steps closer he was able to see more clearly that someone else was there. Then through the spray of the falls, Jesse saw a young woman sitting alone beside the pond. If he had not seen her reach out her arm to command the dog to come beside her, he would have thought she was of a fantasy.

Her beauty made him stare at her. She had a clear tan of the outdoors and her dark red hair shone in the dimming light. She had one long braid that ran down her back, which she tied with a braided loop. This beautiful woman, dressed in a long skirt of tanned buckskin leather, beaded with turquoise and silver, looked up at him in surprise.

Her cotton, white blouse was homemade, but the boots she wore were not. She had remained seated but now released the dog that stood alert, then walked between them, being protective.

The woman rose and walked to the dog, reached out her hand and touched her fur. Was it the way she put her soft hand on the dog that stirred him? They met each other's glance and his eyes stayed on hers.

As Elizabeth stepped forward away from the mist, she was able to see the stranger more clearly. There was white dust on his dark hat, and his vest was open. He had dropped the reins of his horse, and the horse stopped where they lay. He took another step toward her, and the only sound was from his jangling spurs.

A real western man, was her first thought. He had dark hair, a small black mustache, and a clear, blue color lit his intelligent looking eyes. He had sun- bronzed skin on his face and throat, and his rolled up shirt sleeves revealed the tanned skin of his arms and hands.

Was it his manner, the tone of his voice that she was trying to recognize? Elizabeth tried to hear with his every word that he was someone out of her past. Then she realized she was not really hearing what he was saying. She looked at him in surprise.

"Hello. I hope your dog is friendly. And . . . I mean, well, I'm sorry if I startled you." Jesse managed to say.

She stared at him, wishing he would repeat those words. She had only met one other person in a month that spoke English and that sheepherder's English was mixed with some Spanish. She continued to stare, and as Tigue moved against her she was moved back to the reality that this person did not come for her. Disappointment shook

162

her. Tigue gave out a low growl, feeling the pressure she put on the dog's back to help herself gain composure. Again he spoke.

"I am looking for the Kimiah tribe of Indians, which is supposed to be camped here for the summer months. Can you help me?"

By now Elizabeth realized she needed to answer the friendly man that had shaken her so badly.

"Yes, I can help you," was her soft reply. "I will take you there." Her unsteady voice gave him a clue about how upset she was.

"I hope I have not caused you to be frightened of me," he spoke. "I assure you I mean you no harm, and I desire to know how I can help you."

He approached closer to see the expression in her eyes and to be sure that he was not the reason she appeared to be ill. When he moved, the big dog stood quickly between them. Elizabeth spoke a word to Tigue and the dog again stood beside her.

"I will confess I did have a start when you rode up. I was glad you approached slowly and warned us that you were here. Sometimes Tigue gets protective of me and I forget to call her off. She is a good dog and safe to be around. She has never been tested in her loyalty for me because I have been safe here with my adopted Indian family." She had spoken with a stronger voice.

Jesse asked, "Would you do me the pleasure of riding my horse to the Kimiah camp?"

"Oh thank you, maybe that would be best. We could arrive there before dark if we move along at a fast walk. Will you ride one of the other animals?" she asked him with a smile.

"Yes, I have brought an extra riding horse. First let me help you on Skipper. He is very quiet and you will like him, I am sure." Jesse went to bring up Skipper and the other horse.

"This is thoughtful of you, Mr. _____." She realized she did not know his name and felt awkward about asking. Jesse rushed forward, pulling the horses quickly after him.

"I'm Jesse Cannon," he said, holding out his hand to her. His gaze met hers and again he believed he beheld the most beautiful woman he had ever met. Her awesome beauty took his breath away.

"Call me Eizi," was all she said. Elizabeth came near this stranger with his dark blue eyes and honest mouth. He was much taller than she and, she thought, surprisingly good looking in a rugged way. His unshaven face held a firm jaw. She could not tell his age, but she guessed older than she would at first thought.

She took the hand he had extended to her and found it warm but rough. She took the reins he was holding and prepared to mount the horse. Before Jesse regained his composure she had her foot in the stirrup, so he moved up to help her into the saddle.

He was impressed by the manner of this young woman. She had captured him with her trusting and warm friendship and most of all her dimpled beauty. Finally he spoke.

"OK, Miss Eizi, up you go." The feel of her closeness and the warmth of her made him shake slightly as he lifted her onto the horse.

"You lead," was all he could say. They traveled away from the cliff and from the sacred burial grounds. Quietly they moved out of the thick trees and along the rock-strewn walls of the canyon that had shown a lot of different strata in the rock. Elizabeth could see he studied the color changes and she wanted him to talk. For some reason she wanted to know more about him, so she inquired of him.

"What do you think about when you see this wall?"

"It is unusual at the most. I can see that it represents periods when the region hosted oceans, deserts, volcanoes, mountains, and rivers larger than the Mississippi. As we have moved deeper into this valley, I am impressed with the vastness of the canyon—the changing colors, such as that patch of green hosting the bright cardinal monkey flowers, and then the brown crumbled rock/earth mix. This beginning of the Payette range is so rugged. I have not seen a wilderness area I have liked so much."

Jesse realized he was talking a lot and looked at Eizi for her reaction. She only smiled her dimpled smile in a weary sort of way.

"You are weary; I can tell," said Jesse. "We must get to your camp. How far is it?" Eizi was happy that he cared about her health. He was a very kind man, she noted, and responded to him.

"This is just one of my spells. They usually come and go. Do not worry about me, Jesse. I am doing better. Resting like this on such a fine horse. The villages are a mile down the valley."

She pushed the horse forward. They came along the summit trail and viewed the valley below them, hemmed in by a range of lofty peaks. There was a smoky haze like a purple cloud that lay on the waving grass.

Jesse smelled the smoke from the fires of many camps. There was a breeze blowing and he inhaled the musty scent of horses not far away, then spotted them this side of the village.

Eizi had stopped her horse as she too enjoyed the scene below them. She turned to look at Jesse. His face was bronzed by the setting sun and he was smiling.

"Not even a painting by a fine artist could catch the feeling on canvas of this contented primitive life. Or the thrill it gives me to see this. There is the smell of the fires of camp and the horses on the edge of the grassy meadow. It is a dazzling sight," he exclaimed.

Eizi was happy with his remarks, as they expressed her thoughts, too. She never tired of seeing the peaceful village from this spot . . . her home in this wilderness. Now she knew a little more about this stranger and his appreciation of her Maker's handiwork.

"Yes, I love this. It is the best view of the valley." She replied to him. With the sky reddening in the West, the two pushed on so they could get down to the valley below before dark. They moved toward a small herd of grazing horses that gave way to their intrusion as they rode by them. Eizi spoke.

"The Nez Perce possess more horses than any Indian tribe in the West, and it is because of the rich stand of grasses, plus they breed for lines that have stamina and speed."

"Horses get to you, don't they?" he asked. "I have noticed you have a very good time on Skipper, and he seems to like you."

He looked at her response and could read the pleasure in her eyes when he spoke of this. She replied, "I love them."

Jesse could tell she was proud to be a part of this nation and that they had treated her well.

"Tell me how you happen to be here," he asked this mysterious young woman riding along beside him.

"I owe this tribe my life. They saved me when I was in an accident," she replied. "I have been happy here and have been treated like a guest. Come on now, or we'll be late for the evening meal." She smiled and pressed the horse into a fast-moving gait.

They threaded their way through the wigwams and rode around the people who were milling about. The people stared at Eizi's visitor, but greeted her as if her return was long-waited. Jesse was sure they would have a great evening, and he longed for a good night's rest—knowing he would find it here in this peaceful village, among friends.

Chapter Seven

Sleep had come slowly for Jesse last night as he was plagued with anxious dreams That left him unsettled in spirit. The day broke clear with a gray, washed sky that slowly turned blue over the rolling hills. Jesse rose early with the rising sun and went to the stream to wash and get water for his container. He saw a few fires being built as he returned to his bedroll and gear and put the water jug back on his saddle.

Filling his coffee pot and adding enough coffee for three, he walked to the nearest smoking fire. There was an older Indian man and a woman working over the well-burning fire. They greeted Jesse with a welcome sign and invited him to put his container in the glowing embers.

Jesse smiled. It was a warm sign of friendship for him to be invited to share the early meal being prepared. These Indians were very different than the impression given to him before he came out West.

There can be no doubt that the people of this tribe attempt to live a noble life, and they are honest and brave—or that respect is important to them, Jesse noted.

From that place at the fire Jesse could see much of the village. He saw Eizi's tent and recalled that it was just that——a tent, so much different than the teepees of stretched skins over the tall poles.

She must have brought the tent with her, he thought. Did she choose to live here? He thought about last night, when he helped her from the horse and handed her into the hands of Ina,' the grandmother.

Her dwelling was in the middle of five of the village's largest tee-pees, just steps away. He had realized that Eizi's lodge was yielded to the exclusive possession of her and under no circumstances was an intrusive foot permitted to approach the dwelling.

The Nez Perce were a just people, and this pale-faced woman was befriended by all the tribe.

Eizi was certainly a woman of mystery to him, Jess thought. *And a pretty one at that,* he smiled to himself. He hoped today he would learn more of her past.

I am eager to see how Eizi is feeling, but know I should be considerate if she needs more rest, Jesse reasoned. It was then that he realized he had hardly thought of anyone else since their meeting last night.

Yes, I was taken in by her youthful beauty, but I admired her warm friendship and sincere courage to accept me, also. He smiled at the memory of their greeting. In his mind he could again envision her dimpled smile and shining green eyes.

She is the kind of girl I could take care of forever, he mused. *And yet, why do I think that? Maybe I do not know myself as well as I think I do.*

This troubling thought brought a wrinkle on his suntanned brow and he pushed his hat back as he rubbed his forehead. Jesse's eyes were on the tent of the young woman that he had helped home.

The man by the fire touched Jesse on the shoulder and offered him a bowl of food to take.

"Yuta," he said with a smile—meaning *eat with us.*

"Oahu," Jesse smiled back as he took the vessel with a nod of approval. Then the three of them began to eat the morning meal near the warmth of the fire.

As the morning sun directed its rays on Eizi's tent, she woke up because of the brightness.

"Oh, it must be late," she said to Tigue. The faithful dog was sitting up facing her, her tail hitting the ground in a show of happy greeting.

"Yes, you can go out," she commanded the dog. In a quick turn, Tigue darted out the opening, bounded toward the stream, and ran out of Eizi's sight.

Eizi sat up slowly, and when she did, a smile lit her face.

"No headache!" she said aloud. "It is amazing what Ina and Fox Medicine can come up with to help me sleep. I must go tell her now." She began to ready herself for the day.

She groomed her hair, rebraiding it, and reached for her best catch. It was then that she realized she was taking a lot of extra care to look nice.

"Why am I doing this?" She had been thinking of Jesse and their meeting. The image of this man was too powerful to be ignored. She breathed a deep breath as she did not understand the pleasant effect he had on her. She dressed to ride, putting on the split skirt she had been wearing when she came here from her home.

Home . . . mustn't I find out where that is? What am I afraid of? Star talked as if my home could only have been nice. Eizi was shaking a little as she finished tying her boot-strings and she knew that if she kept stressing over her past she would become sick again.

She was looking forward to being able to ride to the lake with the waiting stranger. She had seen him out by the fire with Black Bull. She'd watched Jesse run his hand over his brow as if to wipe off the frown that had just appeared there. She wanted to go to him and make him laugh, to take away the worry from his handsome face and have it replaced with the tenderness she had seen there last night.

As quickly as Eizi stepped out of her tent, Tigue was there, as faithfully she always, seemed to appear whenever Eizi was preparing to leave the village.

How this golden angel knows my every move, she wondered. Jesse was observing the two from a distance. Tigue stood up slowly, happily swinging her tail, her brown eyes alert with expression as she came to her mistress.

Jesse watched Eizi's soft touch on the head of the dog and heard the greeting as both of their reactions spoke of love and excitement. They walked toward him. He rose and met her half way, and when he handed her a cup of his coffee, their eyes met.

Eizi realized there was intelligence and kindness in his gaze. She broke his focus on her with a nod and a greeting.

"Good morning, and thank you," she blushed, looking from his blue eyes down into the dark cup.

"I think I like coffee; it smells so good," she bubbled. She drew the cup to her lips as he watched her. Then, feeling like he had been staring, he spoke.

"You look well-rested. Is your head clearer? And what do you mean by 'you think you might like coffee?'"

"Yes, I feel a lot better. It's a beautiful day for a ride. Will you accompany me?" she asked, changing the subject from her health and completely evading his question of her memory.

Why am I not willing to speak of what happened to me, she asked herself. *Maybe today, I will begin talking with Jesse about what I can remember, and this will help me heal*, she thought.

They rode together to the crest of the ridge near the cliffs. Eizi had promised Jesse another beautiful view. Jesse could tell she loved to ride out like this. She wore a well-kept, wide-brimmed hat that fit her very well.

The single braid of shining hair that hung down her back looked redder than he remembered it from last night. Maybe it was the morning sun's gentle radiance on it. The sombrero made her look like royalty he had read about in a Spanish story. The blouse she wore under her beaded deerhide cape projected a mixed mystery of who she was, which caused him to nearly stare.

This morning Eizi had chosen an older mare to ride, which she called Florrie, meaning *flower.*

The horse was quiet and obedient and this gave Eizi confidence during her recovery, even though she was a good rider. She had saddled up with her own saddle and, hardly visible on its well-worn skirt, was the initial "B."

With much affection, she spoke often to the mare as they rode, especially when the barefooted horse stepped on sharp rocks along the trail. The yellow dog trotted softly beside them . . . always there.

About noon they reached the top of the summit near the jagged peaks covered with streaks of glistening snow. These showed pure white against the blue summer sky.

It was a raw, new country and Eizi was a part of it by choice. Jesse saw the smile on her happy face as she looked at the vast country that stretched for miles.

They moved the horses down the trail to the small, clear stream where they dismounted and watered them. Tigue waded in up to her belly to drink, then went splashing downstream, chasing a small fish.

They laughed at her jumping and splashing like a young pup. Jesse found a log for them to sit on and encouraged her to rest there while he tied up their mounts. When he returned and sat next to her, she was unusually quiet. He looked again at her pretty face, her mind deep in thought. In a few minutes he questioned her.

"Eizi, do you desire to go back to your family now that you are able to travel?"

170

It was a few minutes still before she answered. Jesse believed that she had not heard him speak and was about to inquire if she felt well. Eizi's mind and emotions were playing with the thought of how deeply she did feel about finding out about her past.

Was she free to get to know Jesse in a more intimate way? Should she pursue a serious relationship, and what was it that was holding her back?

I am content here, but when I am challenged, I wonder what it is all about. I won't really be free till I have answers. I know I can't just fret about it until it makes me ill again, she told herself. She looked at Jesse's concerned face, and addressed him.

"Yes, I know I need to move on, but it was odd to find myself involved in the lives of these people. It was as if a part of me was missing and I felt as if I were in a dream or cast in a strange play.

"Every time I prepare to leave here, I get sick. Maybe I am not ready to know the truth. Every day that I wait I remember more of my past, and I am stronger. I do not know what else I am waiting for, unless God has more for me to do here among these people.

"When I saw you yesterday, I thought you were a person from my past. I tried so hard to recognize you, but when I did not, I became very upset. Yes, I wished I had been rescued by a friend that I do faintly remember . . .

"Oh, I have been well-cared-for here. I am so grateful to Ina' for nursing me back to health—and now most of my headaches are gone."

Jesse watched Eizi as she moved her hand to the scar on her temple. He reached for her hand, which fingered the healed spot, and held it in his. With his other hand, he pushed back a strand of red hair from her face, rested his fingers on her brow, and gently smoothed the wrinkle of sadness that had just formed there.

Eizi tingled with his touch from her face down to her breast. She sat unable to speak for several moments.

"Why did you do that?" she finally asked him.

Too late, Jesse realized his action was far more intimate than he'd intended. He too felt a warmth run through his being. He quickly released her hand.

"I am sorry; I meant no disrespect, I wanted to comfort you, and I interrupted what you were saying. Please forgive me," he begged.

"You were about to explain why you have stayed here this long . . ."

"Oh, yes," she began, speaking in a soft voice. "I realized I was in the grip of something greater than myself. After many lengthy talks with Star, I realized that God only was in control, I was to wait on Him and to be content within His Will.

"I recalled scripture as we read the Holy Book that Star shared with me. The book of Psalms was our favorite to meditate on. Through it, God gave me assurance that I was never alone, that I never am, even for a moment's time, away from the mind of my Heavenly Father."

Eizi felt Jesse react to this statement. He moved like someone had shaken him. Eizi put her hand on his arm to steady him.

"What is it, Jesse," she asked.

Jesse detected a change in her voice when she said his name, and being further moved by this, he took her hand in his. He knew that touching her would quiet him, and it did.

"Yes. I mean, *no,*" he replied, gazing into her eyes. "Oh, let me explain Eizi. I understand what you are talking about, as I had, up to a few days ago, been fighting that battle, too.

"I was advised by a wise person to let go and let God into my life. Since then, God and I have had several talks. I believe He knows my heart and I have given my life, again, to Him. I promised Him that I would continue to search, but that now I would turn my quest over to Him.

"You see, it is the same with me as with yourself. I want God's will in my life."

Jesse enjoyed sharing this with Eizi. Eizi could see Jesse had carried a heavy burden in his adult life and his unburdening it to her just now made her feel like she was special.

"Have you found peace here in this country?" She asked with a wave of her hand about them, indicating the country they were in. His gaze would soften with tenderness as he looked at this delicate young woman sitting beside him. His words began thoughtfully.

"I have found contentment out here in this wilderness as I travel. I am content sitting here with you. I feel no tension in staying at the Indian village. If I were welcome, I would like to stay several days and get to know the people," he concluded.

Eizi felt a tingle of excitement as she heard his request, but she felt compelled to ask him, "Jesse, what about your quest? You seemed so urgent about it just yesterday."

Jesse was hesitant before he answered her.

"I'm not sure, but it will keep. For five years I have put this journey to find my brother off. A few more won't matter. I plan to gather more information at the Kimiah camp before I travel on."

She seemed accepting of his answer. When he asked her to tell him what she *did* remember about her past, Eizi began thoughtfully.

"I can remember the loss of my mare and the band of wild horses with the dark stallion who caused my head injury. I think I had some help in this as Star and Ina saw the tracks of the wild herd near the large lake where they found me."

She told him bits and pieces of what she remembered, including a dream she'd had of the black stallion being captured by ranch cowhands and an odd impression that the stallion had at one time belonged to her.

She always had tears in her eyes when she thought of this. When Jesse saw them falling from her cheeks, he put his arm around her shoulder in comfort.

"Eizi, forget about the bad times and all of this unhappiness. The stallion was like a heavy snow that piles up or a gale that soars through the forest, or the occasional forest fire. These are all things that those who live in this part of the West have to accept as a matter of course. Sometimes it's a hard and lonely place," he said, trusting that this would encourage her.

She nestled against his chest and relaxed into the comfort of his words. In this remote place overlooking the high mountain range, Jesse tightened his arm around her while the afternoon sun warmed their backs.

The evening hours back at camp were an enjoyable time. Jesse and Eizi had a delightful supper with Star and Wakanka Ina.

Star had just returned from a successful trade with another small band that was a day's ride from camp. This group had needed horses, so they were able to trade with them for hunting rifles and supplies. It was a festive celebration of old and new friendships.

The newly adopted family had accepted the stranger easily and Star detected a fondness for him that she had not seen since her father had been with them. Jesse roasted some quail that Tigue had flushed out for Jesse to shoot on their hunting trip today.

He enjoyed telling Star all about the hunt that he and Tigue had enjoyed together. They were sitting with the large yellow dog between them, each stroking her large head. With a twinkle in his eyes, he began the story, using his hands as he talked.

"The quail's *Ave Maria* is heard in the hush of dawn. We know they roost in the tall grass. I was able to read their location from the cock of Tigue's ears. We know she can find the grouse! When at last she stopped—stock still! And ready I am as I shoulder my gun. Then the cock grouse drums his defiance!"

Jesse began hitting a rock with a stick. Star laughed. Then Jesse continued.

"Tigue cocks her head as she notes his direction. Suddenly, a rustle in the grass! Tigue jumps forward at the movement—moments too late as the quick bird takes flight."

He throws his hands in the air, and again Star giggles loudly. Jesse, watching Star's face, continues.

"It is quick, I say. It is a long way out, and it is getting dark. Then one shot I take." Jesse points with his arm extended like a rifle.

"Then we see the bird fall, and before I can get the gun down, Tigue has it in her mouth and is returning it with a smile on her face and a wag in her tail." He finishes with a shrug.

"Oh yes, I too have seen her smile! And I thought I was the only one who could see this," Star claps in excitement. They both laugh when Tigue wags her big tail in agreement, too.

Eizi can hear them laughing over the story. She smiles listening to them. Ina' watches the fond reaction and speaks to Eizi.

"My daughter, what do you know about this man? You must not tell him your desires until you get to know him better," she says. "What if he is like Star's father, who left her when there was trouble?"

Her voice is low, and in the twilight they talk in the Indian language for Eizi only to understand. Eizi looks with kindness to the Wakanka and it is then that she fully understands the meaning of the Wakanka grandmother. She has spoken with love and concern for both her children. Eizi responds to her wise words.

"Wakanka my Ina, I will heed your words. Please know that I would do nothing to harm Star." The two smile at each other and go about their task of preparing the evening meal.

Star likes this Jesse, now her new friend. She talks with him, trying out more of her newly acquired English language, and finds him willing to ask the definitions of words in her native language. Jesse enjoys the talk of this smart Indian girl. He realizes she must know more of Eizi's past that she has yet shared.

He thinks he must ask Star more about how they found Eizi and the journey they had together. He hopes to gather information that can help bring back her memory. This is foremost in his mind every time he looks at the beautiful woman with the auburn hair and feels the need to know more about her.

Jesse was going to suggest to Eizi that they retrace the journey. He wanted to volunteer to go with her on this journey, and was willing to put aside his plans to find his brother until she was safe at her home.

When Jesse had the chance after the meal, he approached Eizi and told her of this desire. Her reaction surprised him.

"Oh, no!" she replied in great protest. "I am safe here and happy, too. I could not leave Star right now. Ina' has not been well. It could be old age, and the trip has been hard on her. Until I know more about this concern, I know that I am needed here."

Eizi looked at Jesse's face and knew that he doubted her reasoning. *Was it her own guilt that gave her away?* She did not evade the truth very well and it was easy to see she did not face up to her problems. Caught in a wave of uncomfortable explaining, she reasoned— *I do not need to apologize for my decision.* Her eyes met his gaze.

Jesse saw her blush, and as her breath became short he did not want to press her on the matter right now.

"Eizi, we will talk about this later," he said, reaching for her hand. Then he continued, "But there will come a time when you will see the need to face the heritage of your past, just as I recently did.

She got up from her place by the fire. "Yes, I wish you to tell me about that some time, but right now, come on. Let us join Star and the others."

She reached for his hand. *Was it to have him join her now, or did his touch comfort her?* Eizi did not know, and right now she did not care to answer the question that was bothering her troubled heart the most.

Across the village two pairs of eyes watched every move the white woman with the red hair had made.

"Yes, that is her, the white woman we saw at the lake," one warrior remarked. He had wide, slanting eyes in a narrow, bony face. His jet black hair hung down to his bare shoulders. The younger nodded and knelt down by a small fire they had made in the place where they were staying the night.

"It is good that we have deceived these Kamiah fools to accept us as Nez Perce so we could study our prey," he answered. His dark, treacherous eyes were roving over the campsite, where the young people were participating in their games.

He had a narrow forehead, with his hair cut off so short he looked bald. The two were an evil, nightmarish looking pair.

"Let us get some rest now, so we can leave early and retrieve the war bundle we hid in the trees near here. I do not feel good without it," he said in a low voice.

"Yes, we can find a place to watch and wait," the older Blackfoot Indian replied.

"We must catch them alone. Never underestimate the white dogs; they scrap fiercely for survival. Not like these yellow Kimiah cowards," he said, like a person with a grudge to settle.

The next few days Jesse spent at the camp were some of the most relaxing times of his life. He felt he was getting to know Eizi's friends.

He learned with surprise that Star and her grandmother were considered very well-to-do here in the village. They had many horses and other items to trade for all their needs.

He found Star a very warm young girl with a look in her eyes that wasn't much different than his cousin's in St. Lewis. They were about the same age and he supposed that this accounted for the resemblance. He mentioned this to Eizi.

It was then that Eizi asked Jesse to go on a fishing trip with them down to the river so they could be alone to talk. They saddled up and were on their way by mid-afternoon. Star was riding a horse she called Coyote, a bald-faced horse whose color seemed to change with the vegetation of the landscape. He was an older horse and was very devoted to her, as she was to him.

Eizi rode one of Ina's favorite mares, a wildfire of an Appaloosa and aptly named. The horse was quick and alert. The tack that Eizi had when she came to the village fit the small animal very well. They were a smart-looking pair.

Jesse realized that Star and Ina' had probably given her the horse. The weather was warmer, and the still air near the fork of the outlet allowed the music of nature to be enjoyed. This song of the river was loud as the waters played on rock, root, and rapid. This looked like a good place to fish Jesse thought.

Jesse and Eizi were watching Star play with Tigue along the bank running into the shallow water of the fork. They had found a log on the edge of the stream where they sat with bare feet dangling in the warm water. Jesse could tell that Eizi had something on her mind because she had not once met his eyes.

The afternoon sun cast a glow on her braided auburn hair. He wondered if he should tell her how beautiful she was, and was about to speak when Eizi began asking questions about his brother Ross. She wanted to know when he first came to the Northwest, how often he came, how long he stayed, and where Jesse thought he was going to locate him.

All this talk of Ross surprised Jesse. He was hoping Eizi had made a decision to find her way back to her home. He answered all that he could and told her what he had found out from Helen.

Yes, the wise men of the large Nez Perce village had told him that they had traded with Ross. Others knew of him living here, even though that was more than three years back," he told Eizi, watching her face light up.

"Oh, I knew my suspicions would match what Star has told me," she exclaimed.

"What has this to do with Star?" he asked. "What suspicions do you mean?"

"Don't you see? Ross was here when she was born and he disappeared about the same time Star lost her mother so she came here to live with her grandmother. Besides, Star said her father was a fur trader," she answered.

"This is your suspicion—that Ross is Star's father?" he asked, looking at her in disbelief.

It was a while before she answered. A sparrow could be heard chirping his clear, tenor chant. She moved closer to him and reached for his hand, then for the first time today looked him in the eyes.

"Jesse, think about all the possibilities. Would your brother teach his child English? And about knowing the one living God? Would he see to her livelihood for many years since he has been away, as someone has? They have plenty. You know they are considered well-to-do here."

"If this is so, who do I go to for more information on his whereabouts?" Jesse asked.

"You must ask for a hearing with the tribal council," she replied.

"Yes, I will do that when we return. Thank you for helping me," he smiled. He held her hand and the acknowledgment from her lips was all he needed as she gave him the warm, dimpled smile he had seen her show with Ina' and Star.

Trust was beginning to build in their relationship, along with admiration. This gave Jesse a surge of happiness he could not remember having for a long time.

Chapter Eight

In the bright morning just after the sun melted the fog of daybreak, Jesse rode along the river. Dew-sprayed flowers sprang to life from the damp, warm sand along the bank, which was lined with green grass.

The memory of yesterday was still with him in detail as he recalled Star playing along the river with Tigue. *Could Star really be Ross's daughter?*

The leaders of the tribe described Ross as Lewis, the fur trader, who might still live up the East Fork of the main river—about two days' ride, they had said. *To think we have been that close for the past week! What will a reunion with my brother be like,* he mused.

Skipper stopped and raised his head, which caught Jesse's attention. He came out from a grove of trees on the trail to the lake to see Eizi and Star on the lower trail, riding at a fast gallop.

The dog Tigue was bounding after them. He began waving to get their attention. Then they saw Jesse and reined their horses up to the higher trail, where he overlooked the lake.

"What are you doing here?" he inquired.

"We thought you would be glad to see us," Star replied, as she got off her horse. Her youthful, oval face and delicate features came with a soft voice.

Jesse walked up to Wildfire and took hold of her bridal as Eizi dismounted. Then he reached for the reins of the horse. Their hands

179

touched and her eyes were on his face in time to see a most satisfying smile of welcome. He held her gaze there for a time, then turned to answer Star.

"Oh, I am," he smiled noticing her tone, and appreciating the fact that she had ideas that were clear and expressions that were simple.

"We have something to tell you, friend Jesse. Eizi and I have chosen to go with you on your te-meg to find your brother. We have acquired extra horses and prepared supplies. We can leave at first light."

Seeing the surprise in his face, she added, "You do want us to go don't you?" His mouth fell open, then changed to a slight smile as he heard the clever way she put the question.

"*You* go with me into the wilderness? Through things that are unknown, in possible danger, and not sure exactly where we are even traveling? My dears, it could be a dangerous journey."

"Life is all risk," said Star. There are those who embrace risks wholeheartedly and move forward," Star replied with shining, eager eyes.

Jesse looked at Eizi, who had as yet said nothing. He could tell she was enjoying the looks Jesse stood in amazement at the reply of the young girl.

"I suppose you put her up to this. You said you loved to go to new places and meet others?" he quizzed her.

"Ue Tu, not this time," she replied with her dimpled smile.

Jesse, always struck with Eizi's natural beauty, studied her for a moment. She looked at the lake, which was glistening like a gem in the last rays of afternoon sun. He too was taken by the beautiful scene, and together they quietly shared these moments.

Impatient, Star cleared her throat, waiting for an answer. Jesse then shrugged, looking to Eizi for some help. He did not know how to answer the young girl's request. Star broke the silence.

"As for the danger we could encounter, we will fight to protect each other," she declared with the bravery of a young girl. Jesse listened in amazement, and Eizi put her hand over her mouth to keep a laugh from escaping it.

"Now, listen here, young girl," Jesse began. Just then Eizi put her hand on his arm to stop his outburst.

"Jesse, could we ask you to think about this and let us start back to the encampment in case we do leave early?"

"Yes. It is time to return," Star stated, noticing the man look into the eyes of Eizi and seeing his expression change to one of softness infused with natural feelings.

The sun was beginning to glow behind the fringes of pines that bounded the western hill.

"Let's go home," he said with a smile as he helped Eizi remount her horse, then went to get on Clipper. He noticed a quietness he had not perceived before as the air was usually filled with the carols of many birds.

There were only some blackbirds that took flight down by the lake. Eizi turned her head in that direction and called for Tigue to come. With a whine, Tigue reluctantly obeyed the call.

It was clear that the large dog was still sniffing the strong scents she was uncertain about. These were not the small animal scents she went hunting for, but were the scents of other, more dangerous animals. The others were leaving, so she bounded up the slope to join them.

A shadow moved away from behind a tall pine tree at the far end of the lake. The very angry Indian was moving in a stomping action. As the savage raged within him, it caused his nostrils to dilate and his eyes to glare like those of a wild beast that is prevented from taking his prey.

After a hastily eaten breakfast the three riders and the large dog got an early start, as they had planned. Dawn was breaking and the soft ground underfoot was hardening as the sun dried it.

Thin lodge pole pines grew far enough apart to let the pack horses through. It was a trail that had been wide and bold and cut by many wagons during the early gold rush days.

They made good time the first day of their *Te-meg*, as Star had called their journey. The day was warm and Jesse planned for them to stop early near the spring at the mouth of the East Fork. They skirted a mass of high peaks and cliffs and paused on a slope near the North Rim. This made them miles closer to their destination and on a trail leading up to the headwaters.

Eizi, delighted over each meadow of summer wildflowers, enjoyed the beautiful, brilliant colors all around her. Along a small stream that ran through this meadow, purple ironwoods stood tall against a wall of willows.

"Sometimes it takes ten years for a tree to reach maturity and for some plants to produce seeds, such as the Subphylum seeds that are large and meaty. They are as good as sunflower seeds to eat," said Star.

Eizi stopped her horse to view the scene while Star was speaking. With a strange look on her face, she replied softly.

"I read somewhere that in these mountains in the springtime as many as a dozen wild plants may burst their buds on a single day."

"Where did you read that?" Jesse inquired.

"Yes, where do I remember that?" She questioned herself in a distant voice.

"I believe it was a school, where a friend of mine, named Molly, *and I*—were in a classroom. There were many wildflowers in pots that we were tending. I can see it as plain as if it just happened yesterday."

Wide-eyed she gasped. "Jesse, I am remembering! My friend's name is Molly Newman. But that is all I can recall," she said with sadness.

"Eizi, do not feel bad. Your memory is coming back to you a little at a time, as Ina' said that it would," Jesse encouraged as he touched her arm.

Eizi had a sparkle in her eyes as her dimpled smile spread with pleasure across her pretty face. She returned his touch as she placed her finger on the corner of his mouth near his small mustache.

"Since I first saw you, I have wanted to touch you there," she said.

"It is only the start of many good things to come," Star interrupted. Tigue barked and they all laughed.

"It is time to move on," she added, turning her horse, Coyote, toward the well-marked trail.

For more than a mile they rode along single-file near the steep bank of the slow-moving East Fork, looking for a good place to cross. It was late afternoon when they suddenly came to a group of old, weather-grayed log shanties.

Along the riverfront there was an old fish-smoking rack and there were several tie-up places for the horses.

"We're at the fork we will follow to the headwaters," Jesse said. "But here we have an excellent place to camp, so let's get across at the sandbar."

They set up camp near the buildings and secured the horses in the meadow, letting several graze while others remained tied. The night was clear, so they did not pitch the tents. Jesse started a fire and placed two kettles on coals where the evening meal was soon cooking.

It was a flat valley floor that joined the long-gated range about a mile away. Jesse liked this place for the night because it would be hard for anyone or anything to sneak up on them. He felt safe here.

A steep cliff rose up straight as a tall pine tree on one side, bordered on the other by the main river, where a gray heron was attending to his unfinished fishing. Star looked upstream into a small, dark hole where a trout was rising, making a ring in the clear water.

"Oh, look, Jesse, a big one!" She pointed to the ripple moving upstream. Other than it, there was only slow-moving water here at the opening.

"Can we go after it?" she begged, jumping up, barely waiting for his answer.

"We have plenty of time before dark. I see no reason why we can't try," was his half-grinning reply.

"I'll get the pole and line." Star turned away, and never did a doe bound with more natural motion across her path. She hurried over to the pack lying by the panniers. Jesse saw Eizi smile after her.

"She has a vibrant zest for living," she said with fondness. Eizi spoke to him with love in her voice about Star. He knew it was more than gratefulness for saving her life that she felt. They had developed such a fondness that Jesse knew it would be all but impossible ever to separate the two.

Jesse wasn't sure he would want to separate from Star, either, as he, too, thought a lot about the girl's future.

"You two have fun, and I will wait here with the animals at camp and prepare our supper. I suppose Tigue will stay also," she added, with a hint of inquiry.

"We won't go too far," he replied, hurriedly catching up to Star. Higher up near the headwaters, the fork was narrow, deep, and fed by cold springs that gurgled out under its loose walls of tall willow.

They stepped quietly upstream from the black hole. In its rushing depths Jesse could see a shadow—rubbing its sides against the dirt bank.

Star was so excited she could hardly contain herself. Jesse showed her the shining trout, lying unaware of his fate. Letting their line float down between the screens of slim willow sticks, they wait . . .

A great trout rolls lazily over as he sucks down the gnat. He takes it with one fast gulp. Then the line goes tight, and the tug on it is great. Star raises the pole in an effort to place the hook solid in the trout's mouth.

The fish rebels with a huge jump and with an open mouth in an effort to expel the hook, then try another. Star screeches in delight as she holds the fish on the line. The battle continues for several minutes. When the fish tired, Star backs up slowly to bring the fish onto the shore.

Jesse captures it, then holds it up for her to see. They both are laughing and still excited as they put the fish, kicking, in the basket. A dull misty haze settles down around the camp as dusk begins to be replaced with dark shadows.

Eizi had spoken to Tigue two times when a low growl rolled from the dog's throat. She had a tenseness and an alert head that had alarmed a sixth sense in Eizi. Because of this, she picked up the Sharp 45 rifle that was some distance away and stood holding it, listening.

Was it too quiet? Then she heard the call of a loon, followed by another call. The calls were in different tones and they came from where the forest was dark beyond. Then the laughter of the two returning from their fishing trip was a welcome to her ears. Jesse, surprised to see Eizi carrying the rifle, was walking toward her.

"Is everything all right?" he asked as he rushed to her side.

"Oh, yes, I just don't like the creeping darkness," she replied, not wanting to alarm them without good reason.

"What do you have in the basket?" she asked Star.

"Just breakfast," Star replied walking down to the river to clean the fish. "And one is enough for us all," she said proudly. They laughed at her reply.

Jesse took the rifle Eizi had been holding. He took Eizi's hand and together they walked toward the fire with his fingers entwined in hers. His touch gave her a warm feeling, and her fears faded away—for now.

Tigue walked beside them, but Jesse noticed a tenseness as her lips rose up in an unfriendly manner. Then the dog stopped and strained toward the quiet, dark pines on the other side of the meadow. Eizi spoke to her to catch up and Tigue obeyed.

After supper, Jesse spread his bedroll near the fire and Eizi and Star put down their furs for sleeping right beside him. The huge fish lay over the coals on the drying stick where they left it for the night. Then they prepared themselves for a good night's sleep.

Before their eyes closed they shared some talk of their past, at least what Eizi could remember of hers. Star questioned Eizi.

"Don't you wonder if someone is out there asking for you to be safe, and for the moon to light your way home?"

This left them both speechless. Finally, Eizi smiled and replied, "Yes, I do." With a look to Jesse, she knew they both remembered that she was asking the same questions Jesse had ask when they first met.

That look held his eyes to hers. A yelp of a coyote broke the still-ness. Tigue raised her head, but only a slight whine left her lips. Eizi put her hand on the head of the big dog and was glad Jesse had de-cided they would take turns staying awake tonight.

"Just a precaution," he had remarked, not wanting to alarm them.

Chapter Nine

The first rays of dawn flashed over the Eastern hill-side. A lazy hawk circled in the windswept, cloud-less sky as the early risers watched it catch an updraft and rise into the glowing sphere.

"There is something almost mystical about the mountains," said Star. "My Ina' says they can give you answers, but I tell her it is the Lord that speaks to her," Star said as she rode along on Coyote.

An orange and black butterfly flew over Star's head, then lit on her shoulder briefly. Star smiled and with a nod acknowledged its flutter as the beautiful creature flew away.

Eizi smiled to Jesse. To her, it was incredible that they were on this journey together. How comfortable they were with each other as she felt the strength and safety she had felt at Jesse's side all week. She looked at this man whose dark hair straggled across his forehead from beneath his broad-brimmed hat. After the last two weeks of being together at the village, they had become good friends. Their closeness with Star was growing, and Eizi believed that even if they did not find Ross, Jesse would take responsibility for Star's livelihood.

Now Eizi knew that she too must face what lies ahead and make decisions about her future. Her time with Jesse was just beginning, just as her time with Dalton had come and gone, leaving only a faded memory.

Was it too late for Dalton to be an intimate part of her life? She had only just recently remembered him, that he was her close friend. *Would she feel differently when she saw him and could recall all they had once meant to each other?*

Riding through the wildflowers in the mountains of Idaho was a wonderful experience for Jesse He believed that if given the chance this was something he could do for the rest of his life. He had seen Eizi as a new person away from the life of the tribe. She was an amazing, western woman and it was hard to believe she had ever been a part of the quiet, primitive life.

He was looking at her beautiful copper-colored hair as it glowed in the early morning sunlight. She had not tied it back and a few strands hung forward nearly covering her tan cheeks under the tall, flat hat that shaded her face. He thought a lot about her and she was again in his dream last night.

Last night Eizi talked to Jesse of the people she remembered in her life. She asked him questions about his childhood, his family, and his dreams. Getting to know this kind, Christian man was exciting to her. There was a draft of warmth that they both felt.

The Sawtooth Mountains of the Payette range were split by the Salmon River that flowed from the east. The pioneer surveyors jotted down in their notebooks distant lakes, watersheds, and high points in this wilderness range. However, the unexplored country sported few details for mapmakers.

Jesse got out the map drawn by an Indian Chief and examined it again. It was good to have Star along as it was amazing how well she remembered this trail. Star—*this child amazed them both!*

This morning as they enjoyed the fish for breakfast Star had asked Eizi questions about her home and family. They were questions that had surprised them both. Eizi believed Star was not cooperative in giving more details of her home, but maybe she really did not know many of the answers. Jesse was also right when he said many questions Eizi must answer herself.

The trail cut sharply upward along the side of a shallow gully that sloped from the top of a deadline ridge. There were three blazes notched out on the gnarled trunk of a pine where the trail made a sharp turn.

They were discussing this directional sign when a snarl came from the throat of Tigue. Jesse reached for his rifle—pulling it out of the scabbard all in one motion.

"Let's ride!" he yelled, as he directed the two to move quickly away from the shallow trail. The character of the steep trail changed abruptly as they loped through groves of aspen and massive pine.

Pulling the pack animal was slowing them down. Jesse was looking for a place to stop and make a stand—*if they had to.* Just then the loud sound of a spent bullet hitting a tree nearby alarmed him greatly. He heard a lot of other rifle fire going on up the trail.

"Get into those rocks ahead," he called to the two frightened riders in front of him. They obeyed and quickly dismounted behind them.

Reaching for the rope of the pack horse, Eizi helped free Jesse from one obstacle. Then with his rifle in his hand, Jesse hit the ground running for the opening they had come through. Big rocks on each side provided the safety he needed.

Was it possible that someone was trying to kill him? He wondered. There was a high, steep cliff behind them that provided good safety. Unless an attack came from down in the canyon, the trail they came up was the only way the attackers could get a shot off at them.

They heard many more rifle shots not too far away. Jesse detected distinct gun sounds going off that were different from the first rifle shot that threatened him. Soon the gun battle ceased and it was silent except for the nervous movement of their horses.

The next sound they heard was of a lone horse moving quickly toward them. Tigue, alert, had heard it, too, but she did not growl. Only a single bark came from her anxious mouth.

"Hello there!" a man called out to them. "I come as a friend, and I believe you are safe now."

Gazing down the trail they saw a tall rider approach with his free hand in the air. He rode mostly straight up, but with a slight tilt forward in the saddle that seemed somewhat familiar to Jesse. He was built trim with a dark beard—a man in his early thirties. The black hat he wore nearly covered his dark blue eyes, but they looked right at Jesse as he rode up to him. Jesse pulled his hat from his head to reveal a warm smile on his face.

"Ross, it *is* you!" he shouted with surprise.

The two men stared at each other for several seconds. Ross said, "Jesse? It can't be. How did you find me?"

"Yes, it is your brother, and I have been looking for you for weeks. Why haven't you contacted me before now?" Jesse replied with anguish.

"Jesse, I am sorry, I have no excuse. After I lost my wife I went to pieces and wanted to be by myself. How long has it been," he asked with his arms out and his hands in the air.

Jesse grabbed his arms and, looking at him face to face, replied, "Ross, it has been too long. I am angry with you, but I am also so glad to find you."

Immediately, the two brothers hugged each other, both laughing with joy on their faces, yet showing a few tears at the same time. After some slapping on the back they finally turned to where Eizi and Star had joined them and were also revealing their joy over the happy reunion.

Tigue barked, wagging her tail at Ross, and they all laughed. Jesse started to introduce Eizi, but was interrupted by Ross's stepping toward Star and exclaiming, "Louise, it *is* you! You are beautiful!" With tenderness and caution, he took his daughter in his arms.

"I would know you anywhere. You are the spitting image of your mother." Ross held his daughter away from himself, where he could see her soft and luminous face that filled with a kind of marvelous joy and surprise.

"Father!" Star said looking at Ross in disbelief. "You *are* alive. My Ina' said she believed you were dead. I would have come to look for you before, but for that!" She did not know what else to say.

"Do not fret my little one. I am the one who should have come to the village before now. Please forgive me," Ross asked with a pleading smile.

Star sprang back into his arms with a small giggle and the two held each other and did a little dance together. Jesse and Eizi watched them and shared their joy and happiness. Jesse reached for Eizi's hand and as he took it, she moved closer to his side. He leaned over to speak to her.

"You were right, and I thank you." When Ross and Star turned toward them, Jesse introduced Eizi to him. He acknowledged her with gladness, and when Star told him about their new friendship this summer there was a light in Ross's eyes. He said to her, "It is so wonderful that Louise has had such a nice person come into her life. I must call my daughter by her Christian name, and I hope you will, also. God must have sent you to her. I am glad to meet you, Eizi. Is it short for Elizabeth," he asked, looking closer at her pretty face.

A frown appeared on Elizabeth's forehead. She touched the scar near her hairline and replied, "Yes, in fact I believe it is!" With a smile, she continued.

"Oh, you have it all wrong, Ross. God sent Star to me. Or *Louise,* as you call her," she corrected herself.

Glancing to Jesse she said, "It looks as if we both have new names." Then she said to Ross, "You see, your Louise saved my life.

"Really?" Ross asked, and looked with surprise for a reply from Louise. Then Louise told of her Ina' and her going to see why Eizi did not return to camp that night.

"We found her the next day near the far side of the lake hurt, with her memory gone. But we wouldn't' have found her unless Tigue had barked to get our attention. Eizi was still unconscious and could not call out. It was a miracle of God that we found her," she added. They smiled, and agreed how blessed they were to have found each other.

"We all have a lot of catching up to do," Eizi said, "but I wonder if this is the time and the place to do it now. Who was that shooting at us?" she inquired, still shaken by the attack. "And what do they want from us?"

Ross realized Elizabeth was quite upset. He stepped near her, then answered.

"I saw two renegade Shoshone Indians laying a trap on the trail about an hour before you came up it. I realized they were up to no good, dressed in their war paint and all. I skirted around them to see who they were planning to ambush. I saw you on the far ridge and as you turned to come this way down the canyon, I knew it was trouble.

"About that time, they must have seen me and one of them took a shot at you. I surprised them with a return shot and am sure I wounded one. We had a shooting match for awhile, and then they took off, probably to take care of the wounded.

"Thank you for saving us from a possible disaster," said Elizabeth. "I knew Tigue was not happy with what she knew was in the area, but I could not see much sign to warrant any extreme caution," confessed Jesse.

"Yes, let us get on these horses, find the pack animals, and get you to my place as soon as we can." Ross reported, smiling at Louise and Elizabeth. He was angry at himself for not being more concerned about their being frightened and upset.

"Your place? You mean the old home where we lived? Are we that close," the young girl asked with happiness. Ross nodded in reply and helped her onto her horse, Coyote. Then he went to help Elizabeth.

This very beautiful woman was also very brave he noted. He steadied Wildfire and gave her a hand up. Jesse, already mounted, went to get hold of the pack horse's rope. With a nod they acknowledged they were ready and expected Ross to take the lead to his place, where they hoped to find the safety they so desired.

On top of the far ridge, two pairs of eyes watched them travel up river.

"He's a sneaking, crawling skin trader, and we'll get him—along with the rest of 'em," the older Shoshone said in anger. A long scar from a cut slanted upward from his cheekbone into his dark hair.

"Come on, we need to find a place to rest and treat that wound," said his companion.

"I have heard he is a first-rate hunter and can scent danger as a hound scents deer, so we will have to have a plan," chided the smaller Indian holding his arm. With great effort he mounted his horse and they disappeared into the dark forest.

Chapter Ten

The high ridge gave way and dropped sharply to a lower edge of the big meadow. After crossing the fork that spilled into the big river, they came to the log structure that was Ross's home.

He had built his lodge next to the river bank and had excavated dirt into a wall around the edges. He used heavy driftwood logs as posts along the front that held up a long roof. There was only one window that was framed with heavy shutters where a rope hung on each end, making it easy to shut.

The door was massive as two half-logs fortified it. Part of the house was newly built, but Louise had seen this type of lodge structure that her tribe occupied in the winter meadows.

"This is a swell place, father," Louise stated as she hurried by, eager to get there. When they rode up in front of the house, a large black dog with a rolling tongue came bounding up to Ross.

He was as big as a wolf, but carried himself with an easy movement and the wagging of the tail showed he was very happy to see his master.

"Hello, Buster!" Ross greeted him as he dismounted.

"Did you watch things here while I was gone?" Ross petted his head as Buster's eyes glowed with happiness.

"Louise, come here, please. This is my faithful companion for the past four years. 'Buster, meet Louise,'" he said with pride.

"Oh father, he is so grand. Where did you get him?"

Louise dismounted and came to the dog, who eyed her. His ears stood up alert. Then with a friendly whine and a wag of the tail, he lowered his head close to Star's hand. She reached out and touched him lightly. Buster went to her side and sat close. Ross answered her question.

"I got him as a pup from a lost Indian who needed lodging for the winter. It is a long story, and I will tell it after supper. She took the black dog's head in both hands and spoke.

"I am glad we can be friends, Buster." When she said his name, he stood up and wagged his big, shaggy tail and looked at her with those big, brown eyes as if to say, "I accept your friendship."

"Father, how do you think he will treat Tigue?" Louise asked in the voice of a concerned young girl. Even as Louise spoke, Tigue gave a low growl as she came up to the wolfish-looking dog.

Buster walked stiffly toward her. His tail wagged as he sniffed noses with her, then looked carefully at his master as if to ask what he had permission to do next.

Ross knelt to ruffle the dogs' ears and spoke to Buster.

"You treat your guests nicely—and the rest of these fine people, too." The dog whined, as if replying to his master in agreement. The big dog made one bark and darted off in an instantly toward the river with Tigue following him.

Louise and Ross laughed and watched them go. Let's get off the horses and make our guests at home. Come, all of you, and welcome. My home is yours, such as it is," he added.

Elizabeth watched Tigue disappear over the rise to the water. She could not remember when she had been away from the protection of the big dog.

Jesse saw the look in her face and recognized it as alarm. He quickly got off Skipper and went to Elizabeth's side. He took hold of Wildfire's reins and held out his other hand for her to dismount. She looked into his kind eyes.

The smile on his face left her a little breathless. She realized he was trying to comfort her. She gave him her gentle yet shy smile in return. Their hands grasped one another's as he helped her gracefully dismount to stand beside him.

Elizabeth was lovely. He realized he liked her very much and yet he knew he needed to treat her with respect. His eyes looked deep into hers as he said in a low voice, "Miss Blazier, we are home for now. You go inside and I will take care of the horses."

As the slanting light of the setting sun flickered through the tall trees, it cast a golden glow on the two standing there. She kissed him softly on his cheek, and said, "Thank you, Jesse." Then she turned and went inside the house.

Seeing Louise in his home gave Ross the first happiness he had had in four years. He did not know why he waited so long to go to her. He had reasoned that she was so young, and he thought he could not have raised her by himself. Therefore, he felt it was best to leave her with her grandmother.

Louise's hair fell in long, dark braids down her shoulders and back and parted neatly above a low, smooth forehead. In the conversation he had with her while they prepared the meal, he enjoyed her youthful spirit, her childlike humor. He noted that she had more wisdom than most adults. It was then Ross realized that she had been taking the place of an adult in taking care of Ina' grandmother. He had a lot of making up to do for her, and knew he had deprived her of her childhood by not being there for her.

Everybody needs special language for special groups and she seems to have it, he realized. He had seen her with Elizabeth and with Jesse. Her charm was natural. Her reasoning was far beyond her years. The grandmother and elders of the tribe had done well in raising her. He had remembered his wife telling him the older women were the center of all things strong and good as they maintain the peace within the lodge.

"I love Louise very much and will spend my life taking care of her," he silently vowed. Then he thanked God for giving him another chance to be a good father.

"Louise, you have a spirit I like; perhaps it is a gift of youth, but I believe you are a very caring person, and I love you." He said to her, as he gave her a quick embrace and a light kiss on her cheek. Louise beamed her admiring eyes at him before she replied.

"Father, I am glad you are found." It was a beautiful night for their celebration dinner. Night birds down by the river were singing their songs. They built two fires in front of the lodge along each side of the table they had put outside. The two dogs sat in front like sentinels on guard.

Ross suspected that the two warriors were still in the area by the way the dogs reacted to different sounds they could hear in the night.

Ross told the others he could smell woodsmoke in the air before they built their fire. They would have to talk about protection for everyone, and be extra careful not to go out alone.

Dinner that night was a sumptuous affair, planned as a celebration for Louise. They sat down to a lovely table set with a large bouquet of flowers next to the lantern, which gave sort of a magical effect to the occasion. The venison steak, cooked with potatoes and sourdough biscuits, smelled delicious. Elizabeth found some dried apples and had made a delicious pie.

"Anyone that can cook that well would make a great wife, Bets," Ross teased Elizabeth as he finished off a large piece of apple pie. Elizabeth smiled, tipped her head studying Ross's face as he continued to eye her with delight. He tipped his coffee up to her in a toast before he lowered his gaze and poured more coffee for all. Elizabeth felt something more intimate in the compliment.

"Perhaps I am reading something that was not there, but it was the look I got," she smiled to herself at the expectation it gave her. It was a festive time for all, and Louise wondered if she could be any happier than she was at this moment with all those she loved around her.

"Friends are for pleasure, comfort, and wisdom," her grandmother had told her. She had it all. Pleasure showed in her eyes and a wide smile showed on her lips all through the evening. She looked at her father and realized that maturity made his face more interesting. Time had exaggerated the stubbornness firming his jaw line. He carried himself with confidence, but often a frown graced his brow when Louise was sure he was remembering the past. Uncle Jesse had told her that Ross was making a name for himself as a fur trader and was living the kind of life he always wanted. Louise wondered where she would fit in, and then with her childlike faith she said a silent prayer that God would help her father make the correct decisions that would affect all of their futures.

Just over the ridge, sitting beside a small fire, the larger Indian spoke. "we will get to steal her soon. The time is right. The Wasechu will make a mistake." His voice was mean and crafty.

"Yes, that yellow wolf won't always warn them. I will capture her myself, and we will get the white woman to sell to the warriors in the valley near Montana."

A tremor of passion stole over his length as he spoke. His upper arms and chest were sculpted with the image of the tribe's sacred bird. Dressed in garments of soft hides, he sat cross-legged near the dying fire. His ebony gaze rose over the rise and he pointed to the Isemluks as it rose over the trees on the ridge lighting up the wilderness.

"Tomorrow will be soon enough. It is a sign; the evening light has told us," he said with passion. They began their ritual around the fire. When the Indian is about to go in quest of the great brown bear, they paint themselves and perform all the rituals that they do when they make war on a neighboring nation.

This quest, they believed, would be easy and they would return to their village with more horses and gifts for all. Their wait had been long and now, tomorrow, they had a plan to make good.

Chapter Eleven

The cool, refreshing water soothed her as, waist-deep in the river, Elizabeth continued her bath. She saw Tigue asleep on the bank not far away under a tree and thought, *Just a moment longer I will linger here in this beautiful place. The canopy of the encircling trees gives me a private place where I can relax for a while longer.*

In a short time she realized she was alone. This gave her a start, for Tigue would never leave her unless she gave her permission to do so and she had not heard a sound in that direction.

The wind had come up slightly. Maybe Tigue has gone to investigate a scent that is new to her. I am sure she will be right back, she thought as she climbed the bank where her towel and clothes were.

A rustle in the underbrush caught her attention. "Come Tigue," she called, hardly glancing in that direction. When no dog came, Elizabeth became alarmed. Quickly she finished dressing, picked up her jacket, and hurriedly started back through the trees. Moving at a run and glancing in each direction, she again called, *"Come, Tigue!"*—this time raising her voice nearly to a shout.

She heard several calls that sounded like bird calls and then a sound behind her. Just then a large hand wrapped around her forearm stopping her dead in her tracks, taking her breath away.

"Jesse!" she gasped before the large hand covered her mouth. She felt herself being dragged backwards off her feet. One of her abductors placed a cloth in her mouth and secured it by tying a strap around her head.

"Indians! Oh, God, I pray, help me," she cried as her heartbeat raced at panic pace. Elizabeth screamed, but she only made a strangled sound. They tied her wrists and then, together, lifted her up on a horse.

One of them scrambled up behind her and took off at a fast pace through the trees, away from the cabin. Ross looked up from his task when Buster raised his massive head and growled a low, long warning.

"Where is Elizabeth?" he asked in alarm. Jesse replied, "She went with Tigue to the river to bathe. It is shouting-distance to there. Why?"

"Let's go look for her. Come, Buster," he said, picking up his rifle.

With his hair standing straight up on his neck, the big dog darted off ahead.

"Do you think he heard something?" Jesse asked in a nervous tone. Not waiting for a reply, Jesse began to call out, "*Elizabeth!* Tigue!." A lot of barking began as Ross ran into the trees where Buster was making the noise.

"Buster has found something—over here," Ross yelled. They came to where the black dog was standing over Tigue. Buster was sniffing at the fallen dog's body and a whine escaped his throat. Then he began licking at a small wound that was bleeding from Tigue's head. Ross dropped down to examine the animal.

"Where are you, Elizabeth?" Jesse yelled, staring at the dog. Then he bolted down to the river. He saw no one in sight.

Fear gripped him as he ran along the bank looking for a clue. He saw tracks that he knew to be Elizabeth's boots alongside of some large, soft, shoe tracks. There were fresh, unshod horse tracks.

He stood there staring, knowing in his heart what they showed him. Just then Ross came up to him carrying a bloody arrow.

"Indians!" he exclaimed. "This spent arrow went right through a soft spot in Tigue's head. I stopped the bleeding. She is too weak to walk. Let's go take her to the cabin for care and prepare ourselves to follow these kidnappers."

"They took her in broad daylight." Jesse said in a shocked voice. "I was responsible for her safety."

"Yes, now come out of it, man. We will find her, but we must hurry. Time is so important," Ross said as he shook Jesse's shoulder.

They turned to pick up the injured Tigue and hurried to the cabin to prepare to rescue Elizabeth.

Louise saw them coming and opened the door for them. "What has happened? Where is Elizabeth?" she quizzed them in alarm.

"We think she is all right," her father began. "Those renegade Indians kidnapped her, but we will get her back. I know they want her for trading and so they will not harm her. I promise we will get her back," Ross reassured his distraught daughter.

"This is awful. Yes, let us go at once to find her," she cried.

"No, not you. I need your help here. You are needed to care for Tigue, and to be here if Elizabeth comes back. Will you do that for me?" He asked this as he held Louise tightly to abate the sobs she was making.

"Oh, yes, Father, what can I do for Tigue?" she answered after a moment of recovery. "I will help you pack what you need."

At once the two began to gather supplies, and as they did Ross talked to his daughter about how to nurse Tigue with some healing leaves. He told her to keep all the doors and windows locked and to stand guard.

Her countenance changed and her chin went up. She indeed looked brave.

"I will stand guard," was her reply. Ross smiled at her and went on changing clothes for this hunt of the renegade Indians and Elizabeth's safe return.

When he finished, Louise gasped as she looked at him. Her father looked like an Indian himself. He had removed his shirt and replaced his boots with moccasins. He carried a bow and quiver of arrows and hung a bag around his neck, but carried no rifle.

"Father, be careful!" she exclaimed. She gave him a hug and opened the door for him. Jesse brought up the horses and Ross gave Buster a command to remain, then mounted his own horse and took off at a gallop. As he looked back, Louise was closing the shutter on the window and Ross knew he could never again leave his daughter.

The trail was easy to follow and it went in one direction. *Too easy,* Ross thought.

"They must have a plan, and it is either to ambush us or to go to a place where they can hold up—one they are sure we will not get into," Ross said to Jesse. Then he continued.

"If it is the latter, I know where they are headed. It would be a good plan, but I can get there quickly and they will not expect me.

What I need for you to do is take the horses the long way and wait for a signal from me to move in.

The two brothers talked of the plan and before long they came to the place where Ross planned to continue on foot. Ross brought out a hand-drawn map and finished with a talk about what might happen.

"Remember, when you come to the large trees you must proceed on foot and with caution. If they try an ambush it will be near the old cabin," Ross lectured. "I do not want any thing to happen to you."

He held out his hand, which his brother took. With a look of affection, they gave each other a firm handshake.

"I know Elizabeth means something special to you, and I feel she has come into Louise's life at a very important time. I feel—I owe her a lot, too. This is the only way we will get her back. Go with God," Ross said, and slid down the steep mountain on foot. He was soon out of Jesse's sight.

Elizabeth tried to notice each turn in what was a faint trail, although they were traveling at a fast pace. She hoped to get free and didn't' want to get lost in the wilderness. The grip that the large Indian had on her was painful, as was the gag in her mouth. The cruel Indian with a savage-looking scar that ran from his eye down to the bottom of his jaw tightened his grip on her. Elizabeth felt her flesh crawl with his touch.

As frightened as she was, she could only imagine how Louise and Jesse were reacting to her disappearance. She had time to think about her beloved dog and prayed that she was unharmed. She could not figure out how these two evil ones had surprised her, except that she had not been careful enough.

Soon they came to a wall of a dug-out barn that looked as if it had been built in a hurry. The leader jumped off the horse and hauled her down beside him. The other injured Indian took their horse and rode on down the trail without a word.

Before she knew what was happening the scar-faced Indian picked her up and carried her inside the building. It was a musty place with only the door for an opening. He put her down and motioned for her to stay back, and then he kept himself between her and the door.

After a long wait, the one in charge must have realized that the injured warrior was not going to join them. He tied Elizabeth's feet up and set her down on a pile of trash. She watched while he began to take down a rock wall in the back of the room. There was a tunnel behind the wall. He made the opening big enough to go through, then came over, untied her, and pushed her through the opening with him following behind.

She watched him with a wary eye as he lit a torch. With the well-lit torch, they went further into the tunnel to where its corridor opened into a large room.

He pushed her inside and shut a makeshift door to lock her inside. In a short while the light from the torch disappeared down the tunnel.

Elizabeth, left in darkness until her eyes adjusted, could see slivers of light coming through some cracks. How long the light would be there she did not know. If she was to do something, it must be now. This, she knew, would be their hideout and they may even plan to stay here for days.

"God, help me to be calm," she breathed a prayer. Her nerves cried out, *this must be a terrible dream!* She fell down on her knees and began to pray.

"Lord, prayer is a relationship. Ours is built on love and transparency. You know my situation. I have a great longing to be near you, God, as I ask for your grace and mercy. Please, grant me knowledge as to what to do next."

Left alone in the dark mine, Elizabeth felt the fear of the darkness replace her fright that the two very dangerous Indians might soon return. At least here she had time to devise a plan.

Do not let fear move in and interfere with a plan of what to do next, she reminded herself. She had just prayed for this, and she knew that courage came from her Lord.

"Do not let me take too long to find it," she spoke out loud. She was not a coward. She would act.

Keep control, she said to herself as she walked around in the room. Then she realized she was in a mine and that the rubbish there could be of use to her. She wrapped her arms around herself as she felt the chill from the dampness creep around her.

She thought of the old camps she had been around that were near her home, and of the troubled, turbulent lives of pioneer miners. *It looked as if a miner may even have lived here.*

There might be some way she could build a fire. Better yet, a torch! Yes, a torch to light her way. Way? To where? Think, Elizabeth! There had to be another way out.

Rummaging through the pile of trash, she pulled out several pieces of oily rags, then found a long, narrow timber, which she wrapped the rags around and began looking for something to spark a fire with.

She could use the flint she always carried in her riding skirt pocket. Excitement began to build as she prepared the material for the sparks she could make against the old rusted machinery.

Putting some pieces of a rat's nest on top of the pile, she made attempts to ignite the soft materials. After a few endeavors, the fire was going strong. She thrust the rag torch into the fire, and before long it burned brightly.

Yes! Just what I need! She picked up some more rags to see her way through the tunnel and, with a prayer for guidance, went to the back of the long room. Groping through several cave-ins, she finally found the main tunnel.

She watched the torch carefully so she could replace a new fuel rag in it when needed. As she proceeded down the tunnel it became wider and she quickened her steps. Just before the last oil rag burned up, she saw daylight at the end of the tunnel.

"Praise you, God!" she exclaimed loudly. Waiting for her eyes to adjust to the light, she stepped out into the bright sunlight.

The sun was behind her and she knew it was still early day.

"I must hurry on. My captives may check on me and I will need more time to stay ahead of them," she worried.

She hiked on up to the top of the ridge, and then turned to look back. The far mountains, covered with the blue mist of the morning, outlined the peaks of the Payette Mountains and these would be her landmarks. Ross's cabin was just this side of them.

She needed to get to the top of the crest to see her way out of this long, deep canyon. When she crossed a well-used path that went down to a creek, she hoped it would take her to the far end, to a summit she could see in the east.

This direction she traveled for about an hour, looking back occasionally. *What a trauma she had been through! All this stress and fear— what good was it in her life right now?* She questioned these things, and then she began to relax as more time passed.

This gave her an opportunity to notice that some of the bushes' leaf looked golden in the sunlight. The bluebell flowers were beginning to bloom into tall, delicate spires along the path.

Blue is rare in nature, she thought. The sky and lakes have most of it. She smiled at this thought and realized that the path was broad and covered with small leaves and grasses. The smell of mint made her search for the lavender. It was then that Elizabeth realized that most of her memory had returned to her. She jumped for joy.

"Yes, thank you! I believed many miracles would be mine today, and You have granted me my most desired wish. Thank you, my Lord."

"Oh, good, water. I am so thirsty!" she exclaimed, as the stream was just below her in a small gulch. On closer approach, Elizabeth saw that the stream was beautiful, a silver streak with violet shadows and wide blue patches of reflected sky. In the warmth of the afternoon sky she fell down on her knees to drink her fill.

"Oh, thank You, God, for this good water," she said as she lifted her eyes to the sky. She sat there reflecting on the sparkling water. *Was she the first one to drink here? she mused."* Alone meant being the only one. It was solitude. *I wonder if Dalton is feeling alone also?*

Elizabeth remembered his loving look at her when they shared beautiful moments in beautiful places like this. She smiled at the thought of him. Her heart raced as she remembered his kiss and embraces on the last night they were together. Then she wondered why she would think of Dalton now.

Why did he come to my mind instead of Jesse? It will be Jesse that will rescue me, she believed.

I am feeling lonely and still a little frightened after the near-brush with death or, worse, being traded as a slave, she shuddered.

She looked over her shoulder, scanning the valley she had just traveled through. She got up and continued her climb to the high ridge.

As Ross walked on the side of the mountain above the old cabin, he thought about the enemy ahead.

These are the worst kind of renegade Indians, but I can't let what happened to Sweet Song crowd my judgment. Oh Lord, help my anger subside so I can be alert and quick," he prayed.

Ahead he heard a sound of bushes breaking and the sounds of horses' feet hitting rocks, even before he saw the injured Indian leading two horses into a thicket. Unsuspecting that Ross had climbed the rock ledge, the Indian was not looking for trouble.

Ross knew he had the advantage, but did not want to take a chance that the kidnapper could still get away.

The black soot that Ross had applied to himself from head to chest gave disguise behind the dark trunks of the tall, shaded pines. Quickly he reached in his pouch and secured the hairpiece on his head.

When he was sure his dress for this hunt was proper—he let a low growl escape his lips. It caught the Indians' attention and the horses began to jump around. Then a growl so exceedingly fierce and natural proceeded from the beast-like figure, which let it be partly seen by them from behind a large tree.

At first the Indian believed he had seen a real fierce beast growling like a brown bear. Just as the Indian drew his bow, the horses bolted from the frightening bear sounds that they imagined were coming closer. When the horses dashed forward, he lost the hold he had on them.

They disappeared in the sober darkness of the forest, nearly knocking over the Indian and causing him to lose his unspent arrow. He drew another arrow to put into his bow, but too late. The man in black sprang like a tiger toward him and, on the attack, let fly his weapon— the axe buried deep in the Indian's chest. His cry was heard echoing throughout the forest.

Walking up to the fallen man slowly, Ross spoke.

"Why did you wish me harm? I only wanted to defend myself. Now I'll have to come back and bury you." He stood over the Indian and bowed in prayer.

This tragedy brought back memories of when he lost Sweet Song, and he felt grief. After a while, he turned to go back and join his brother.

Things look pretty quiet here, Ross said to himself as he came in view of the old mine. This dugout building was where he was to signal Jesse. He whistled two sharp hawk calls and Jesse answered by another shrill call, loud and clear.

As he approached he saw Jesse, moving from one tree to the other, taking his position closer to the door. Ross covered him, with his bow ready, but the door did not show any signs of opening.

"If the renegade was going to try to keep us from coming inside he would have showed himself by now," Ross assured Jesse. He advanced to the front and pushed the door open, signaling that he would go in first.

Once inside he saw that the room was empty and he opened the door for his brother.

"Where did they go? Is there another way out of here?" Jesse asked in alarm.

"Well, let us search." He signaled for Jesse to cover him as they went deeper into the mine.

"Look here, this wall has been taken down. There is a small opening that was made here."

Working together, they made it bigger and slid through into the large room. They saw that a torch was made and searched for material to make them one. They would search deeper and needed a light to read all the signs that Ross would need to follow.

Ross pointed to the tracks in the soft, damp soil of the floor.

"See the boot prints of Elizabeth? And those are the soft large moccasin tracks of her abductor."

"Yes, these will be easy to follow, and we won't have to search other tunnels. We will make good time." Jesse said excitedly and rushed ahead of Ross.

"Wait. Slow up. This may be too easy," Ross warned, too late as Jesse was moving like a madman. It was a fast-moving pace for Jesse and soon he saw the daylight at the far opening of the tunnel.

He was frantic. Fear ruled his mind that the Indian would take off with Elizabeth before they could catch up.

"The Shoshone Indian has taken her." In his anger he lunged forward through the opening. The sun hit him full on and when he put his hand up to shield his eyes, something hit him hard, knocking him back.

Jesse felt himself falling backward on the ground. Sharp pain racked his head. He felt warm blood run down his face into his eyes. He lay there stunned, unable to move or yell out. Then everything went black.

"Jesse, can you hear me?" Ross rolled him over and gaped at the open wound on his forehead.

"Oh, my God, please help us!" he cried out. Ross quickly applied a heavy cloth to the cut to stop the bleeding. He used his belt to secure it tightly around Jesse's head. Then he tried to make him comfortable.

A slight movement from Jesse caused Ross to again ask if he could hear him. A long moment went by, then Jesse moaned and replied a barely audible, "Yes."

"Jesse, we need to keep this tight against your forehead. You must not move; you may have a concussion. He hit you where your hat band is or he would have scalped you. I think you will be all right." Ross told his brother.

"Then you must go after them," Jesse replied. Ross answered with a slight smile, "Jesse, Elizabeth is not with him. I think she escaped earlier and is on her way back to the cabin. She is probably an hour ahead of him, if he is following her at all."

"Are you sure?" Jesse questioned.

"Yes, let me go out to check. I'll be right back." Ross left quickly. When his brother left, Jesse struggled to rise. The pain nearly made him pass out.

I cannot let anything happen to Elizabeth. I must not stop Ross from going after them. He cannot find out that I can't see, he mused to himself.

"Oh, God restore my sight," he whispered in anguished prayer. Soon Jesse heard footsteps.

"Ross what did you find out?"

"It is what I thought. They went in different directions. That renegade is going over the mountain the hard way, and probably we will not see *him* again," Ross replied. He began checking on the bandage to see if the bleeding had quit.

"Ross I am OK. You need to go after that culprit to make sure he will not cause any more trouble. I will lay here for a while until this headache is not so severe. You know it is the right thing to do, Jesse pleaded with his brother.

"You may be right. I have some medicine for your pain here in my bag. It may make you sleepy. I think you will be safe here."

Ross left him the water bag and put his rifle near him.

"Now, promise you will lie very still?" Ross asked, touching his brother on his shoulder.

"I promise. Now go quickly, and God speed," Jesse bravely replied.

The way north led up into a narrow canyon. To get over the ridge quickly, he needed to climb straight up. Ross could not see the Indian climbing because of the steepness of the incline, but small pebbles fell in front of him and he knew he was there.

Without hesitation, Ross began to climb the mountain. The way he chose was rugged and broken. In spots it was nearly impassable. The course he choose lay up the ascent and still continued, hazardous and laborious, as Ross moved swiftly along the dangerous crags like he possessed the power to move on air.

He continued scaling the mountain like a man with a mission. Just as Ross had planned, the Indian had not heard him It was very steep here. They both seemed to be standing on air.

Hearing the steps behind him, the Indian whirled. Pulling his knife out of the pouch, he scraped the rock on the uphill side, which threw him off balance.

The rocks under his feet gave way as he fell. The knife brought gushes of blood as it stuck deep in his chest. With surprise in his eyes, the savage gave out a cry, *"Neztu!"*

He screamed and slid downwards to his final destruction. Ross stared one hundred feet below him as the fallen body lay on a rock ledge. He watched for a long time and saw no movement from the Indian. He felt a wave of pity for him as he fell to his knees and bowed his head, where he remained until he'd finished a prayer. Then slowly he rose to return to his brother.

Chapter Twelve

Elizabeth's break at the stream gave her time to study the surroundings. This canyon was very beautiful. The rosy rock cliffs extended upward and as the sun touched the rock masses of these walls, they glowed with its rays.

She had read something someone said about how nature gives to every season some beauty of its own. This was sure true of this canyon, and to add to it, she had seen artifacts scattered throughout the canyon. There appears to also be a mystery about this place. The canyon seemed to have its secrets.

She remembered that the last tribe to inhabit this area, recorded as the Anastasi, hunted and grew corn for food. They lived in these canyons a century ago.

Yes! I am remembering my school days and I long to go home as soon as I get back to the cabin and say my goodbyes to Louise—if I can. She felt anxious about this.

Going farther along the trail, she saw animal tracks—many of them. Then she smelled the musty scent of horses and realized that horses made most of the tracks in the soft earth. How she longed for the companionship of her horse!

Oh, Princess, why was I riding you that day? She whispered to herself. *At the ranch there were many other well-trained horses that I could have chosen to ride to the Kamiah camp.* She shrugged as she walked along talking to herself.

Don't live in the past, Elizabeth. Get going to the future. The words of her friend Shadow came to her. He had also said, "We are not always held responsible for the things that happen to us—only for our reactions to what has happened. This is what God looks at. Do these actions glorify Him?"

It's such a fine thing to think about at a time like this, she thought. With a renewed spirit, Elizabeth began the long walk to the top of the next ridge. She was still thinking about home and about who would be in her future.

When she reached the crest, she had a good view of the valley below. Sighing softly, she said, *Those Indians are not pursuing me! This is an answer to my prayer for safety.*

She began to relax and walk along at a slower pace. She could see the valley opening into a small pass that would lead her out. First she needed to reach that rock outcropping. That is where she would rest.

Walking in these boots was not as good as walking in the moccasins she had back at Ross's cabin. The odor of horses again reached her senses. It was so strong that she thought the runners could be just over that ridge. Then she heard the beat of hooves on the rocks. *Was she being rescued?*

Making herself more visible, she climbed upon the highest point of the rock formations. When she could see down the trail, she gasped, "Oh, my!"

A small herd of horses was running up the ridge and would soon be upon her. She was glad she could have protection in the rocks—away from their frenzied running.

"They are part of the wild brood," she said excitedly. Elizabeth watched as the lead mare swung her head in the direction of the rock outcropping. It was her way of keeping the others in line. She had a pretty head and a silken mane and tail. What good care she appeared to give, just as good lead mares provided this for the entire group they were in charge of.

An entire herd of horses in motion is a marvelous thing to watch, she thought, as she viewed the lifting of their hooves into full flight. There were mares and foals alike—surging up the steep open hillside toward her. It looked like a stampede as they seemed to fly headlong toward their goal.

As they approached, the wild horses slowed, then, as led—they stopped and milled around. With them came the dust, and the blowing of their noses. Only yards from her, the lead mare stood shaking her head violently.

A young horse colt stood stiff-legged, with head and ears alert, looking directly at her. Elizabeth realized she was the one on examination here. She spoke gently.

"Whoa, *whoa*." She repeated the greeting several times, then, raising her hand out to them she continued to talk softly. Just then the colt turned away from her. Elizabeth's heart sank. Then a whinny came from the center of the wild group.

A few horses milled around in a circle and again she heard a low neighing sound.

The voice of the friendly one—which one was it? The rising dust and glare of the sun caused her to shade her eyes so she could see more clearly. She viewed a small, red horse holding her head high and shaking it. The whites of her eyes showed clearly—large and curious. She had a star on her forehead and a small strip of white blazing down her nose that gave her a distinctive look. She was still wearing the halter.

"Princess," Elizabeth cried softly. "It *is* you! Come here, Princess," she commanded, reaching out to her.

When Princess took a step forward, the boss mare tried to frighten her to go back. Elizabeth spoke up.

"I am not afraid of you, and neither is Princess." She now gave all her attention to Princess, who had stopped moving her head about, her, ears back, listening. The horse turned toward the familiar voice and nickered again.

Elizabeth reached down and pulled a sprig of dried seed from some shrubbery, held it out to her horse, and took another step toward her.

"Now that I have your attention, little one, I say, *whoa*."

She continued to speak as she slowly approached. The horse took the seeds from her hand, munching them quickly. Elizabeth petted the horse's neck. Then, with her other hand she took the end of the long scarf she had around her neck and tied it to the broken bridle that was still on Princess.

She secured it tightly, letting the horse know she was caught.

"I sure hope you remember your manners, little captive, and do not try to pull back." Elizabeth continued to talk quietly to the horse as she secured the other end of the scarf to the other side of the mare's bridle. She moved to the side of Princess and spoke.

"Now all I have to do is swing on as I put this makeshift rein over your neck. But first I need to say a prayer."

Still holding the mare with a firm hand, Elizabeth bowed her head and whispered, "Oh Lord, help me, I pray. You have said that I need to trust You with my heart, and *lean not on my own understanding* . . . to acknowledge your ways, and that You will direct my paths."

When she said this, Princess nuzzled her arm and sniffed the familiar skin of Elizabeth's face. With a smile, Elizabeth put her arm around the horse's neck and, returning the affection, pulled the new rein over his head.

"Now or never!" she said as she jumped on, securing herself on the horse's back by tightening her legs around the horse's belly and grabbing a handful of mane.

Immediately she turned the horse away from the herd and at a fast trot they went up the trail. A stomping and whinnying noise was all she heard behind them, but she did not look back as they went over the ridge, disappearing from sight. There is danger and fear and excitement that come with two blended species, such as this woman and horse.

If Princess wants to run where the trail is smooth, Elizabeth remembered, *I will let her wild nature show.*

There on the red mares back that day, she had no fear. *There are times when I know Princess will look out for me. Our passions are rooted in our hearts and souls and I was privileged to discover them at a young age in my association with riding horses.*

On Princess's back there is balance, trust, and calmness. She needs that release through her body before we can become partners.

"And if ever a time I needed a partner, Lord, You have provided," she said with feeling. It was then she realized that this is why she had compassion to work and bring change to a free spirit such that Princess has.

To be captive is to resign to one who has been well-cared-for. Bringing about change in this mare has set off a transformation in me. It enables me to find strength and assurance in my faith that I did not know existed.

Elizabeth smiled to herself as she remembered many of the great times she'd had on horseback. They rode along like this into the late afternoon stopping only for water at the stream.

Elizabeth watched the sky darkening in the west. They needed the right place to wait out the coming storm before reaching the summit.

"That point near a wooded steep cliff might afford protection for us, Princess," she said as she urged her on at a trot. The sky, filled with great black thunderheads, looked cold and metallic. Lightning flickered from them to the valley below. "The storm is upon us, Princess; we must hurry."

Soon rain whipped her face and pounded at her with tiny, angry fingers. Her light jacket quickly became soaked as the rain fell steadily. They came upon a dramatic limestone pyramid overhanging above a lake. It was a breathtaking sight, although the storm gave off a black gloom behind them.

The overhang they were looking for was more than adequate. It actually acted like a cave opening where there was room for both of them to stay inside. Dismounting quickly near the trees, she acquired several larger pieces of burnable wood and hurried into the protection of the cave with them. She ground-tied the horse near the back wall. Shaking from the soaking, she huddled around her quickly made fire. Steam rose from them as they felt the warmth of the flames. Taking off her jacket, she held it up close to the fire, being careful not to let the now-roaring flames catch it. The ferocity of the storm was fully upon them now as they heard the wind strike and make a moaning sound in the trees. Then with a roar came the torrent of rain.

"This will indeed be a long night," she said to Princess. "I hope to get dried out so that I will quit this shaking."

Outside the cave the rain fell in torrents, lightning flashed, and thunder cracked. With his head into the wind, the lone rider was sure he smelled smoke as he reached the narrow end of the lake.

"Hopefully there will be a friendly face that goes along with the warm fire I am looking for in that protected area." he said to his horse as he urged him to the top of the limestone mountain.

In a letting up of the falling rain, the glow of the fire allowed Elizabeth to be brightly illuminated before the cave. As he approached, his horse nickered. A soft whinny inside echoed the call.

Well, we just announced our visit, he said to himself as he pulled his mount to a stop and gazed upon a face lighted by the glow of embers.

"A rider is out there," Elizabeth whispered. Her heart started racing as fast as the frenzied wind. "Maybe we have been rescued," she prayed, then with an anxious step she approached the shadowed rider, who had dismounted from his horse and was leading him inside.

"Is that you Liz?" he gasped in disbelief. Then the smile he remembered broke across her face.

"Dalton!" she cried as she ran into his open arms. When they parted, he moved with her toward the fire. He pulled his horse under the protection of the cave, where Princess was. After he took off his rain gear, he turned to her.

"Let me look at you—are you all right? Where is your gear? How long have you been out in this," he asked her as he looked around. Then, taking her hands, he realized that she was shaking.

"You are cold and still damp. Here, put on my coat."

He removed his jacket and put it around her shoulders. It was warm from his body heat and felt good to Elizabeth.

"Thank you." She went back into his arms to hug him again. He received her with a sigh and they embraced for a long moment.

"My love, I have missed you so much! Why did you disappear? Did I give you that much of a scare when I asked for a commitment?" He began these questions, then realized her condition was not good, and she might be suffering from the cold more than he realized.

"Forgive me; you need more warmth." He left her side and re-trieved his pack. "Here, sit near the fire with this bedroll. The heavy blanket is comfortable and you need to sit down."

Helping her onto the blanket, he tucked her into it, then on his knees he fed the embers with more wood and stroked the flames into a warm fire. Then he took some supplies out of the other pack and took a water pot and held it out to catch rain water. When it was full he set the container on the coals of the fire to heat. Only then did he sit down next to her. She was still shaking and he drew her close with his arm around her. Just having someone near her after what she had been through was very comforting, and she liked the comfort Dalton had given her.

"Liz, I will fix you some of my *energy tea*. It is horse mint and yarrow I got from the first tribe of Indians that I stayed with when I was looking for you. Then we can eat some hot soup and you will feel better."

Looking at his handsome features caused her to be lost in the tenderness and warmth she saw and felt there.

"Thank you again. I have missed you, too," she replied.

"I have a lot of explaining to do. There were some incidents that I could not help, however," she began. Then she told him of her being found by Louise and her grandmother after being hurt. She explained why they took her back with them to their village.

She told of Tigue coming out of nowhere and saving her when she lay injured and had suffered the loss the of her memory. When she showed him the scar on her head, he held her closer. His fingers trailed across her scar with a tenderness that made her tremble. Then she smiled at him and reached for his hand. When she kissed his fingers the sweetness of the moment touched him.

"Oh, then, were you lost from this storm, too? I am afraid that is what happened to me. How far are we from the encampment of the tribe where you are staying?" he asked anxiously. "Oh, I am not lost. I am on my way back to a cabin where my friends Jesse and Louise are. We were on a journey to find Jesse's brother and Louise's father. I thought I could make it before nightfall—but the storm—" her voice trailed off as she began to shake violently.

"Liz, you are sick! Let's get some of this tea down you." he put the tea leaves in the hot water, poured her a cup, and brought it to her. He insisted on feeding it to her. She sipped most of it while he talked to her about how he came to be here.

"I had to come find you! I missed you so much. Liz, I want to make you happy. All my happiness dwells in you. You don't get choices about things like this in life. You fall in love with the people you fall in love with," he told her quietly.

"How do you know this is right?" she asked cautiously. "Because I love you," he said, praying that she heard him as he watched her eyes close. Gently he laid her down on the blanket and soon she was fast asleep.

His worry over Elizabeth was so great that he could not eat anything. *My life would be empty if anything happened to you, he spoke softly,* more to himself. He replenished the wood on the fire. Realizing it was getting dark, he then went to tend the horses.

Elizabeth stirred only once. Being lost in the tone of the crushing storm and the fatigue from the fright of being a prisoner was too much for her. Warmth was returning to her, so she welcomed the sleep. She opened her eyes to see Dalton sitting against his saddle and he was dozing in an upright position. She smiled at his concern for her and remembered that this was why she liked him from the first time they had become friends. She had been fond of him for so long, but had never allowed her feelings to move forward.

It scared me before knowing how much I liked you, Dalton. But maybe I was not ready for a commitment, and that is why I ran away from any healing I needed after the accident. So I've closed out all my past, she confessed in her mind.

A stir from the horses woke Dalton. Instantly he was at her side, staring down at her beautiful, green eyes that were gazing back at him.

"You feeling better?" he asked with concern. It was all he could do not to gather her up in his arms and tell her again how much he missed her and that all he wanted to do was to make her happy.

"Yes, I am." She assured him, a little flushed, as she gave him her best smile. She felt his compassion for her. *Oh, those eyes he had!* She thought they went with such a handsome face.

"And I am hungry," Elizabeth smiled as she sat up.

"You stay there. I will serve the soup I have made." he declared, moving to the fire. He poured the soup into a cup and returned to her side. "Here, we will have to share, as I only have one cup." He smiled and wondered if she remembered them drinking out of a single cup when they were very young.

"Just like old times," she grinned, taking some of the soup, then offering him the cup to drink. She smiled as she watched this admirable person who had come looking for her. Was it fate that he had found her? She believed not.

"Oh, dear God, thank you!" Elizabeth prayed silently. Trying not to let her teeth chatter, she began to tell him why she was out in this wilderness by herself.

"I will tell you the short version of how careless I was to be allowed to be kidnapped by two renegade Indians this morning.

"Kidnapped!" he exclaimed in alarm. Then as he looked at her he knew nothing bad had happened to her.

"I will tell the rest, Dalton." She held up her hand and began again telling him all she knew of her abductors since the first attack on the trail.

"When they left me alone in a mine, I found another way out that led to this valley. Then Princess came back to me. She was with a herd of wild horses down the trail that I came across. It was a real gift of God. I know because I prayed for help, and He sent you to me, too."

Dalton sat down beside Elizabeth and reached for her hand, then he said, "Elizabeth I prayed for you just this morning in a specific way. I asked Him to supply your need."

"Yes, she said. "I know it was because of His answer that I am safe, I know He sent me Princess and you." She replied smiling, those emerald eyes sparkling at him. They talked for a long time about people at home. The only time he left her side was to fill the cup with more soup and to build up the fire.

Elisabeth realized he had been searching for her from the time she was missing from the ranch, and that he did this four or five days a week. This touched her very much and she reached for his hand to hold it.

Dalton, quieted by this and as silence held them, took her shoulder and pulled her to his side and placed a kiss upon her full lips. When they parted, she smiled at him and snuggled next to his chest. They drank tea into the evening and she asked Dalton about Molly and the baby.

He told her all he knew from the times he had returned for supplies and fresh horses.

"Molly is fine. The baby will arrive about the time we should be back," he stated as he watched her brighten with the news. She brushed a strand of hair off her face. Dalton pressed his lips against her forehead and murmured against her skin.

"Liz, I'm in love with you." He wrapped his arms around her and she seemed to melt in his embrace. She was soft and sweet but he was not one to give in to strong emotions, especially if the results would hurt the other person.

Rising slowly he said. "You must get your rest Elizabeth," he sighed and knelt beside her as he placed her head down on the bed and covered her frail body with the blanket.

"The rain has stopped, and we need more wood for the night. I'll be right back," he assured her. She watched him disappear into the darkness and knew he had to leave just now. He had told her his heart. Would she realize what her heart already knew? Shaken by his kisses, she considered all these emotions would be hard to forget. Then she closed her eyes, and with a smile on her lips—she slept.

Chapter Thirteen

Good morning, love, Dalton called to her. "You look much better today." He smiled to reassure her that the dreams she had last night were not going to be recollected in her mind. "Would you like to go down to the lake and refresh yourself?" He asked as he pulled a clean cloth and a comb from his saddlebags for her. Then he held out his hand to help her up.

She gave him her hand, then rose, looking at him with a smile. "Even the emerald has returned to your beautiful eyes," he added. She was watching his every move; from his first expression of seeing her awake to the long strides he took to come to her.

"He has that rugged/attractive look," she thought. Then she wondered if her smile showed what she was thinking and this caused her to blush as she grabbed the towel and comb from him.

As she left the cave, she turned and said, "You were there for me last night. Thank you." He returned her gaze with a slight upward turn of his mouth and replied, "Elizabeth, I would fly to the moon with you." "And I would wish upon a star with you," she replied with a hint in her voice of remembering.

"It looks like a great day to travel and return to Louise and Jesse," she added. Dalton watched her go.

"Thank you, God. I believe she will be all right," he breathed in silent prayer as she moved down to the lake. Dalton could see a glow of warmth being breathed into her as she skipped along the trail in the early sunlight.

"Does she talk too much about this Jesse person, or am I just listening to find a problem that is not there? She has not known the man long enough to get involved with him. Yet, she is very beautiful," he said to himself with a frown.

Dalton looked at the range of sharp, rugged peaks piercing the clear, blue sky. They made this wilderness a summer paradise. Down at the lake, the water's surface had a smooth glitter of silver as the breeze rippled the water. There was a soft sound of bird songs as they rustled in the treetops.

He saw a gaggle of geese circling as they checked out the lake for landing. "Elizabeth," he yelled, "I am going hunting for our breakfast." He signaled to her, pointing to the other end of the lake. She replied with a wave of acknowledgment and continued down the path of newly fallen leaves that glittered with drops of rainwater in the bright morning sun.

When she finished with her morning catharsis, she found a game trail and began following it to the end of the lake, where she thought she would join Dalton. This was such a beautiful place. The tall peaks that surrounded the lake on three sides were cone-like on one, and pointed on the other side.

It was an unimpeded view of this highest peak, with nothing beyond it but clear blue sky. The scattered clouds were in the east, moving away quickly with a slight movement of the wind. Any activity of a rustle of the leaves startled her. Then a sound like a hoot, such as an owl makes, added with a cluck, broke the silence. along with another call.

The trail showed scratching and caused some turned over leaves to leave the clue. She noted that they were tracks belonging to a hen or tom turkey. Relaxing a little, Elizabeth approached, thinking she might see a bird roosting in the trees.

Earlier she had heard its shock gobble and knew it was in trouble. Suddenly this big, black-feathered bird came at her, barely flying off the ground, its wings flapping as it was half-flying in a frightened hurry.

"Something had definitely scared that turkey and it wasn't me or it wouldn't have come toward me," she believed. Dashing behind a large tree, she waited, listening. A shot rang out from the end of the lake and a splashing of water told her Dalton had bagged a goose. She started to step cautiously back onto the path when a tightening in her chest told her—"beware, and danger is close."

A rock loosed by something, thumped and rolled to the lakes edge. The tree above her shook and she knew something just went into it.

Were there more turkeys roosting there? She asked herself this question. *But why do I feel frightened?* Peering out, she saw movement, but she still remained behind her hiding place.

Another rifle shot down by the lake echoed throughout the canyon and seemed to shake the animal in the tree. It became wary and suspicious as it jumped and crouched on a lower branch, now in Elizabeth's sight. The lynx's cruel and wild face looked at her as a known killer would. She was frightened, because Elizabeth knew it had ferocity and speed.

She did not know whether to yell for help, or continue to hide. She became very anxious of the animal as it continued to gaze in her direction. Its catlike face looked framed in a ruff of hair, with ears that rose alert to tufted points. Its coat was soft gray overlaid with a few darker spots revealing a chunky build ending with a short bobtail. It continued to stare at her with gleaming malicious eyes.

"My scent has caught its attention!" she said in fear, as she questioned what to do next.

"Should I run . . . or yell . . . or look for a weapon and wait?" Suddenly the lynx hit the ground running. It circled the big tree and stopped and crouched low, snarling. No fear showed in its eyes, only pure hatred. She hesitated for only a heartbeat, then in an instant Elizabeth dashed around the tree holding up a club she picked up from the ground.

She was ready to use it if the cat sprung. The yell she let out would have frightened off most animals, but not this hungry predator. She became immobilized. The lynx came toward her with quick, measured predatory tread. It hesitated, and she did not know why, unless it was in surprise of her noisy actions.

Hearing a loud, ferocious growl coming from directly behind it, she realized that the cat had heard it earlier. The cat whirled to meet an animal that began to bark and snarl fiercely. It was twice the cat's size and it moved to attack before there was time for the cat to retreat.

"Tigue!" Elizabeth yelled in surprise and alarm. In a split second the big yellow dog showed her fangs and grabbed the lynx by the neck, holding it in her strong jaws. She shook her head in a mad frenzy and swept the cat off its feet. A deep gash in the cat's neck spilled blood all over them. Then with a whirling shake the wolf-dog let go of the predator. The cat somersaulted in the air and fell hard expelling its breath as it hit the ground. Slowly it got to its feet and let out a muffled snarl as it backed away.

Elizabeth did not know where it came from as a loud rifle shot permeated the air. The savage animal fell in its tracks and lay dead on a bed of pine needles. Tigue reached Elizabeth's side and put a large paw upon her side. Elizabeth dropped down to caress the happy dog.

Tigue looked up at her with a flash in her eye and a happy, rolling tongue. "Tigue, where did you come from?" Elizabeth asked, with tears streaming down her face. Alert, alive, and challenging, she looked at her mistress like she was looking right through her wondering why she had tears running down her cheeks. The big tongue licked the side of Elizabeth's face trying to wipe away all the tears. She wagged her tail happily at her master, as if to say—*I'm really glad to see you.*

Dalton ran up to them and, seeing tears run down Elizabeth's face, drew his knife. He was shaking in alarm but he hesitated, and asked, "Elizabeth, are you hurt? He did not understand that the dog had saved her life.

"I am crying because I am so happy! I have Tigue back," she said reaching out for Dalton to join them in their happy embrace. He put his arm around Elizabeth, held her and shared the happy reunion with the two of them. "I need your comfort," she cried to him.

Dalton drew her closer and smiled down at the animal that looked like a wolf except for her friendly face. "So this is Tigue," he softly replied, then he led them back to camp.

The ride to the fork where Ross's cabin stood was long and tiring for Elizabeth. Neither of them spoke for a long time. The shadows from the cottonwoods and the rocks created dark looking pools in the water along the river in the late afternoon.

Dalton knew Elizabeth needed time to herself. He believed she did care deeply for him, but her not returning any mention of love to him made him question his future with her.

"Well, time will tell, and after what she has been through, I am not going to press her," Dalton concluded, thinking about all she had told him of her journey here. Upon arrival at the cabin, the two dogs had their happy reunion, and the barking certainly announced the arrival of Elizabeth to Louise. She came bounding out the cabin door and in one bounce was in Elizabeth's arms.

Tears filled their eyes as they hugged and cried about their concern and love for each other.

"Oh, Eizi, I have been praying for your return. I knew when Tigue was gone she would find you. Are you OK? Tell me all about it. It was awful, I know. How did you get Princess? Did this man bring her to you? Father killed the two that took you away from us," she added with pride.

Then, realizing what she had said, she stopped as a gasp escaped Elizabeth's breath. "Oh, are Ross and Jesse safe?" Elizabeth asked in alarm.

Ross interrupted and stepped up to try to make it all right.

"Here Louise, let me welcome our friend," he asked, holding out his arms to Elizabeth as he took her tenderly into his embrace. He always felt the same thrill of having her so close. Then he spoke to her with emotion.

"Elizabeth, God is good. He has brought you back to us safely." Then he released her, and turned politely to Dalton. When Elizabeth found her breath, she stepped forward and took Dalton by the arm to meet Ross, who held out his hand to greet the tall young man.

"Dalton, this is Ross, and Louise—my friends that I have told you so much about," she said. Then she asked with impatience.

"Where is Jesse?" There was an added silence, but it was Louise that answered with caution, "He is inside. He has been ill."

"Oh, can I see him? What is wrong?" Elizabeth asked, confused.

"Yes you can see him, was Ross's reply. He will be so glad you are safe, but first let us get your horses taken care of and you can freshen up. It will give me time to fill you in on his condition,"

Ross knew this moment might come, and had known in his mind he had to tell her of the loss of Jesse's sight. He did not want her to blame herself about what the kidnapper had done to his brother. There was no easy way to tell her, so he began to tell her what had happened, leaving out the fact that he had killed her abductors. Then he ended with the injury that caused Jesse's blindness.

"Jesse is blind? No, *No.*" She repeated in alarm. She reached out for some support to stand; she had suddenly become very weary. Ross was at her side immediately to steady her with his hand on her shoulder. He should have known she would have taken it hard. He was pretty sure she had serious feelings for Jesse. Elisabeth sat down on the bench outside the house.

"Can I see him now?" she whispered.

"Yes, when you have recovered from the shock," Ross replied, still remaining by her side. Louise brought her some water and sat beside her. Elizabeth felt comfort in having her there for support. Many thoughts ran through Elizabeth's mind, including her part in this tragedy. After a short recovery, Elizabeth quietly approached Jesse's bed and touched him hesitantly on his fevered head.

"Jesse, I'm here," she whispered to him. He moved his head toward the voice but did not open his eyes. His face was hard, yet it was sad, too, and this touched her. She sank to her knees, saying a silent prayer for him. She realized he was burning up with fever and she began to dip the washcloth into a basin of water, squeeze it out, then gently place it on his forehead near the wound.

She touched the bruises on his head near the open cut. Just looking at it made her shudder. The sound of his labored breathing filled the room while she continued to dip the cloth in the cool water and return it to his face. After awhile his eyes fluttered open and he grabbed at her arm, his hand shaking.

"Speak to me," he commanded squinting at her shadow.

"Jesse? It's Elizabeth, and I'm back safe. Do not worry anymore," she sighed. "Just get well."

"Elizabeth, you took so long—I couldn't find you. Are you unharmed?" His voice was barely audible. He fell back on the pillow unable to say any more.

"Yes, Jesse, I am fine, I will be here for you to help you regain your strength," she reassured him. Ross came in the room and said to Jesse, "Here, take this willow bark tea to drink." They held his head up while he drank.

"I will nurse you back to health Jesse," she said softly. Ross left the room knowing his brother was in good hands. This gave him time to get some badly needed rest. Elizabeth sensed Ross's need and was glad she had the knowledge and skill to help. She continued to bathe Jesse's head with the cool cloth as she watched him as he fell asleep. *Was this what it was like when I had my concussion?* She remembered that time in her life, and Star had said to her, "Sometimes God allows winter to come even though we long for perfect summer nights. This is going to take faith, patience, and watchful care, but with His help and guidance, we will prevail."

Elizabeth breathed as she continued her careful vigilance. Jesse's head felt like it was in a vise, the pain was throbbing, and agonizing. The cold sweat and sickness continued making him so sick he could not stand. A deep, overpowering fatigue continued to plague him, but the worst was the darkness. He could see shadows in bright daylight, but it was mostly darkness.

It has been four days and I am not any better, he mused. *I hate this weakness, I have never been sick a day in my life. I have been taking my despair out on Elizabeth, but I must discourage her from any future with me if I continue to be blind.*

He agonized over his next move, even as he placed his head in his hands and wept silently. Then a prayer escaped his lips, "God, help me to make the right decision, there are many lives affected here." He rolled over in the bed and slept a deep sleep that had escaped him sense his injury.

The next day, Ross came out of Jesse's sick room and went outside to find Elizabeth. He found her standing alone near the sparkling stream. He could tell she was sad. Just seeing her, he felt the sheer ache of her loneliness. He had been alone too long, and he knew that after having her here in his home he could never continue to live alone. He was rubbing his brow where an old scar was when Elizabeth saw Ross coming toward her. She noticed the worried expression he had.

Here was an extraordinary man who had looked beyond the mask I wore as a confident outdoors woman, to a lonely person who was reaching out—only to feel rejection. If it were not for his companionship, I would have not known where to turn.

All this she felt, and now *she* wished to cheer him up. She smiled sweetly to him and realized her heart was beginning to thud.

Careful, Elizabeth, she cautioned herself. Ross saw this gentlewoman smile and his worries left as he watched her relax. His heart went out to her and he began to sift the problem around in his mind.

I would like to see Bets happy and smiling again. Yes, I would spend my whole life making this happen, but I must back off as it is too soon. I would not impose my feelings on her at a time like this.

He stood close to her and spoke quietly. "Young woman, I believe Jesse is on the mend."

"Yes, his fever is over, but he needs to see a doctor about the loss of his sight," she said with concern. She had realized Jesse had been changing a lot toward her. He had been happy to see her at first, but things were different now. The change was so gradual that it was permanent before she realized it. Now Jesse wanted only to be alone.

"I believe he is well enough to travel to Idaho City if we take our time getting there. We could make one long stay at the Kamiah summer camp, if you wish. Besides, aren't you and Dalton anxious to return to your homes?" Ross asked.

"Yes, we both are, but I wouldn't stay long at the village with Dalton along," she sighed. "I do believe the change would be good for Jesse, though. He is so depressed," she added. Ross heard in her voice the sadness he knew she felt about leaving Ina' and Louise.

"OK, let us tell the others as soon as they return from their fishing trip. We should leave in two days. I will find good health care for him and I promise to let you know how he is doing. You will get a letter from me every week, young lady, I promise," he repeated. In his heart he wanted to say, "I want to keep in touch with you, Elizabeth. You have been so kind and have helped me through this time. Believe me, I hate to see you go."

He hesitated as he watched this pretty, western woman meet his gaze. He knew he must let her go back to her home and sort things out. He could not speak his heart, not now. She could never be his now and maybe they both knew this.

And what of Dalton, her long time friend? He was obviously in love with her. "There is so much to pray about," his heart cried unto his soul.

"I am going to miss you, too," she spoke so softly to him that he might have missed it if he hadn't been standing close to her.

"And I have enjoyed your hospitality," she added as she reached up to straighten the collar of his denim shirt. Before she lowered her hand she touched the curl of his shining, dark hair that fell over it.

"I wonder why I wanted to do that?" she questioned herself. He reached up and caught her hand and held it for a lingering moment. The warmth of the touch, felt by both of them, caused her shoulders to relax again, and a tentative smile played around her mouth. This quiet, handsome powerful man gave her a challenging gaze—perhaps looking for some answers.

Overlooking the Kimiah village from the ridge, Elizabeth would never forget the scene of the hundreds of chimneys lifting their fingers of smoke toward the evening sky. Viewing the peacefulness of the village as they approached it on that warm still night, Elizabeth realized it was such a stirring sight.

"What will I say to my friends and to my beloved Ina' grandmother?" Elizabeth murmured. *I was one who could not find peace in the home where I grew up, and yet I had had a spiritual peace that the*

Lord had given me here. She knew that if she would grasp it she could have the peace within herself that she longed for.

When she joined the Kamiah tribe they helped her through her sickness and yet together they supplied needs for each other. It was here that she began to know the true meaning of peace and contentment in loving.

"Through strain is gained strength. Not my will, but Thine, Lord. Through life and through all of the adventures I meet along the way—joy or sorrow, success or failure—let me set my face to do Your will." She recalled the prayer she had said during her stay here:

"Just as you helped me then, Lord, help me say goodbye to these whom I love. How I will miss them!" Elizabeth prayed again silently, a tear falling down her cheek.

Two days later, they arrived in Idaho City to find that a stagecoach would be leaving for Naples in two days. Dalton went to secure two tickets for traveling home.

His mind was still on the journey here as he watched Elizabeth's concern over Jesse, plus the time they spent at the Kimiah tribe's summer home where she said goodbye to her Indian friends. The scene of Elizabeth saying farewell to Ina'—he believed he would never forget.

He was sure he'd heard Elizabeth say she would return. At the cabin, Ross had spoken of the special relationship Elizabeth had with these Indian people. He had said, "She seemed to be born with the blessings of God to show a special love, while she was there in their midst.

She did not wait with folded hands as she could have done while recovering there. She has learned that when God said to go—that is what Elizabeth did. I so admire her," he had added.

Well, I will take one day at a time with you, my love, Dalton spoke to himself, as he mounted the steps of the boarding house where they all had rooms.

The following night, Elizabeth's steps revealed her disappointment when she left Jesse's room.

Ross had assured her that they would find the doctor Jesse needed, but she looked so lost. She was looking down ward, as if in thought, and began walking out to the nearby meadow.

Watching her from across the street, Ross had been waiting for her. True, he had needed to be alone after they received the bad news from the doctor. He felt the old sadness, the melancholy tracking through him and, in order to not let it get the best of him he had gone out to pray.

But the Lord and I have sorted out what must be done and now I must exercise faith. I can see something is wrong with Elizabeth and probably the report has hit her hard, he supposed.

I must say something to lift her spirits," Ross thought, so he began walking toward her.

Elizabeth looked up and saw Ross coming as she studied his profile sharp against the falling sun. She had been thinking about him and she turned hesitantly toward him.

"This incredible, brave man standing in the fading light," she noted. Then it was impulse more than anything else that made Elizabeth hold out her hands for him to take when he greeted her.

Ross took her hands tenderly in his, then held her at arm's length because she took his breath away. They stood for several minutes that way, looking at each other.

She liked the approval she saw in his eyes. Ross noted that she had caught up her hair in a lace snood and some loose curls danced around her ears. She wore a new green blouse that was exactly the color of her eyes. The new travel skirt showed her slim figure well.

Ross worried she was not eating well. It was all he could do not to gather her up in his arms to comfort her—*no,* he knew he just wanted to hold her.

I must use caution, as tenderness is what she needs now, he scolded himself. Elizabeth smiled at him, looking into those dark, blue eyes that were searching hers. He wore the dark pants, denim shirt, and a leather vest she had seen him pack for the trip. His dark, slightly curly hair bore the crease of the large-brimmed felt hat he now carried in his hand.

He was clean-shaven for the first time since she had met him. Part of his face was suntanned, but the light skin of his newly shaven jaw line revealed wide cheeks and a smooth mouth.

The crease from his smile was deep and she realized that Louise had this smile also. As she studied him, the image of Louise was so plain. Elizabeth had a desire to touch him there on his face, near his lips. He released her hand and offered his arm as they began to walk out to the tree-covered point that overlooked the town.

The point was comparatively lonely and they made a beautiful portrait against the colorful sunset. The leaves aloft were signing a golden glow from the reflection of the setting sun. Ross found a log and, placing his vest down on it, motioned for Elizabeth to sit there. He sat down facing her and began to talk.

"You must go home, my dear, and give yourself time to sort through all we talked about at the cabin. Jesse will improve, and after the surgery he may gain back most of his eyesight, just as the doctor said."

"Yes, you are right, Ross. So much is up to Jesse and the Lord. It is nice of Helen to offer to help and stay with Jesse during his morning hours. This will give you time to get Louise in school and get settled in a different place." She tried to smile as she reflected upon all that had transpired since they arrived in town.

Elizabeth is always concerned about others, he noticed, and he watched her finger a curl from her face with a nervous hand. Cast upon her pretty face was a shadow of a frown.

A heaviness rose in Ross's chest as he felt this strong emotion within. He seemed to know what she was thinking, so he spoke frankly.

"You will be just as missed, my dear. I promise to keep you informed." They sat there for a while watching the colors in the sky change. The sun was brilliant—orange, pink, and red ran along the horizon in long strips, like lines of colorful clouds.

He reached for her hand and whispered, "I will miss you." She flushed as she looked at his face. Not knowing what to say, she changed the subject.

"The influence of Narcissa Whitman and Mrs. Spalding at the school they started was a blessing for Louise. There are several other Indian children going to this school, too, and I know she will adjust just fine."

"Yes," he agreed, "vision is what most people never see, and you had some of this special concern or otherwise you would not have come to the Kamiah summer camp. They are fine people, I . . .," he stopped.

She put her hand over his, "Ross, tell me about your wife, Sweet Song. What was she like?" Ross breathed a soft sigh and a slight smile left his lips.

"She was very kind—like you, Elizabeth," he said, looking at her. Then, thinking a moment, his eyes grew distant and he talked for a while of their years together. It wasn't until Ross felt a slight shiver of cold go through Elizabeth that he realized it was late and the night air was chilling her.

"We have talked enough, and must get back," he said. His arms came around her to help her up.

"No," she spoke in a soft voice. "It has been good for us both." She spoke against him, as she rested against his warm chest.

"What would have been good was to have saddled Princess and Jake and gone for a late evening ride," she said.

"I've seen you with your horse and you two are connected," he teased with a smile. Somewhere deep inside a knot he had carried for four years fell away. He touched her cheek with his finger turned her head toward him.

Touched that he thought of her and her love to ride, she thought, "He knows me quite well just in the weeks we have been together," she realized.

She gave Ross that dazzling dimpled smile and her red hair glowed in the fading shadows. Ross was grinning and his blue eyes twinkled. They stood there together, then she hesitated as she felt his hand on her shoulder. Tenderly and with caution he held her, and then kissed her waiting lips.

The kiss lingered as she closed her eyes, letting his lips deepen upon hers in warm fervor. Before he pulled away from her, she looked at his face.

"I will remember this as long as I live," she believed. Then she asked, "Ross, why did you do that?"

She was still standing close to him, shaken. Ross replied, "Because I wanted to. Call it a farewell kiss for now, Bets, In-eah . . . Go safe!" He took her by the arm and they walked back to the house in silence.

The summer sun was high in the evening sky, giving a warm, golden glow that beamed through the window of the stage coach door. Elizabeth's crimson colored hair seemed aflame beneath the brilliant sun. Heat shimmered over the dry, yellow grass as the squeaking, jolting wagon gave them no rest.

They had just crossed the high pass in the mountains and were looking down on a wide valley a long way below them. They could see many small rivers and streams that flowed into the great Snake. These tributaries looked like pencil drawings on a map; they were so far away.

Dalton wished there had been a train they could have taken to make this trip. Most of the long journeys he had taken were in the East and he always enjoyed riding the trains. These towns west of their ranch were remote and small, and he had no reason to go there. The roads, such as they were on, were often washed out, rutted, or blocked altogether.

The discomfort they suffered riding this coach did not give them much of a chance to talk. He looked at Elizabeth, searching her face, smiled, then his gaze narrowed. Dalton knew Elizabeth had tired as he watched her shift back and forth trying to get relief. He admired her for not saying a word about her discomfort.

"I know she would rather be riding her horse, but the trip home would have taken twice as long. We are expected by anxious parents who have not seen either of us in months," he thought, as he leaned back and tried to get comfortable.

Every valley the stage rode into, reminded Elizabeth of the summer camp with the Kamiah people. With a deep, painful ache, she missed Louise and their long rides across the green meadows to their favorite waterfall or fishing spot. She missed the evenings around the fire as they taught each other their languages and the fun exchanges of the skillful work of weaving or tanning a beautiful piece of leather.

Then the most important thing she missed was telling new friends at the camp about their awesome God.

"I can't do God's work, as He does the seeking. All I know is that He has chosen me that I could embrace Him. All I can do is inform others what He has done for me."

Yes, she believed that her faith had grown while she had been here—the patience, provision, and bringing of others into her life. Aloneness wasn't an issue——not to mention the healing. He had blessed her with by restoring most of her memory.

This was the reason the farewells she had with the young girl and her father were so heartbreaking. Elizabeth knew that this day would have to come, and she had to go back alone and leave the people she had learned to love. They were people who had shared with her their beautiful poetry and legends.

"I have the memories, but they are not enough, Louise, you are my sunshine and Ross I remember my first memory of you. You picked me up when I fell, although much of my pain was heartache, and loneliness. You were always there, but I wasn't prepared for the power of love."

She sighed, and a tear formed in her eye. She did not want Dalton to see it, so she kept her head turned away.

By nightfall she was dozing against Dalton's shoulder and he put her linen duster around her to ward off the cool air that was coming into the open window. They would be traveling all night, with only one stop for fresh horses, before reaching the crossing.

After an uneventful night, the sky grayed and dawn would soon be here. The stagecoach followed the bank of the small creek that had no towns along its path. *This is really a remote area. I wonder why I like it here so*, Dalton pondered to himself.

It must be because this valley is my home. Maybe that is why Liz seemed to be unhappy at her folk's home. I should promise we will spend more days in the surrounding towns.

I hear Hailey has a grand hotel going up and with natural hot springs. "It is not unusual for someone so young, like Elizabeth, to want to be with others." his mom had told him last spring.

He dreamed of Liz and him being together. He wanted to really court her. "I know I do not have much time for this before we are weathered in for the long winter months. I had better make plans," he thought. Dalton smiled as he snuggled down next to Elizabeth and the two cushioned each other, allowing them to sleep the rest of the way to the Crossing and then home.

Six weeks later, Louise came running into Helen's restaurant. "We're going to see Eizi!" She burst into loud dialogue as she was gathered up in her aunt's arms.

"Well, aren't you the bearer of good news," Helen smiled at the young girl now sitting on her lap. Helen could not believe the change in the child in just a few months of school. Elizabeth had helped her very much in giving her a sense of where she belonged.

They had had a closeness of spirit and the change had happened in a very lovely manner. She believed it was their mutual trust and faith in God that had given them the ability to adjust. They had talked about how much Louise had missed her Ina.

The new friends in school and the learning itself had done the trick in combating her longing to be with the people from the tribe—and Elizabeth.

"Are you leaving during the break?" she asked the child. "Yes, next week. Will you take care of Tigue and Buster for us," she asked, looking at her new aunt. "I will bring them by. We are taking Princess with us. Elizabeth has missed her so."

Helen grinned at the manner in which Louise was always affectionate over the animals. Ross had told them it is a softness in her that went with the heart her mother had. This was also the reason Elizabeth had left Tigue here with the child. Then the young girl was off her lap and waving good bye, saying something about riding some horse for the last time. Helen could hear her singing as she mounted the horse.

"Mid pleasures and places though we may roam, be it ever so humble there is no place like home. Home, home, sweet, sweet home. There's no place like home," her young voice sang out.

Ross opened the gate that led into the spacious barn yard of the Grover ranch. Abruptly he turned and swung himself back into the saddle.

Determined to pull himself out of the blue mood that had unexpectedly engulfed him the last two weeks, he had agreed to make this trip with Louise. As they reached the corrals, Ross spoke.

"I'm not so sure this surprise visit is a good idea. I am not sure anyone is home." He admitted only to himself that he had been missing Elizabeth for weeks.

Yes Betts, what a change you've made in my life. You have replaced all the broken parts. How patiently I have waited for your love, he pondered with a smile at the memories of her. Then his daughter spoke and he came back to today.

"Oh, I hope she's home. Where would Fizi go?" Louise inquired. Ross continued to look around but saw no one. They rode into the tall, dry grass to tie up near the barn. The door was open and two figures were standing in the opening. A man and a woman were in an embrace, but Ross could not hear their conversation. He turned away with a slap of anguish when he recognized who it was.

The pressure in his chest increased and he knew he did care. Soon a man on a horse left the barn at a full gallop. It was Dalton. The woman was Elizabeth. Inside, Elizabeth was not aware that anyone was near. She was emotionally shaken.

She had a deep well of compassion for Dalton, but she had to tell him she was not going to marry him.

"You are free," she told him. Then she embraced him and said a sobbing goodbye. He rubbed away a drying tear from her cheek with his thumb, then Elizabeth stepped back from him and squared her shoulders and walked away. She heard him mount his horse and leave in a great hurry. Elizabeth left the barn by a side door and went in to the house. When she was inside, she heard a knock at the front door and went to see who was there.

It was now five months later:

Through the kitchen window at the ranch, Elizabeth studied the Sawtooth Mountains as they loomed up against the blue, spring sky.

"The storms of winter are over, the snow up high is receding," she said to her mother. Her mother barely looked up from her task at the table. Elizabeth approached her.

"Here, let me help you," she spoke as she sat down next to her mother waiting for a reply.

"Yes, you need something to do, Elizabeth. You have hardly been out except to check the new colts. Even Dalton has quit asking for you to accompany him to the Crossing to get the mail.

The pass has been open for a month and you have no excuse not to take the wagon and go over to the Russell ranch. You have lost interest in making linens and quilts even! I am not sure this is good for you. You seem so restless. What is it?" her mother asked with concern.

"Haven't you heard of spring fever?" she replied, not meeting her mother's eyes. "Hmm," was her mother's only response.

Elizabeth did not know why she could not tell her mother about her sleepless nights and the dreams that seemed so prevalent. Often when she would walk back from being with the horses, the force of her loneliness took her breath away.

In her thoughts were the talks that Ross and Louise and she had shared together. It seemed easy to share one's hopes and dreams and disappointments with them. Yet sharing them with her mother was so difficult. Why did she think of Ross and Louise so often and look forward to those weekly letters?

Some vague feeling stirred in her heart as she recalled the strong, yet gentle grasp of Ross' arms around her and the sweetness of his kiss that last night in Idaho City. She remembered when he kissed her goodbye. She'd resisted the urge to close her eyes. She needed to see his face, to remember it exactly as it was.

He had murmured, "I'll miss you, Bets." As she recalled this time they had together, emotion flooded her heart, warm and real.

"Well," she whispered, "I have my memories." Her mother just shook her head. She gazed out on the quiet scene through the large window, seeing the ever-changing trees with the new, bright green buds. The receding snow on the mountains was now showing green grass in its melt.

In the evening Elizabeth sat out on the porch, quietly lost in her own thoughts of the people that were in the dreams that plagued her. She would lie awake for hours. When she did sleep, she would lay dreaming of all her friends at the Kamiah summer camp—Ina' Louise, Ross—and Jesse and Tigue, too. Do they miss her—she wondered?

The short visit Ross and Louise had given her last fall was just that, very short. She barely got a chance to talk to Ross. He never seemed to want to be alone with her. "I wanted to share my dreams with him, and take the time for Ross to tell me his dreams," she softly spoke. In the dream last night someone was walking away from her. She could not tell if it was Dalton, but it might have been. She did not call after him, and thought that it was odd if it was not him, who could it have been?

"Dreams seem so real, and yet, Lord, are you trying to tell me something? I have asked You for Your guidance in my life, and I have always been willing to go. Yet, I am hesitating. Give me a sign," she prayed as she walked down the path that night toward the barn. The sky filled with a million stars, brightening the night. They seemed no different than the spring nights of all the years before—except it was the clearest night she could remember in her midnight strolls this year. Then it erupted—the brightness of the falling star lit her path and lasted for about ten seconds.

"Oh!" she cried out with a smile, and felt joy in her heart that she had not experienced all winter long.

"If you had one wish Ross, what would it be?" She questioned, "and what would you do differently?" Then she realized she must not go on like this.

The next week Elizabeth hooked up the horse to the wagon so she could go pay a visit to Molly, James, and the new baby. She hoped the mail from the Crossing would be there.

She had arrived at the Russell home at about the same time Dalton did. He seemed glad to see her but there was a quietness to his greeting with her. He acted differently, and seemed estranged as she could sense it.

After he asked about herself and her family, he handed her their mail, then he excused himself and went out to look for James. Among the letters to their ranch was the weekly letter from Ross. Elizabeth tore into it and began reading the familiar writing; it read:

My Dear Elizabeth,

Late tonight as I watched the stars in the heaven, I saw a falling star that reminded me of the many things important in my life that I have let fall. I have missed many God-given blessings in my thirty years. You are one of these. I will not let another day go by without telling you how much I miss you and that Louise and I keep you in our prayers daily.

I have written to you faithfully in the last four months but those letters were all about others, and not about us. I want to write you if you are free to correspond with me in this way. Please tell me of yourself. Are you happy? Do you get out much? I understand you are no longer seeing Dalton. I want to see you. Can you come down to the City and spend some time here, and soon? There are many things I need to say to you when I see you. Please come. Again, I miss you.

Affectionately, Ross

Just then, Elizabeth heard Molly come to the door and welcome her in. Elizabeth put the letter with the other mail and hurried inside. She turned to Molly and inquired of her.

"What was all that about Dalton? He hardly spoke to me." Molly did not know how to answer. She took the baby and laid her down in the crib, then she took Elizabeth's coat.

She led Elizabeth to the large, cushioned leather couch. When they had seated themselves, Molly took her friend's hand and spoke.

"Elizabeth, Dalton is seeing another girl in Naples. I think he is serious with her. He goes there every week and it is not just to bring back supplies."

Elizabeth sat there looking at Molly, her face flushed, and her lips slightly parted like she was going to say something, but couldn't. Then a smile spread on her face and even Molly caught the contagion to smile, being glad about Elizabeth's reaction to the news.

"I am so glad for him!" she began. "Who is the lucky girl?" "You know her. She is the young woman who helped me with my wedding dress. Lydia and I have also become good friends," Molly answered with a sparkle in her eyes.

"You seemed almost relieved and not at all surprised by the news about Dalton," she added.

"Yes, I am not surprised at the miracles God works. I have been praying for answers in my life and I just got one door closed forever." She hugged Molly as she got up from the chair to get her coat. Molly stared at her.

"Are you leaving so soon? We just began our visit."

"Yes, I must get home to pack. Remember last week when you ask me to accompany you and James to the county seat at Idaho City? I have just accepted the invitation. We will have a lot of time to visit on the trail. So, bye for now!"

Elizabeth hurried out of the house to untie Princess for the journey home. She couldn't wait to tell her mother about her decisions. On the way, she hardly noticed the beauty around her, but could only see Ross's dark, blue eyes and the way he looked at her the night he kissed her.

Funny about life, she mused. *I had to come home to find out my place was back there with Ross and Louise where I had spent the summer—the best summer I have ever had in my life.*

Elizabeth felt excited. *Now I can share my feelings with everyone. I may shout, 'I'm in love with a wonderful man!'* She did yell it to the mountains and just hearing her voice echo on the hills made her happy.

The big yellow dog began to pick her way more carefully as she continued her journey. She was hungry, limping and shaken as she came out of the scrub brush. She headed across a stretch of open meadow covered with new sprouts of early flowers that was a postscript to a hope for more warming sunshine.

The day was warm for spring and the thirsty dog was now on a parallel line to the big stream that cut into the flat land of the valley.

She went to the edge of the bank and drank the cool water that refreshed her and helped erase her hunger.

She trotted through the undergrowth, hoping to find small animals or trapped birds there. The birds set off some alarming notes and flew ahead of her. After a time of hunting, with evening drawing near, she began to look for a place to sleep for the night. Her stomach was heavy and she had begun to have pain. Having experienced this birthing before, she made a deep nest under a fallen tree, then pushed some dried plants around inside it. This hole would protect her young. Having finished this task, she fell down and slept fitfully until the time was right. Then, through the night, she birthed her litter of pups.

When it was over, she nuzzled them near her. Then she slept again. About midday, awakened by human voices Tigue got up to investigate.

"Come on, Eizi," called Molly. "Or you will have to walk the last mile into the city," she teased.

"What are you looking at?"

"I'm not sure, but I thought I saw something—a glimpse of an animal with a yellow tail and a striped head," she replied to Molly. She motioned for her to come over to where the trees began.

James and Molly crossed the stream where the horses were drinking and quickly joined Elizabeth in her quest. Just on impulse, Elizabeth called out, "Come!"

Tigue merged into the open, wagging her tail. She let out a slight howl, then came bobbing to Elizabeth's side to lick her hand.

"Tigue, what are you doing out here? Oh, you are hurt, and you look awful," Elizabeth said, kneeling down to stroke her head. She reached for her so she could examine her, but Tigue backed away and bounded into a thicket, then stopped and turned to them before she went out of sight.

"What is she doing?" Elizabeth cried.

"I think she wants us to follow her," James said very suspiciously. They walked into the brush, where they lost sight of her.

"Where are you, Tigue, come," her mistress command. But there was no response.

"Easy, we will find her," James spoke.

"Shhh, I hear a noise, over by that fallen tree." They all hurried to the ditch near the tree. They bent down to peek into a well-made nest that held three puppies and a proud mother.

"Oh, they are so beautiful!" Elizabeth cried. "Louise told me she was expecting, and this is a wonderful surprise.

Tigue greeted them with a wag of her tail as she scooted her body closer to the three hungry mouths so they could nurse.

"I have heard that the wolf will go off by herself to have her young," James stated. They watched as she fed them while they talked about each pup's different characteristics; two of the father, Buster, which were dark, and one that was yellow striped, like Tigue. When the nursing was over, with excitement, they picked them all up and loaded them in the wagon.

"So this is Tigue," James said in amusement, shaking his head. "Yes, the same dog that saved my life more than once," was Elizabeth's proud reply. "And I can't wait to show these pups to Louise."

James picked up the reins and hurried the team into town while the women fussed over the new offspring.

"Look, the miners are moving in already!" exclaimed James as they came into the edge of town. In the spring, many tents flanked the main street of Idaho City. There were some new structures being built.

The noise and bustle of the busy men fascinated the travelers. As they passed the mercantile store, Elizabeth studied the patrons inside. Molly saw her searching look.

"Where do you think Ross is this time of day? I know Louise is in school. We are a day early from what was our original plan," Elizabeth spoke excitedly. Then blushing at her anxiety, she thought, *Am I deeply in love with him? Is this what love is?*

"Let's stop at the restaurant Helen has purchased. It is called Gertie's and is just up the street. Helen will know where Ross is."

Inside, the cafe was nearly empty except for some persons sitting at the bar drinking coffee.

"I am fascinated with this place and the people here," James thought, looking around at the newly remodeled interior.

"This is so good what Helen has done to the old building. I'll bet she is glad she moved here to open her businesses."

He continued looking around to see the old wood blackened by time, smoke, and grease, now scrubbed clean and mated comfortably with the cream, colored walls. The large stone hearth was warm and friendly, and the low tables and benches, snuggled around in a relaxed way. The bar was beautiful, displaying a one piece, aged pine log—polished with a shine.

James listened to the voices and the conversations, and he noticed they were a mix of accents. "This is what makes the growing West so interesting and I guess why I came," he spoke to Molly.

"History in the making," she replied, smiling at him and directing him to a seat near the fireplace.

"I think Helen named this place after the one in Dallas. She and Jesse went there on their way to see a doctor for his eye surgery last fall, then they moved here."

Elizabeth spied Helen near the back and went directly to her. "Hello, Helen," she greeted her.

"Why, Elizabeth, we weren't expecting you until tomorrow. What a nice surprise!" she said as she stood, then gave her a welcoming hug.

"Wow, I like what you have done to this place, Helen. From a waitress to an owner, how do you like the switch?" Elizabeth asked.

"Thank you, I love it! The stake I gave that old minor really paid off," she replied with a smile.

"And Jesse is comfortable here," she added, looking at this pretty girl with uncertain thoughts as to see how she felt about Jesse and her marriage.

"Helen, I am so happy for you both," Elizabeth replied with a sincere voice.

"I'll bet you are looking for Ross," Helen said with a smile.

"Yes, I am anxious to see him, is he in town?" She blushed as she asked.

"I believe he is not that far from the outskirts of town, but it would be better if you rode my horse up the road to where he is working. I just tied Beauty up out back. Do take her as she needs the exercise. It will be dark soon and the ride will save you time getting there."

She told her where to find the site where Ross was working. Elizabeth told Molly and James to go on to the boarding house and get settled, and that she would meet them there later. She hurried out the door, got her duster out of the wagon, gave Tigue a command to stay, and went around back to find Beauty.

Riding out to the site, the horse ambled along the steep road as the sun was setting over the summit across the canyon. With the sun reddening the sky in the West, Elizabeth began her own private race with the sun.

She nudged the horse on at a faster pace, and they cut across to a trail that went in and out of pine trees into a stand of aspen. There was the fragrance of blooming Syringa bushes, and she saw bright fuchsia Indian paint brush waving in the evening breeze.

"What a pretty spot," she thought. The trail made a curve and a gradual climb to a flat place on a ridge. Just a short climb away, Elizabeth saw Ross standing by a newly erected log house. In his hand was an axe, but he dropped it when he saw her coming and began walking toward her. Elizabeth stopped the horse and watched him move quickly toward them. He greeted her with an easy grin of surprise and welcome.

"Elizabeth!" he began, holding his arms up for her to fall into. She slipped from the horse into his arms. Ross was right there—all six-foot-six of him. He seized her to give her a big hug.

Ah, she felt good in his arms. He sighed a sigh of relief. *It was about time she came to him,* he thought. He caught her scent, which was like delicate rose petals in the dew. It weakened his knees and made his heart beat faster. Elizabeth found comfort with his arms around her; they made her feel protected and hopeful that they could live their dreams together.

"I thought you would never get here," he began as he held her, "but you are early. I am so sorry I was not in town to greet you," he babbled.

"Shhh," she ordered as she placed her fingers over his lips. "Do I have to kiss you to get you to be quiet?" She was so beautiful as she flushed red over her brazenness.

Ross thought, *Kiss you is what I wanted to do since the first time I saw you.* Oh, Bets," he breathed through her hair, drawing her closer. He dropped his head down to hers and his face grew anxious as his eyes rested on her gaze with his. She lifted up her chin, revealing slightly parting lips to him. He placed a lingering kiss on her sweet mouth that caused her heart to thump quickly.

Warmth swept through her like a soft, summer breeze. The young lovers remained enveloped in each other's arms as the sun dipped over the ridge, drawing a dusky haze around them. She parted from him, being aware that the lingering kiss had become quite passionate.

I asked for this lovemaking, now I had better control it, she reminded herself. The sweet words Ross said to her were words she longed to hear, and this attention was what she had dreamed of from the man that was in love with her. Yet, she was taught respect for each other was important.

She pushed away slightly and Ross responded by releasing her. He looked at her and spoke.

"Bets, I thank the Lord for planning my life, and for sending you back to me. The Lord works in marvelous ways. I didn't even have to look for you, and I certainly do thank Him."

Ross touched her face, then ran his hand through her thick, red hair. The last rays of sunlight shimmered over it.

"I never thought I would feel this way again. But I have found you! Marry me, sweet Bets. I love you. Louise and I want you in our lives forever. Say you will," he pleaded.

"Oh, yes," she replied, as emotion flooded her heart. She threw her arms around his neck, and gave him a loving embrace. He picked her up and spun her around. They laughed the laughter of young lovers. She was breathless as he pressed his lips against hers.

"One more kiss to seal that promise," he demanded. When they parted, Elizabeth looked beyond Ross and saw the large log home on the hill.

"Ross, what are you doing out here?" With a twinkle in his eyes he answered her, "You have spoiled my surprise, my love. It is a home I have been building for us and Louise. Now let me show it to you."

He took her hand in his and they walked up the hill to the house. It was an exciting adventure to see the home. Ross had built it cleverly and well. She saw the room that was to be Louise's. Her heart swelled at the thought of having sweet Star Dancer for a daughter.

To me she will always be my Star Dancer, and I will love her with all the love mothers could, she silently vowed. Peacefully, they sat on the grassy hillside with his arm around her. It was a beautiful spot and the twilight illuminated the view and softened the raggedness of the serene landscape.

They watched a gaggle of snow geese fly by, listening to their springtime songs of honking. The V formation they made stretched across the dimming horizon.

"They're coming home," Ross spoke with emotion. Elizabeth felt the same feeling that Ross did.

"Yes, coming home, such a good idea," Elizabeth agreed as she snuggled closer to Ross's side. She wondered about the difficult journey of the hundreds of miles those birds had flown to come home. She had completed the first part of her journey and believed it was *not* a matter of planning. Like the geese, it was a matter of what was and what will be—and the fact that she needed to say in her heart that whatever she did, it was God's plan and leading.

"God, you know the future . . . and because of this I am just beginning this exciting journey of my new life," she breathed this silent prayer. The solitude of aloneness that Elizabeth had felt, she knew now only the geese could understand. She had found her place in these Idaho mountains, and it was right here. Here, where there were wishes yet unsaid, but a lot of love and longing in two hearts that beat as one.

She continued her prayer, "Thank you, Lord, for an incredible journey. I once was lost, but now I am found."

To order additional copies of

the
journey
series

Have your credit card ready and call:

1-877-421-READ (7323)

or please visit our web site at
www.pleasantword.com

Also available at: www.amazon.com

Printed in the United States
16070LVS00002B/201-216